Here are some c
characters you'
in

THE CAPTAIN'S TIGER:

An attractive widow on the make and her young son who knew the score but wouldn't play the game.

The cantankerous mail room chief who liked to skin executives alive.

A cynical war correspondent whose sleuthing was complicated by exiles from Café Society.

Two party girls who got a riotous sendoff after a weekend in New York.

An important civilian whose connections and Presidential Citation led to nothing but bitter frustration.

THE CAPTAIN'S TIGER is full of Jerome Weidman's genius for strong characterization, masterful dialogue and superb storytelling.

the captain's tiger

JEROME WEIDMAN

Author of "The Price Is Right"

MB

A MACFADDEN-BARTELL BOOK

THIS BOOK IS THE COMPLETE TEXT
OF THE HARDCOVER EDITION

A MACFADDEN BOOK 1964

MACFADDEN BOOKS are published by
Macfadden-Bartell Corporation
205 East 42nd Street, New York, New York, 10017

CONTENTS

INTRODUCTION 7

MONSOON 17

AN EASY ONE 25

EXAMINATION 32

A DIME A THROW 38

EYEWITNESS 43

PHILADELPHIA EXPRESS 49

DEATH IN THE FAMILY 56

DUMMY RUN 59

THE THIRD ALPHABET 68

JOUST 76

MY AUNT FROM TWELFTH STREET 81

GALLANTRY IN ACTION 85

EVERYBODY AND HIS BROTHER 94

MOVABLE FEAST 101

HOUDINI 109

THE NEAT MEXICANS 115

A LODGING FOR THE NIGHT 124

THE PLEASURE OF THE PRESIDENT 134

SEND FOUR MEN TO HANOI 144

SOMETHING FOR LUCK 157

THE BOTTOM OF THE MOUNTAIN 173

INTRODUCTION

Several months after we entered the war, in the uncomfortable days when the German submarine campaign against Allied shipping in the North Atlantic was enjoying its greatest success, I was sent to England on a government mission. The journey was exhausting and perilous. I did not know, when I left New York, that it was going to be. By the time I found out, it was too late to register the objections that would undoubtedly have gone unheeded even if they had been made at the appropriate time. Neither I nor my mission was of sufficient importance to justify an air priority.

In accordance with complicated but precise instructions, I went from New York to Canada by rail. There I was met in a blizzard by an official of the British Ministry of War Transport, to whom I presented my credentials. He gave me a number of documents and put me on a train bound for the Maritime Provinces. After a tedious day-and-a-half trip, during which I caught a bad cold, I arrived in a Canadian port. Here I was met by another official who took some of my documents, presented me with others, and left me, in a small frame hotel that could easily have been a prominent part of the set for a film of one of Jack London's more lurid stories about the Yukon, with instructions to relax and wait.

I could not relax, but I did wait and, toward evening of the fourth day, the BMWT official called for me in a car. He took away several of my documents, gave me a few new ones, drove me down to the waterfront, advised me to do something about my cold, helped me into a small launch, and waved goodbye in the gathering darkness. Night fell rapidly as we chugged and bumped our way through the floating ice in the harbor to the ship that was to carry me to England. It was completely dark when I was put aboard, and we were at sea when I came up on deck in the morning for a look around. This did not take long.

The S.S. *Celtrover*, which was not her name, was a vessel of some thirty-two hundred tons, and even a man whose training and predilections ran to pavements could circle her decks, from stem to stern and back, in eighteen seconds flat, as I soon found out. She had been built in 1893 to carry freight on the Baltic run and, as a concession to one of the owners who liked to go to sea with his wife every now and then for his gout, two passenger cabins had been constructed aft. In 1915 the *Celtrover* was armed and converted into an auxiliary cruiser and, in 1933, when she was forty years old and had served her stockholders and her country well, she was junked.

After Dunkirk, when the U-boat successes against British shipping were helping to pose the grimly dubious question of England's survival, the Admiralty issued a desperate call for every hull of British registry that could float. Since this is the approximate equivalent of calling to arms every citizen who can breathe, a considerable number of ships was able to meet the Admiralty's rather basic requirement. The *Celtrover* was hauled from her muddy pasture on the Clyde, hurriedly if inadequately refurbished, and sent back to sea.

The fact that, when I came aboard, she had run for nearly two years without mishap through the submarine-infested waters between Alexandria and the Mersey, was not in the least reassuring. In addition to her long record of honorable service, the *Celtrover* had a permanent list of fifteen degrees, a maximum speed of eight knots, no running water, a larder that seemed to contain nothing but beans and a thick, gummy soup made from frozen cabbage greens, twelve passengers in the two cabins originally built for the gouty stockholder and his wife, three lifeboats that had not swung free of their davits in twenty years, four hastily improvised gun pits fitted with weapons that jammed even in practice, a flank position in the convoy we were to join the following day, a mutinous crew, and one toilet that worked.

My tastes are not even remotely sybaritic. I was born in a slum, and the homes I knew in my youth were indifferently equipped with sanitary facilities. I found the inconveniences of the *Celtrover* staggering, but far from lethal. It was impossible to shave or bathe. The cement floor of the single toilet was constantly awash with a thick, grayish slime, the accumulation of years of uncleanliness dissolved by salt water leaks from several pipes and a porthole that refused to close. The food was unpalatable and indigestible. You could not brush your teeth or wash your hands without the desperate conviction that your body had gone completely numb from your gums up, or your wrists down. It was impossible to buy or borrow or cadge a drink. And even if there had been room, in the cabins built for one but now shared by six, to change your shirt, the strict order from the bridge was that everybody was to sleep in his clothes and his life belt. Everybody did, for twenty-two days.

8

It was not the accumulation of discomforts that upset me. What I found disturbing was the fact, obvious even to me and underscored by everybody on board with whom I talked, that if the *Celtrover* got us safely through the North Atlantic to England, it would be only with the help of God. Assistance from any other quarter, the Royal Navy, the crew, the passengers, the equipment of the ship, seemed a possibility so fantastically remote that it could be safely disregarded in any computation of betting odds.

The crew was mutinous because its members had not received so much as a day's leave to visit their homes since they had joined the ship, even though the *Celtrover* had touched U.K. ports several times during the past two years. Also, the ship, despite its size, was undermanned, and the living quarters available for the crew were even worse than those provided for the passengers. During our first boat drill, which was held at eleven o'clock on our first morning out, I noticed that, in addition to life preservers such as the passengers wore, several members of the crew carried on their hips a flat oilskin package. After the drill I asked one of the deck hands what these packages were. Submersion suits, he said, made of thin rubber. The waters of the North Atlantic at this time of year, he explained, were so cold that, if you were fortunate enough to find yourself a floating survivor after your ship was torpedoed, you would probably freeze to death within ten minutes. The submersion suit would keep you reasonably warm for several hours, no matter how cold the ocean. I asked when these suits would be issued to the passengers.

"Passengers?" the deck hand said acidulously. "Look, chum. There ain't enough of these things to go around among the crew."

The other passengers were even less reassuring than the crew. Each of the eleven was a D.B.S., or a Distressed British Seaman, a merchant mariner who, after being torpedoed, had been fished out of the ocean by a passing vessel and carried to the rescue ship's nearest port of call. These eleven men were being returned to England, at the expense of His Majesty's Government, for new assignments. None of them had met the others before he was put aboard the *Celtrover*. They had a good deal to say to each other. I did not want to hear any of it, but the *Celtrover* was not the sort of ship on which you could be alone and, besides, I was bunking with five of them. I heard it all, several times.

Since all of them had been torpedoed at least once, most of them twice, and four or five had been blown into the sea with unbelievable regularity, always at different intersections of longitude and latitude, there was, almost literally, no square inch of what, in their interminable bull sessions, they called

9

the Western Ocean that might be regarded, by a person hunting desperately for straws of reassurance, as a safety zone: a strip of sea into which U-boats could be counted upon not to venture because to do so was either foolhardy or unprofitable. Speed, my fellow passengers said, was the only protection against submarines, and the *Celtrover*, which could do eight knots when hard pressed, was crossing in a six-knot convoy, the slowest type, designed especially for revived derelicts like the *Celtrover* that had answered, from their muddy beds of retirement, the Admiralty's frantic call.

We were for it, these experts grimly assured each other and me. On the morning of the second day, when simultaneously we reached the convoy rendezvous and ran into the heavy weather that stayed with us for three weeks, I was convinced they were right.

Because the *Celtrover* was undermanned, each of the twelve passengers was impressed by the second mate, who doubled as gunnery officer, for gun watch in the pits on the upper deck. I drew three tricks of two hours each, from 4:00 A.M. to 6:00 A.M., from noon to 2:00 P.M., and from 8:00 P.M. to 10:00 P.M., in a pit mounted on the roof of the radio room and fitted with a set of twin Marlins that, according to the worn engraving on their barrels, had been manufactured in 1913 and, according to the gunnery officer, had not been fired for twenty-two years when they were added to the *Celtrover's* improvised arsenal.

"I shouldn't worry about their jamming, if I were you," the gunnery officer said when he was showing me how to operate the Marlins and they jammed. "Machine guns are no bloody good against submarines, anyway."

The watches were mounted, I learned, not to inflict damage on attackers, but to provide the ship with extra pairs of eyes. I used mine industriously during my first watch, from noon to 2:00 P.M., and whatever last shred of unreasonable hope the D.B.S. bull sessions had left in my breast was converted immediately to prayer. From my flimsy aerie built on the roof of the radio room I was able to make out sixty to sixty-eight ships in our convoy. The total varied with each computation because the seas were so rough that it was difficult to count with accuracy. I had no such difficulty with our escort. No matter how often I counted, this total always came out the same: three four-stackers, the all but obsolete destroyers we had transferred to England in the swap for Atlantic bases before we entered the war, and four corvettes.

The appalling inadequacy of this escort for a six-knot convoy of sixty or more merchantmen was pointed out to me by all eleven D.B.S. passengers, each one coupling his demonstration with a stream of bitter and obscene recriminations against

His Majesty's Government for failing to provide him with swifter and safer passage. I assured them, with a conviction I did not want to feel, that they had made their point. It was proved to me conclusively twenty-four hours later, when our convoy was sighted by a U-boat wolf pack. We were under submarine attack of varying intensity for sixteen days.

When our convoy split up—four days before we reached Liverpool, the destination identified in my many and complicated documents as "a U.K. port"—and the *Celtrover* swung into the Irish Sea, I was unable, no matter how many times I counted from the gun pit on top of the radio room, to reach a total of more than forty-eight ships. We had lost to the German raiders about one-third of the vessels we had met almost three weeks before at the rendezvous point near the Canadian coast. In addition, the four tables in the *Celtrover's* tiny dining salon had broken loose from their moorings and, along with the sixteen chairs, had been smashed to bits by the violence of the sea; for the last eight days of the journey we took turns, standing up, eating the thick, gummy soup, made from frozen cabbage greens, out of the six bowls that were all that remained of the *Celtrover's* crockery; I learned to distinguish between the sounds made by a distant torpedo finding its target and the explosion of a depth charge; and I discovered to my considerable astonishment that it is possible for the human nervous system to survive sixteen consecutive days of being scared stiff.

I attribute this survival, in equal parts, to a member of the *Celtrover's* crew whose existence I did not become aware of until the attack by the undersea raiders had been in progress for almost a full week, and to the unquenchable self-interest that is a part, probably a necessary part, of every writer's equipment.

Like most human beings, I suppose, who feel their end is near, I spent much of my time during those bad days, when I was alone in the gun pit, compiling a list of regrets: things I had done in the past that I wanted desperately to do over, opportunities lost, chances that would not come again. It does not embarrass me to record, although I have been told it should, that prominent on this list was the annoying realization that I would never again be able to write a book.

Again like most human beings, even writers, I am loved by a few people. It helped me get through the nerve-wracking hours in the gun pit, while depth charges rocked the small ship and the corvettes dashed back and forth across our bow, like frenzied mothers breaking up a concentration of children frozen with terror in the path of a team of runaway horses, to make and revise and remake and revise again a mental list of those of my stories hitherto unpublished in book form that,

11

since I was about to die and would not again have the opportunity to write a novel, I wanted collected between covers after my death as the final book from my pen. I find it only mildly surprising now that I took myself and this project with great seriousness then.

Although I had published in various magazines almost a hundred stories since the first collection of my shorter fiction appeared, the imminence of death made me so harsh a winnower that, no matter how hard I tried, I could not make the total on this mental list go higher than twenty or twenty-five. I was disturbed by how little I wanted to save, but I hoped, with what now seems an excess of unreasonable irritation, that my posthumous editors would respect the standard I had *in extremis* set for myself and would not, in their misguided affection, try to swell the list. At the same time I realized, with mounting annoyance, that this hope was vain. People who love you seldom make the best editors. There was only one solution. I would have to arrange to be present to make the selections myself.

The day I reached this implausible conclusion, I noticed a boy, who looked about thirteen and upon inquiry proved to be four months short of his fifteenth birthday, making his way rather skillfully, and with apparent unconcern for the buffeting seas and the surrounding detonations of high explosive, across the pitching, slippery deck, toward the bridge, carrying a tray, balanced neatly on the flat of one hand, loaded with all the complicated paraphernalia necessary to an English tea. When I came down from my midday watch I asked a D.B.S. who the boy was, and why I had not seen him before.

"That's the captain's tiger," the D.B.S. said. "Doesn't have much time to hang about. He's kept pretty busy, you know."

I didn't know, so I asked several more questions. The captain's tiger, it seemed, was ship's slang for the boy who served as personal servant to the master of the vessel. His duties were difficult to list or define because they varied with each captain. Some masters didn't like to have anybody hanging about. Others did. Some captains preferred to do things for themselves. Others liked to be waited on hand and foot. The master of the *Celtrover*, a pudgy little man with a crapulous face and a poorly fitted set of dentures, whom I had seen only once, the day before the wolf pack caught us, was of the latter type, I was told. He drank vast quantities of tea, particularly when the going was rough and he was forced to remain almost constantly on the bridge, and he kept his tiger hopping.

The next day, during my noon to 2:00 P.M. watch, the boy looked up and saw me following him with my eyes as he crossed the deck. He grinned shyly. I waved from the gun pit.

He stopped, hesitated for a moment, then scrambled up the ladder nailed to the side of the radio room and, balancing his loaded tray on one shoulder, he asked if I would like a cup of tea. My attitude toward tea is hardly one that could be described as open-minded, and there was nothing about the black, bitter brew that went by that name on board the *Celtrover* to dissipate this perhaps unreasonable point of view, but a man who has been scared stiff for the better part of a week does not always remember his peccadilloes when faced with a display of spontaneous generosity. I said I would love a cup of tea and the captain's tiger, with an exhibition of dexterity the equal of which I had not seen since Houdini stopped playing the Palace, poured one for me, said he had to be getting on to the bridge, and dropped nimbly to the deck without so much as upsetting the arrangement of the crockery and silver on his tray. Later, when he came back for the cup, we chatted for a few minutes. Every day after that the boy stopped at my gun pit on his way to the bridge, gave me some tea and, when he came back for the cup, we talked for a while before he hurried away to perform some errand for the captain.

I was surprised by how much these daily chats helped me. I began to look forward to them. I think this was because the boy, the only person on the *Celtrover* younger than myself, was completely unaffected by what we were going through. I was ashamed to ask him if he was afraid because I felt that to put the question was to confess my own fear, but it was plain that he did not know what the word meant. He had been born in Bootle, a slum area in Liverpool, and had gone to sea as a cabin boy at the age of twelve. He had never been inside a school and, in many ways, he was as innocent as a child half his age, but he had a warm, spontaneous gaiety mixed with a quick, ageless, almost terrifying shrewdness that cannot be taught and has never been learned in any classroom. By indirection, because he would not have known how to express it in words even if I had been stupid enough to ask the question, I gathered that he had not the slightest doubt that the *Celtrover* would survive because he had not the slightest doubt that he would live forever. Death was a concept that had not yet reached him, as it had not yet reached me when I was fourteen. It was helpful and refreshing to recall this at a time when the concept seemed momentarily on the verge of becoming fact.

One day, while he was collecting my empty cup, he asked what I did when there was no war. With that odd and insincere self-deprecation common to many members of my profession—as though I were announcing that I stole pennies from the cups of blind men, not because I liked to do it or because I was particularly adept at it but because I had to make a living—I said I was a writer. It was obvious at a glance that the boy was impressed, even awed, and, of course, at once I liked him better.

He had never before met a writer, he said, although he read a good deal. I asked what he read. He said oh, anything, magazines mostly, and he named a few and asked if I wrote for them. I said no, they were British publications, and I wrote only for American magazines. He said shyly that he would like to read some of my work, and he asked what kind of stories I wrote. I was astonished to discover that, after all these years, I could not answer this question. I stalled for time and asked him what kind of stories he liked. He seemed to have as much difficulty with my question as I had experienced with his.

"Well," he said, hesitating as he balanced the tea tray against the pitch of the ship and looked thoughtfully into the distance. "I don't know," the captain's tiger said slowly, and then his small, pinched face broke into the disturbing smile that was at once shrewd and yet very sweet. "I like them to come out nice in the end," he said.

My heart sank. I remembered that, when my first collection of short stories appeared, a weekly news magazine of enormous international circulation had captioned its review of the book with a single disdainful word: Sourball.

My stories, quite clearly, did not measure up to the standard set by the captain's tiger. I lacked the courage to tell him so. I did not want him to think ill of me. If I got back to America safely, I said hastily, I would send him some of my stories and let him judge for himself. By the time we docked at Liverpool, I had forgotten my promise.

A year and a half later I was sent to England again. Neither I nor my second mission had increased in importance, but the war was going better. The transportation problem was less acute. Air priorities were to be had almost for the asking. This time I flew. I landed at an airport near Liverpool late in the morning and learned that the next train for London would leave at five o'clock. Six empty hours faced me. I remembered the captain's tiger and, with a feeling of remorse, my neglected promise. I thumbed through my pocket notebook and found his address. It was scarcely legible, because I had scrawled it in the gun pit on top of the *Celtrover's* radio room, and I had neglected to jot down his name. I was certain, however, that I could find him without it. He was an unusual lad. His neighbors would know him from my description. I caught a bus into Liverpool, checked my bags at the railroad station, and took a taxi to Bootle.

We stopped in a devastated area that had once been part of a crowded slum. The street in which the boy from Bootle

14

had lived was gone. Weeds were growing in the untidy piles of rubble that had been picked bare of every household article worth salvaging. The address in my notebook no longer existed. There were no neighbors.

At a pub on the edge of the wrecked area, I described the boy I was looking for and I asked when the bombs had struck. The publican shook his head dubiously at my description but he said the neighborhood had been hit during the worst part of the blitz, early in 1941. I made a hurried calculation and, with some relief, reached a conclusion that I still think is sound.

When I met him on the *Celtrover*, the boy from Bootle had not had so much as a single day's leave in two years to visit his home. When the bombs destroyed the house in which he was born, the captain's tiger could not possibly have been in it. And since, no matter where he might be, probably somewhere at sea in the *Celtrover* or another of the ships that had answered the Admiralty's call, he was still young enough to retain unshaken the conviction that he would live forever, there was a fair chance that I could yet fulfill the promise I had made in the gun pit equipped with a set of twin Marlins that were ineffective against U-boats even when they did not jam.

To this book, which contains the few stories I felt I wanted put between covers at a time when I thought I would not again have the opportunity to write another, I have given the only name by which I ever knew the boy from Bootle; and because I am aware that the standard I set for myself is not one he would have chosen or approved, I have added a couple of stories that, whatever their faults, meet the standard by which he judged: they come out nice in the end.

It is a very small and inadequate payment for services rendered in the bad days on the Western Ocean.

JEROME WEIDMAN

St. Petersburg, Florida

MONSOON

The first two days out of Aden, when the passengers complained to one another of the heat, they did it with polite, good-humored smiles. Not to mention the heat at all in the Arabian Sea in August would have been ostentatious, even in those late summer days in 1939, when the clouds of war were so close they were almost visible in the burning, mirrored skies, and subjects for conversation were not difficult to find. On the third day, when the thermometer in the bar went up above the hundred mark and stayed there, the smiles disappeared. Nobody mentioned the heat all of that third day. Everybody talked about the monsoon, which, according to Mr. Madgwick, was due to strike the vessel along about the middle of the next day, the fourth out of Aden and a full week, perhaps even eight or nine days, before the *Baroda* would reach Colombo.

Mr. Madgwick was a small, compact, middle-aged Englishman with a full beard which was shaved around his lips, so his face looked like a fur coat from which a round hole had been gouged, revealing a pink section of the wearer's skin. He was a rubber broker in Singapore, where he lived with his mother, a tiny, fragile, friendly old lady who was stone-deaf. Her son had taken her to England for a gallstone operation, which had been successful, and now they were on their way back to Malaya.

During the first two days out of Aden, Mr. Madgwick had been just another passenger, more odd-looking than most because of the peculiar gap in his otherwise impressive beard. On the third day, however, when the monsoon replaced the heat as a subject of conversation, Mr. Madgwick became the centre of a good deal of attention. He knew a lot about the East. He had lived in the Malay Peninsula for almost thirty years, and he was pleasant and modest while imparting his knowledge to others, especially to the six American passengers, who made no secret of the fact that they had always thought a monsoon was a sudden, violent, and dangerous

17

storm quite capable of breaking a vessel of the *Baroda's* size in two.

"It isn't that at all," said Mr. Madgwick, with a kind smile. "You're thinking of a typhoon, which is a horse of a different color, as the fellow says." Mr. Madgwick had a precise way of wrapping his pink, almost girlish lips around every word he uttered, pronouncing each one with equal clarity and giving such syllable its proper weight, so he seemed to be bestowing on his listeners, in addition to information, a small unobtrusive lesson in elocution. "A monsoon is a wind and nothing more, a wind that blows part of the year from one direction and part from the opposite direction. The monsoon we are heading into, for example, blows across the Indian Ocean from the southwest from the latter part of May to the middle of September, and from the northeast from about the middle of October to the middle of December. Coming from the southwest, since this is August, it will strike us thus." He arranged an ash tray and a half-dozen matches in a pattern on the black marble top of the bar table. "Assuming the ash tray is our ship and these matches are the wind—here." He moved the matches across the table until they touched the ash tray. "You see? A slow, steady, monotonous wind and nothing more. The ship will roll a bit, and I daresay we'll all be jolly uncomfortable for a while until we get used to it, but you needn't worry, really. I've been in it a dozen times or more and so has my mother, and I know. It won't do any of us a tuppence-worth of harm, as the fellow says."

Toward the end of the third day, when Mr. Madgwick's popularity and his authority had been established, he explained about his beard. His mother's deafness had made it necessary for her to learn how to read lips. She was wonderful at it, he said, and could understand almost anyone, except cinema stars who specialized in rapid, lipless patter, but Mr. Madgwick's beard had proved a definite obstacle to their conversation. He hadn't wanted to shave it all off, because he had grown fond of it, so he had compromised by shaving only his mustache and a small area under his lower lip. It looked odd, he knew, but he had become accustomed to it, and, he added with a twinkle in his eye, he was afraid he was starting something of a fashion in Singapore. He had noticed two Dutch planters with similar beards in a club on Pasir Panjang Road before he left, and he was willing to wager a five-pound note against a sixpenny bit that there would be at least a dozen more like it by the time he got back.

The air of quiet authority in Mr. Madgwick's voice and manner when he spoke of the East led the other passengers to consult him about an anxiety almost as pressing as the monsoon: the two Chinese who were also passengers on board the

Baroda—should you treat them as social equals or should they be ignored?

If there had been a group of younger people among the passengers, the question would not have come up. But there were no young people. Even the six Americans were middle-aged. It was an uncomfortable problem to face, especially in the heat of the Arabian Sea in August, and several of the more stuffy English passengers announced that they were going to write to the line's head office in London at the first opportunity. It wasn't that they objected to having Chinese on board, but they did think it was a bloody outrage for the company to saddle the white passengers with the problem of how to treat them. After all, the two Chinese were travelling first class. Luckily, in this particular case, the two Chinese were sensible and, after Mr. Madgwick's authoritative assurance that it was perfectly all right, the problem had disappeared by the end of the third day out of Aden.

Every morning the two Chinese came up on deck together just as the Lascars were finishing their scrubbing, a full hour before any of the other passengers, including the six energetic Americans, were awake. The two Chinese, wearing expensive flannel slacks, silk sports shirts, and complicated leather sandals, would begin pacing the deck for exercise. They would take two of the large, juicy oranges that the Goanese stewards left for morning walkers in a basket near the companionway leading to the bridge. As they circled the vessel side by side, walking firmly but delicately, as though they were anxious not to disturb the other passengers, who were still asleep below them, they would peel their oranges, picking the strings fastidiously from each segment, and fling the skin and seeds overboard on the lee side so that the wind, of which there was as yet very little, would not carry the refuse back to the deck.

At first glance they looked alike, but only because they were both Chinese. Actually they were very dissimilar. Mr. Ton was tall and thin, with deep hollows under his high cheekbones, and his eyes, which were devoid of lashes, were mere slits. Mr. Wiu was short and plump. Both had strong, black, shiny hair clipped close at the temple. It was impossible to tell their ages, but they looked young—somewhere around thirty or thirty-five.

By the time they had walked a mile and a half, checking the distance against the sign on the capstan just under the bridge, near the basket of oranges, the other passengers would begin to come up on deck for their constitutionals before breakfast. Mr. Ton and Mr. Wiu would move closer to the wall, so that the white men and women could have the more desirable right of way against the rail. When they passed

19

the two Chinese, they would smile and say good morning, and Mr. Ton and Mr. Wiu, grinning delightedly and showing their strong, white, handsome teeth, would nod their heads and say good morning in reply. The other passengers never stopped to chat and never slowed or quickened their pace to catch up with the two Chinese so they all could walk side by side. Mr. Ton and Mr. Wiu always walked alone, clearly by their own choice, the other passengers were able to say with relief and with complete accuracy.

In the dining room Mr. Ton and Mr. Wiu sat together at one of the small tables for two against the wall. There were eight of these small tables, but the other seven were unoccupied, mainly because the few wisps of air that were caught by the tin scoops stuck in the portholes above these tables passed right over them and benefited only those people who sat at the large tables in the centre of the hot dining room. Mr. Madgwick, who sat with his mother and the six Americans at a centre table, assured the other passengers that this was perfectly all right. The Chinese were more accustomed to heat than white people, he said, and besides they preferred to be alone. This was undoubtedly true, people agreed. Mr. Ton and Mr. Wiu obviously had a good time. They ate together, with beautiful table manners, and watched the other diners with small, restrained smiles of pleasure.

After breakfast they sat side by side in deck chairs, reading. They would glance up every now and then from their books to nod politely to a passenger who, in passing them, had nodded first. After tiffin, which the six Americans stopped calling lunch on the second day, Mr. Ton and Mr. Wiu would disappear belowdecks for a nap. At three o'clock they would come up, fresh and clean, looking highly polished in more immaculate slacks and more elaborate sports shirts. They would walk slowly and carefully across the games deck, stopping behind the ping-pong table, the deck-tennis court, or the shuffleboard square to watch a game for several minutes before moving on. Occasionally, when a ball or a quoit went out of bounds, Mr. Wiu would retrieve it quickly and, in response to the short smile or nod or word of thanks from the middle-aged player, both Chinese would smile delightedly and bow with pleasure.

They always entered the bar together and they always took the narrow couch which stood under the thermometer, and seated only two. In this way they could be in the room with the other passengers without creating a situation. Everybody in the bar had the feeling that Mr. Ton and Mr. Wiu were not being ostracized and at the same time everybody was relieved of the danger of having consciously to

20

avoid sitting down with them. It was considered a bit of luck that the bar had this fortunate piece of furniture.

At night, when there was dancing on the upper deck, the two Chinese would appear together, impeccably dressed in white mess jackets, and stand against the rail, smiling with appreciation as their eyes watched the sedate dancers. They always retired just before the dancing broke up, so that nobody would be embarrassed by the necessity for not including them in the groups that were going off to have a nightcap. All in all, it was very well done, and more than one passenger said, somewhat pompously, perhaps, that Mr. Ton and Mr. Wiu deserved a good deal of credit for the discreet and sensible manner in which they were handling a situation that could very easily have been unpleasant.

In the middle of the fourth day, the monsoon struck the *Baroda,* as Mr. Madgwick had predicted, and, precisely as he had said, nobody was much the worse for it. The ship rolled a little more, and two of the six Americans didn't eat as much dinner as usual, but that was about all. By morning of the sixth day everybody was accustomed to it.

That afternoon, just before tea, the ship took a deep roll. A marble table in the bar broke loose from its fastenings, slithered across the polished floor, and struck the couch on which the two Chinese were sitting. Mr. Wiu's legs were caught between the table and the couch and his ankle was broken.

Mr. Wiu was terribly embarrassed by the excitement this accident caused. He smiled at the circle of sympathetic passengers, his watery, protruding eyes filling with tears of gratitude and remorse, while the doctor examined him. Finally the doctor straightened up and said it was nothing serious. A simple fracture. The bone had not been completely severed. He would put the ankle into splints and Mr. Wiu would have to remain in bed for the rest of the trip. Nothing to worry about. His ankle would be as good as new two weeks after he landed at Colombo. Mr. Ton smiled and nodded his thanks to the other passengers for their kindness and sympathy to Mr. Wiu as he and the doctor and three stewards carried the helpless, apologetic little man out of the bar and down to his cabin.

Neither Mr. Ton nor Mr. Wiu showed up on deck for the rest of the trip.

The first night after the accident several passengers asked the doctor how the injured Chinese was feeling, and he said irritably that he'd told them once there was nothing seriously wrong with Mr. Wiu's ankle. He had bound it in splints, the Chinese was in bed resting comfortably, and there was Mr. Ton to take care of his wants, which, they should have known by this time, were simple and few. Within forty-eight hours everybody had forgotten all about the two Chinese.

On the fourth day after the accident, Mr. Madgwick took two of the Americans, whose names were Gerard and Winter, down to B Deck. He wanted to show them the engine room, which he knew intimately, this being his sixth voyage on the *Baroda*. They were walking forward, through a section of the vessel that was unoccupied because there were so few passengers on this trip, toward the companionway that led down into the bowels of the ship, when they heard a faint cry. They stopped and stared at one another. The cry was repeated, feeble, croaking.

"It's back this way," Gerard said. "One of these cabins on the right."

The three men turned and retraced their steps. Once more the sound came. The three men stopped, turned again, and ran back to Cabin 709, which they had just passed. Mr. Madgwick twisted the knob and pushed the door open. The three men stopped short in the doorway.

Mr. Wiu was lying half on his bed and half on the floor, clutching the side of the bunk and trying weakly to raise himself. Both his legs stuck out straight and stiff behind him. His pajamas and the sheets of his bed were soiled. The odor in the room was dreadful. On a table beside the bunk, Mr. Wiu's water bottle was lying on its side, empty. A fruit basket was on the floor, also empty, in the middle of a small pile of curling orange skins and yellowing apple cores. Beside the bed were the splintered remains of a cup and teapot from the tray that had slipped from the table. Mr. Wiu's lips were parched and cracked, and there were little blobs of dried black saliva in the corners. His tongue, dry and thick and heavily coated, stuck far out of his mouth, as though the effort of calling for help had exhausted his control over it and he lacked the strength to pull it back into his head.

"Holy smoke!" Winter said in astonishment. "The poor guy's dying of thirst!"

They rushed into the room. Mr. Madgwick stripped the soiled, foul-smelling sheets from the bed and flung them into a corner of the cabin. The two Americans lifted Mr. Wiu gently into drinking position. The water revived Mr. Wiu at once. He clutched at the bottle, but Mr. Madgwick held it firmly and would allow him only a little at a time.

"It looks like nobody's been near this room since he broke his leg four days ago," Gerard said excitedly. "Where the hell is that sidekick of his, Mr. Ton?"

Winter stepped out into the corridor. "Mr. Ton!" he called. "Mr. Ton! Hey, Mr. Ton!" There was no answer. Winter came back into the room and bent over Mr. Wiu.

22

"Where's Mr. Ton?" he asked. The fat little Chinese shook his head weakly.

"These cabins are all unoccupied at this end," said Mr. Madgwick. "The ship is terribly understaffed at this season, and those lazy Goanese will only do so much." He looked down at Mr. Wiu. "Where's your friend? Where's Mr. Ton?" Mr. Wiu's puffy eyelids flicked up and down over his protruding eyes. He licked his lips slowly with his bloated tongue. "He can't talk," said Mr. Madgwick. "One of you chaps run up and fetch the doctor, will you? We'll find Mr. Ton later."

The two Americans hurried out. At the companionway they parted. Gerard went off to find the doctor, and Winter went forward to the purser's office and told him what they had discovered.

"We couldn't find Mr. Ton anywhere," Winter said, talking rapidly. "He wasn't in their cabin, and even though I yelled my head off in the corridor, he didn't show up. Nobody showed up. Not even a steward. That part of the ship seems deserted. Do you know where we can find him? Nobody's seen Mr. Ton since four days ago, when Mr. Wiu's leg was broken."

"You might try his cabin," the purser said.

"I just told you we were in there," Mr. Winter said impatiently. "He wasn't anywhere around. We yelled for him and —oh." Mr. Winter looked at the purser in surprise. "You mean they're not—?"

"No, of course not. Mr. Wiu is in 709 on B Deck. And Mr. Ton is in—let me see." The purser flipped the pages of a loose-leaf notebook. "Mr. Ton is in 550 on A Deck."

"Oh, I see," Mr. Winter said. "I thought they were both— we all thought they were—I mean, because of the way they were always together, coming up on deck together and going down together, we all thought—"

He stopped talking, as though he could not find words to express the simple thought that had never occurred to him or to any of the other passengers.

"We'd better take a look at the injured one and then have a go at finding his friend," the purser said briskly. "Come along."

On the way down to B Deck, the purser told Winter that Mr. Ton was a research chemist who had recently completed some work in the States at Johns Hopkins and was now on his way to a post in Shanghai. Mr. Wiu was an insurance agent who had been visiting the central office of his firm in London and was now returning to his own office and home in Hong Kong. When the purser and Winter reached Mr. Wiu's cabin, they found the doctor in the middle of a crowd of excited, puzzled, indignant passengers. The purser pushed his way through to the bed on which Mr. Wiu was lying comfort-

23

ably, his round, fat face creased in a smile of apology for this new disturbance he had created.

"He's all right," the doctor said to the purser. "He can't talk yet, but he will in a short while. I've given him some broth and some water. It's my fault, I suppose," he said, scowling. "I should have looked in on him, but it's been so beastly hot and it seemed such a minor injury. You see what happened." He turned to the passengers, as though he were seeking justification for his neglect. "In addition to his broken ankle, he apparently received a severe blow at the base of the spine when the table flung him against the back of the couch. Must have caused a hemorrhage in the spinal canal. The bleeding brings pressure to bear on the nerves leading to the legs and causes paralysis. Temporary, of course. Lasts several weeks, perhaps. What's known technically as paraplegia." He seemed to take comfort in the sound of the word. "Very rare, you know. There are no immediate symptoms. It occurs twelve to twenty-four hours after the blow. I never dreamed it might happen in this case. Very rare. Very rare indeed." The passengers nodded and looked at Mr. Wiu on the bed. The doctor turned to the purser. "I had no way of knowing, you see. Besides, I assumed his friend was taking care of him and would let me know if anything was wrong. Damned rotten, deserting his pal like this without letting anybody know. The poor beggar might have been done in if Mr. Madgwick hadn't happened along. Where the devil *is* Ton, anyway? Nobody seems to have seen him since—"

The purser was pushing his way through the crowd to the door. Mr. Madgwick, plucking nervously at his beard, followed. They reached the corridor and hurried up the companionway to A Deck. In front of Cabin 550 they stopped and the purser tapped on the door.

"Yes?" Mr. Ton's voice said. "Come in."

As the purser pushed open the door, Winter and Gerard and perhaps a dozen more excited passengers came hurrying down the corridor and crowded in behind them. Mr. Ton was sitting at his writing table, wearing a silk dressing gown, looking very clean and bright as he ate lunch from a tray and read a book that was propped up on a tumbler of water. He folded his napkin neatly, dropped it on the tray, and stood up to face the crowd in the doorway. Before the purser could speak, Mr. Madgwick pushed forward.

"Look here," he said petulantly, tumbling his words out with indiscriminate haste, not at all like a man accustomed to precise diction. "We've just found your friend Mr. Wiu in a terrible state. Nobody's been near him since he broke his ankle. He hasn't had food or water for almost four days. The poor man might have died."

24

"I am so sorry," Mr. Ton said politely. "That is too bad. But I fail to see how that is my responsibility, which I assume you think it is from the tone of your voice."

The passengers behind Mr. Madgwick gasped.

"You fail to see how— But he's a friend of yours! The two of you are—"

"A friend of mine?" Mr. Ton raised one eyebrow disdainfully. "That stupid, fat, ignorant insurance salesman? I never set eyes on him before I boarded this ship."

For the first time since the *Baroda* had left Aden, Mr. Madgwick was at a loss. He scratched his beard perplexedly and looked behind him at the purser, at the Americans, at the other passengers. Nobody seemed to know what to do or say. Mr. Madgwick turned back to the Chinese, and his full, red, almost girlish lips parted and closed several times, quickly, as he hunted for words.

"If you don't mind," Mr. Ton said with a small, icy, polite bow of dismissal, "I should very much like to finish my lunch."

AN EASY ONE

"What's the capital of Louisiana?" the boy asked.

"Louisiana?" his mother said. "Let's see, now. New Orleans?"

"No," the boy said, laughing. "Baton Rouge."

"Why, of course," his mother said, laughing with him. "Baton Rouge. Go ahead. Ask me more."

"All right. What's the capital of Illinois?"

"Chicago," the mother said promptly.

"No," the boy cried, squealing with delight. "Springfield. Everybody makes that mistake. Everybody says Chicago."

"Oh, dear, that's true," the mother said with a hint of annoyance in her voice. "Springfield. What else?"

"I better give you an easy one. What's the capital of Florida?"

"Oh, I know that," the mother said. "Tallahassee."

"That's right. But that's an easy one. What's the capital of —wait." The boy looked up at the ceiling of the car. "I know! What's the capital of Washington?"

"Seattle."

"No, it isn't! It's Olympia!"

The boy clasped his hands gleefully between his knees and bent over to enjoy his laughter. His mother smiled, her face a mixture of pride and mild irritation, as she put out her hand protectingly to prevent him from toppling out of his chair. The roadbed was not particularly smooth and the train rocked and jounced so hard that all the furniture in the lounge car rattled. It made the lamps shake and caused the lights streaking by in the night outside to shiver wildly. The boy straightened up, his face split wide in a happy grin, and the mother took her hand away.

"I better ask you another easy one," he said. "What's the capital of Maryland?"

"Sh-h-h," his mother said, still smiling, but with a trace of sharpness. "Not so loud, David dear. You'll disturb the other people in the car."

She glanced about with an expression of apprehension that was delicate and yet at the same time curiously exaggerated. There were three men in the car, sitting widely spaced. They were smoking and holding magazines bound in leather covers on which the name of the publication was printed in small gold letters. The three men were not reading, because the boy was talking so loudly that their attention was practically forced in his direction. They watched with small, genial smiles. It was almost a very pleasant sight, and it was difficult to say why it was not utterly charming.

The boy, who appeared to be about nine or ten years old, though small for his age, was dressed as if he were younger. He wore a blue cheviot suit with short trousers that left his knees bare. A stiff white Eton collar spread out on his narrow shoulders and was pulled snugly about his throat with a dull-red tie on which the crest and the initials of a private school were embroidered in yellow silk. His blond hair, a shade or two darker than his mother's, had obviously been combed just before dinner. It was still damp, but the forelock, which had dried more quickly than the rest, was tousled. His legs, which did not quite touch the floor of the car, swung back and forth happily. He seemed completely unaware of the three men in the car.

His mother, however, knew they were watching. She was young and pretty, at least from a distance of several feet, at which the little, hard lines at the corners of her mouth were invisible. She wore long, black, artificial eyelashes, and when she laughed she threw back her head so her beautiful white teeth showed clearly and the tip of her conical, saucy hat brushed the window behind her. She wore a silver-fox cape and a tweed suit with a tight skirt. Her handsome legs were crossed at the ankles, one high-heeled shoe locked behind the other, and she maintained her balance in the shaking chair with one toe pressed firmly into the dull-green carpet. She gave the three men in the car a little self-conscious smile that was supposed to convey embarrassed apology, and almost did. The boy saw the smile and looked apprehensively toward the men. His mother opened her large, square, black suède purse, took out a cigarette, and struck a match.

"Just a little more softly, David, please, dear," she said as she blew a neat stream of smoke up at the ceiling. "You mustn't disturb the other people."

"Yes, Mother," the boy said in a low voice. "I'm sorry." Then, grinning again and louder than ever, he asked, "What's the capital of California?"

"Oh, dear, let me see now. Los Angeles? No, no—wait. Wait, I have it. San Francisco!"

"No!" the boy squealed. "Sacramento!"

He had forgotten the men entirely and, clasping his hands between his knees with delight, let his laughter rock him in the chair. His mother laughed too, much more moderately, and glanced around the car. Two of the men smiled and then, embarrassed, buried their heads in their magazines. The third man, who was sitting obliquely across the car about ten feet away, laughed out loud. He looked at the mother and their eyes met.

"He's—uh—he's quite a boy," the man said experimentally. "Isn't he?"

"Yeh-hess," the mother said, laughing through the word as she broke it into two syllables. "But I'm afraid he's disturbing everybody, showing off his geography this way."

"Not at all," the man said, squirming into a more comfortable position in his chair and dropping the leather-covered magazine flat on his lap. "It's a pleasure to listen to him."

The boy pretended he didn't hear them. He scowled at the flickering lights that whisked by in the night outside, as though he were thinking hard, but out of the corners of his eyes he was watching the man who had spoken to his mother.

"All right," the child said suddenly, his voice pitched high to attract his mother's attention. "I have one. I have one. An easy one this time. What's the capital of Nevada?"

His mother looked down at him. She took a few seconds to concentrate, doing it very prettily, one forefinger poking a dimple in her cheek.

"What's the capital of—" she began. "Oh, yes. Nevada. The capital of Nevada. Reno?"

"No," the boy giggled. "Carson City."

"Oh, now, David, that's not fair," she said sharply, pouting through a cloud of cigarette smoke. "You're studying them in school now and I haven't been in school in years." She

27

smiled across the boy's head at the man. "You shouldn't ask such hard ones," she said, softening her voice to a prettily maternal tone of mild reproof and fanning her long, dark eyelashes up and down. "It's been years since Mother studied the capitals, you know."

The man who had dropped his magazine now threw back his head and laughed boldly, a series of short, hacking bellows. He hesitated for a moment, and looked down the car speculatively. Then he stood up, tossed the magazine onto his chair, and walked over to the mother and the boy. He was a tall, clean-looking man with a slightly flushed face and smooth black hair parted in the middle. He hiked up the trousers of his tweed suit at the knees and stooped down in front of the boy until their heads were at the same level.

"Suppose I ask you one or two capitals, son," he said in a deep, throaty voice. He smiled questioningly at the mother, as though he were feeling his way in unknown terrain, and said, "May I?" She smiled back, fanning her eyelashes again, and nodded. The man grinned quickly and turned back to the boy. "What's the capital of New Hampshire, son?" His voice sounded confident, even faintly triumphant. The boy didn't answer. His little legs stopped swinging and he drew back slightly in the chair. "Don't be frightened, son," the man said cheerfully. "Your mother said I could ask you. What's the capital of New Hampshire?"

The boy didn't answer. He turned to look at his mother, his small face pinched with sudden anger at this interloper who was breaking in on their game. His mother was watching the man.

"Go on, David," she urged. "Tell the nice gentleman what's the capital of New Hampshire."

The boy blinked at her in silence and his grip on the arms of the chair tightened.

"Sure, come on," the man coaxed. "Be a good fella, David. Tell me. What's the capital of New Hampshire? You know it. That's an easy one. What's the capital of New Hampshire?"

"I don't know," the boy said shortly.

"Why, David!" his mother said. "What nonsense!"

"Come on," the man coaxed. "What's the capital of New Hampshire?"

"I don't know," the boy said sullenly. "I told you I don't know."

The speeding train took a curve without slowing down, and the man, poised on the balls of his feet like a catcher in back of home plate, was thrown off balance.

"Woops!" the man said as he lurched to one side. The mother said "Oh!" and put out her hand to prevent him from

28

falling. He caught himself on the edge of the empty chair next to hers and, with the same movement, heaved himself into it. The woman was now sitting in the middle, between her small son and the big, clean-looking man. "Boy!" the man said, laughing. "That was close, wasn't it?"

"I'm so sorry," the mother said. "You might have—"

"Nothing at all," the man said, laughing more loudly. "But that calls for a drink. Will you join me?"

"Why, yes," she said, with a small expression of surprised delight. "Thank you so much."

The man reached behind him and pressed a buzzer. When the porter came, the man looked inquiringly at the woman.

"Scotch-and-soda?" he asked. The woman nodded. "Two," he said to the porter. Then he leaned across the woman, placing his hand on the arm of her chair, and spoke to the boy. "What about you, David?" he said jovially. "A lemonade?"

The boy didn't answer. His chin was sunk so hard into his stiff white Eton collar that it seemed to be cutting deeply into the flesh of his neck.

"David," his mother said in a voice that contained enough sudden irritation to cause the boy to jump slightly. "The gentleman is talking to you!"

"No," the boy said in a gruff voice.

"No, what?" his mother asked sharply.

"No, thank you," he said, scowling.

"David doesn't seem to want to play any more, does he?" the man said affably, still leaning forward so his head was directly in front of the woman, almost touching her silver-fox cape. "He won't tell me the capital of New Hampshire and he won't have a lemonade."

"Yes, he is acting sullen, isn't he?" the woman said carelessly. "I can't understand what's got into him."

The train lurched again and the man's head swung with it. His cheek brushed the woman's silver-fox cape. He sat up quickly and looked frightened, as though he had destroyed by unnecessary haste a small and fragile edifice that had taken much time and patience to build.

"Sorry," he said.

"Quite all right," the woman said, smiling easily. The frightened look disappeared from the man's face. A slow, steady, confident grin took its place. The boy's lower lip started to quiver. He sank his upper teeth into the flesh to hold it steady. "This roadbed is rather rough, isn't it?" the woman said.

"Terrible," the man said. He turned to the waiting porter. "Two scotch-and-sodas, please."

"Yes, suh," the porter said. He bowed and went away. The man and the woman turned toward each other and began to chat animatedly. She told him she was a widow, that she lived in New York, that she had taken her son out of school for a short visit to her mother in Salt Lake City, that they were now on their way back to New York. The man smiled at her as she talked, looking straight into her face, nodding his head to the rhythm of her words, and crossing and uncrossing his legs many times. When she finished he cleared his throat and told her he was in the oil business, that he lived in Chicago, that he made frequent business trips to New York, that he usually flew but had missed his plane and had taken the train instead, that this was the first time he had ever been glad he had missed a plane. They both laughed at this, quite hard, as if it were something that got funnier and funnier the more they thought about it. The boy watched them in silence, his lower lip still clamped in his teeth, his small hands gripping hard at the arms of the shaking chair, his eyes pinched with something that might have been resignation but had enough tenseness in it to look like fright, as though he were poised for a blow that he knew he could not dodge. The porter came back with the drinks, his shining black face broken into a neutral smile as he swayed his way expertly through the car, keeping the glasses level on the small tray in spite of the jarring of the train.

"There we are," the man said, uncrossing his legs and turning away from the woman toward the porter. "That looks good, doesn't it?"

"It certainly does," she said.

The porter pulled over a large smoking stand with a wide metal pan surrounding the ash tray in the middle. The woman crushed out her cigarette while the porter set the glasses down on the metal pan. They rattled noisily with the movement of the train. While the man hunted in his pocket for money, the porter stood with his hands clasped behind him, smiling good-naturedly at the silent boy.

"Did you say a lemonade for the boy, suh?" he asked politely. "Ah wasn't sure—"

"Why, yes," the man said, as though he had suddenly remembered something. "I wanted him to have one. What do you say, David? A lemonade?"

The boy didn't answer.

"The cat seems to have gotten his tongue," the woman said through a scowl of exasperation. "He doesn't seem to know how to talk any more. David, the gentleman asked you a question!"

"I don't want any," the boy said rudely. "I don't want his old lemonade."

The man seemed startled by the boy's vehemence. The mother's face contracted into an expression of anger that brought out the deep, hard creases at the corners of her mouth. The porter saw what was about to happen and spoke before the mother could.

"Ah heard him say the capitals of all those states," he said in a friendly, helpful voice. "Ah wonder if he knows the capital of mah state, Alabama?"

"Sure he does," the man said heartily as he handed the money to the porter. "That's an easy one. What's the capital of Alabama, David?"

"I don't know," the boy muttered.

He stared with hatred straight at the man. His little back was arched stiffly.

"Now, David, you stop this nonsense at once," his mother said sharply. "You do know. You've been asked a question and I want you to answer. What's the capital of Alabama?"

The boy's head jerked around until he was staring directly at his mother. But he did not speak.

"David!" his mother snapped. "I told you to—"

"Ah guess he's tahd," the porter said apologetically. He seemed terribly embarrassed by the curiously tense situation his innocent question had created. "Ah guess he's—"

"He is *not* tired," the woman said angrily. "He's just being sullen for some ridiculous reason. David, you answer, do you hear? What is the capital of Alabama?"

The boy's lower lip quivered noticeably in spite of the grip he had on it with his teeth. Still he did not speak.

"Let's forget it," the man said, no longer making any pretense of geniality. He was definitely annoyed. He picked up his drink and took a long pull.

"Very well," the woman said grimly. "If you're going to act like that, David, you can't stay here." She turned to the porter. "Will you please take him to our section and see that he goes to bed at once?"

"Yes, Ma'am," the porter said. He was not smiling now. He looked vaguely frightened. "Yes, Ma'am."

"Go ahead, David," the woman ordered sharply. "Go to bed at once."

The boy's rigid body relaxed, as though the blow against which he had been steeling himself had finally landed. He slipped off the chair, the jacket of his blue cheviot suit bunching up around his hips and his short pants sliding up and away from his naked knees. He put his little hand in the porter's outstretched big one. For a moment he stood there, staring at his mother. There was no longer any doubt about the look on his small, pale face. As the woman picked up her drink and smilingly touched glasses with the big, pink-faced man, the boy looked at her with eyes in which resigned despair and blind terror were evenly mixed. The porter led him

31

through the lounge car, steadying him against the sway of the pounding train. Behind them the man and the woman were laughing and talking and clinking the ice in their glasses. At the end of the car the porter pulled open the heavy metal door. He leaned over the boy solicitously to help him across the threshold.

"Ah'm surprised at you," he said in a soft, gentle, chiding voice. "A smaht boy lahk you not knowing the capital of Alabama."

The boy's teeth came away from his lower lip. He screwed his face into a tight scowl to prevent it from quivering and looked down at the floor of the car.

"Sure I know," he said in a listless, uneven voice that was almost a whisper. "It's Montgomery."

EXAMINATION

"The doctor will be here very soon," the nurse-receptionist said. "In just a few minutes."

Wayne looked at his wristwatch, which showed twenty-eight minutes after seven. "But he told me on the phone yesterday—he said seven-thirty!"

"I know." The receptionist smiled peculiarly and for a moment Wayne thought she was going to scream. Then he saw that her smile was intended to cover a yawn. "Dr. Manck called me a little while ago and said he knew about the appointment with you. He didn't forget, but he got delayed. He asked you to please wait. He won't be very late, he said." The smile won out over the yawn and she looked more cheerful as she blinked away a faint film of tears. "Will you have a seat, please?"

"Thanks."

Wayne stepped out of the small foyer, in which her desk stood, into the empty waiting room and sat down in one of the overstuffed chairs. As soon as he took the weight off his feet he felt the tiredness in his knees that told him he had been up too late the night before. The receptionist picked up her fountain pen and dipped her head into the circle of yellow light from the desk lamp. She suppressed a new yawn delicately, with her fingertips against her lips. Wayne caught the yawn from her. He turned in the chair to look out the window at the early-morning grayness of Seventy-third Street and the small

32

wedge of Central Park visible at the end of the block. Then he turned back to the room, glanced at the prints on the walls, and picked up a magazine from the small table near his elbow. The receptionist rose from her chair, but Wayne reached up over his head and switched on the lamp himself. The receptionist smiled as she sank back and he smiled, too.

"I guess I ought to apologize," he said, "making you come down to the office so early."

"That's all right, Mr. Wade. I come—"

"Wayne."

"I'm sorry. '*N, e*'?"

"That's right."

"Mr. *Wayne*. I come in early like this quite often. Dr. Manck has a great many patients with important government jobs—war positions, you know. They're always going down to Washington these days or rushing off to catch planes and things, so they have to come early."

"Really?" Wayne said, losing part of the feeling of importance the early-morning appointment had given him. He glanced at his wristwatch again: twenty-five minutes to eight. "How prompt a man is Dr. Manck?"

"Oh, he's *very* prompt," the receptionist said. She looked down at her wristwatch. "A few minutes perhaps this morning, but no more."

Wayne nodded and opened the magazine. His regular doctor, Harry Holdridge, was a friend of his. Harry would have seen him in the evening or on Sunday, when Wayne wasn't so rushed for time. Or he might even have filled in the form and signed it without going through the formality of a physical examination. They had been friends since childhood and he knew that Wayne was in excellent physical shape. But Harry was somewhere in the Pacific now. He had a commission in the Navy, and Wayne had made this appointment with Dr. Manck, whom he had never seen, because Harry Holdridge had turned his practice over to Dr. Manck when he left. As Wayne read, he kept touching the top of his head, where the hair was getting thin.

"That window bothering you?" the receptionist said. "If it's a draft I could close it."

Wayne glanced up from the magazine. "What?" He saw the receptionist looking at the window beside his chair. It was raised two or three inches. "Oh," he said, "no. No, thanks." He dropped his hand hastily from the top of his head. "It's perfectly all right."

"I always like to open it a little in the morning. It's so sort of stuffy when you come in early like this."

"Sure," Wayne said, looking at his wristwatch pointedly. It was now a quarter to eight. He was due at the Army Air

33

Forces Intelligence office at nine. Unless Dr. Manck showed up soon, there wouldn't be enough time for a physical examination, he'd have to leave, and the whole point of this early-morning appointment would be wasted. "The window doesn't bother me. But I'm worried about——"

"He'll be here any minute now," the receptionist said. "Dr. Manck is very prompt."

At eight o'clock the door opened with a bang, and a tall young man in a shapeless blue overcoat came in.

"Hi, Miss Perrin," he said cheerfully. He took off the coat, tossed his hat onto her desk, and looked across her shoulder at the mail in front of her, all in a single complicated whirl of activity. "What's new?"

"Good morning, Dr. Manck," she said, and then, nodding toward the waiting room, "Mr. Wayne is here."

Dr. Manck grinned and beckoned to Wayne with his hand. "Sorry to keep you waiting, Wayne. I had to drop over to the hospital. Hurry call. Come on in and we'll have you out of here in no time." He pulled open the door to the examination room at the other side of the foyer, and, as Wayne reached him, stuck out his hand. Wayne took it. "Glad to know you," Dr. Manck said, kicking the door of the examination room shut behind him. "Sit down. Make yourself comfortable." He slipped out of his jacket and took down a white coat from a hook on the door. "Had a letter from Harry yesterday."

"You did?" Wayne said. "From where?"

"Postmarked San Diego," Dr. Manck said, punching his arms into the sleeves of the white coat. "Didn't say much. He's not allowed to. Just he's going to sea soon and he expected to be seeing action in a little while and he'd write if he could, but not to expect much mail, and I should take care of his patients," Dr. Manck laughed. "Great guy, Harry."

"He certainly is. Swell guy."

Wayne, who was twenty-nine, the same age as Harry Holdridge, was surprised to see that Dr. Manck was also about that old. He didn't know why, but when Harry had told him he was turning his practice over to Dr. Manck, Wayne has assumed that Manck was an older man. It was the phrase "turning over," he supposed, which sounded like something out of a bad but well-intended war poem—turning over the reins of the home front to age while youth went off to battle. Dr. Manck, with his boyishly cheerful face, his loose-limbed stride, and his unruly crop of thick blond hair, looked even younger than Wayne. "O.K.," he said as he hauled the white coat, stiff with laundry starch, down in back. "Where does it hurt?"

"No, no. There's nothing wrong with me," Wayne said. He pulled a folded sheet of paper out of his breast pocket. "It's just I have to get this thing signed by a doctor, saying I'm in good physical shape."

"Oh," Dr. Manck said. He stopped grinning, took the paper, and scowled at it for several moments, longer than was necessary to learn what it was. "What's this for?"

"Air Forces," Wayne said. "I don't come under the regular Army rules. Army doctors, and all that, because it's something special."

"How do you mean, special?"

"I'm not supposed to talk about it," Wayne said apologetically. "I'm going abroad for them on a special thing and they want me to—"

"Going to one of the fighting fronts?"

"I don't want to sound important," Wayne said with embarrassment, because it *did* sound important. "But no kidding, I'm not supposed to talk about it."

"Spy stuff, eh?" Dr. Manck gave a curious little laugh that caused Wayne to look at him in surprise.

"My God, no. It's just that they, well, they—" Wayne stopped. "I'm not supposed to talk about it," he said helplessly. "They instructed me not to."

"All right," Dr. Manck said. "Take your clothes off." He bent over a small basin, turned on the tap, and started to wash his hands. Wayne took off his coat, loosened his tie, and unbuttoned his shirt. "Take them all off," Dr. Manck said, glancing at him over his shoulder. "Strip."

"All of them?" Wayne said, his voice rising. "Everything?"

"The blank calls for a complete physical examination."

"But I'm all right. I'm in good shape. I don't need—"

"That's what I'm supposed to attest to," Dr. Manck said. He snatched a small towel from a pile on the glass shelf over the sink. "Take off everything."

"I mean you've got my records from Harry's office, haven't you?" Wayne said. "He used to check me over regularly. He gave me a complete physical only a couple of months ago, before he got his commission. I don't think you have to—"

"If you want me to sign that blank, Wayne, I'll have to give you the complete physical examination it calls for," Dr. Manck said curtly. "Dr. Holdridge's records are Dr. Holdridge's records, not mine. He's not signing this blank. I am. Shoes, too, please."

Wayne took off all his clothes, piled them neatly on a white enamelled chair, and turned back, naked, to face Dr. Manck. "O.K.?" he said with a hint of sarcasm in his voice. "This all right?"

"Your wristwatch, too," Dr. Manck said dryly. "And lie down on the table, please." Wayne took off his wristwatch and climbed up on the padded examination table. Dr. Manck

35

put the Air Forces blank on top of a white metal cabinet next to the sterilizing machine and pulled a silver pencil from his vest pocket. "I'll fill these things in lightly in pencil as we go and then Miss Perrin can type over my pencil notations later and I'll sign."

"That'll be fine."

"We'll see," Dr. Manck said, making no effort to conceal his own sarcasm. He wound the band of the blood-pressure meter around Wayne's arm. "Drink much?"

"Not very. Just a—"

"I've heard that before," Dr. Manck said, watching the gauge as he pumped the bulb. The air hissed slowly out of the band. "Lot of you young guys who say you don't drink much are just one step away from apoplexy." He pumped up the band again, pressing the bulb gently, and looked at the gauge as the air escaped. Then he removed the band from Wayne's arm and stepped over to the white cabinet to make a note on the blank with his silver pencil.

"How's my blood pressure?" Wayne asked from the examination table. "High? Low?"

"It's all right," Dr. Manck said. He sounded disappointed. "Sit up, please." Wayne sat up. Dr. Manck placed a stethoscope against his chest and listened intently. "Cough, please." Wayne coughed. "Breathe deeply." Wayne breathed deeply. "Slowly, now, please." Wayne breathed slowly. "All right. That's enough."

Dr. Manck stepped over to the white cabinet again and frowned as he made a note on the blank.

"How's the heart?" Wayne asked. "Hear any loose bearings?"

"You needn't get cocky. We'll find something wrong. All you guys who come in and tell doctors you're in fine shape, there's nothing wrong with you, you're in wonderful physical—stay on the table, please. Lie back."

Wayne dropped back on the examination table. He had an odd feeling of mixed anxiety and elation. The physical examination, which he had resented because he felt it was unnecessary and because he was in a hurry, had turned into a contest between him and Dr. Manck. Wayne felt the way he used to feel in high school when, as sophomore swimming champion, he was about to swim against a boy he knew he could beat. He felt excited because he was on the threshold of another victory and yet slightly worried because, until the race was over, there was always the chance that he would lose.

"The teeth are all right," he said. "I wound up with the dentist yesterday."

"I'll look for myself, if you don't mind," Dr. Manck said. "Open, please."

As each item on the blank was filled in, Wayne's spirits rose higher and the look of annoyance on Dr. Manck's face grew deeper. Wayne had a moment of doubt when Dr. Manck wet the soles of his feet to take an impression of his footprints; he didn't remember ever having been tested for flat feet, but apparently they were all right, too, because Dr. Manck made the note on the blank with a small, angry flourish. Finally, when Wayne was standing on the scales and Manck was adjusting the crossbar on his head to measure his height, the young doctor's face broke into a smile.

"All right," he said. "You can get dressed now."

"What's so funny?" Wayne asked cheerfully as he pulled on his clothes. "Find I've got cancer or something?"

Dr. Manck's smile spread, but it wasn't friendly. There was a curiously deliberate expression on his face. He looked almost as though he were sighting a gun. He waited a moment, running his hand slowly through his own thick, blond hair, and then he said, "You're all right, but you haven't got very much on that scalp of yours, have you?"

With an effort, Wayne managed to check the involuntary movement of his hand to the top of his head, where the scalp showed. His fingers fumbled at the buttons of his shirt and he could feel his face grow hot. He finished dressing hurriedly, tied his shoelaces, knotted his tie, and buttoned his coat.

"If you'll give this to Miss Perrin on your way out—" Dr. Manck said, holding out the blank. "I've signed it at the bottom. She'll type in the entries I've made in pencil."

Wayne took the blank and went out.

Miss Perrin raised her head from the circle of yellow light thrown by the desk lamp and smiled. "Everything all right?"

"Yes, great," Wayne said. He explained about the pencilled notes and asked her to mail the blank to his home after she had finished typing them in. "Send my bill with it, too, will you please?"

"Oh, Dr. Manck doesn't bill his patients till the end of the month, Mr. Wayne. There's no rush."

"There might be," Wayne said sarcastically, reaching for the outer door. "A man with a perfect scalp, a head of hair like his—the Army'll be wanting him any minute now. I don't see how they could have passed him up so far and still expect to win the war."

Miss Perrin giggled as she rolled the blank into her typewriter. "Not him," she said. "Dr. Manck tried to enlist the same time as Dr. Holdridge. He has a bum heart."

"Oh," Wayne said with his hand on the knob. He glanced at the closed door of the examination room and had a sudden impulse to go back. He wanted to say something to Dr.

Manck—tell the poor guy that he was sorry. But there wasn't time. He saw by his wristwatch that it was a quarter to nine. If he took a taxi he could just make his appointment at the Air Forces Intelligence office.

"I'll tell you what," he said awkwardly as he pulled open the door. "There's no rush on that bill. Send it to me at the end of the month, when you send out the others, in the regular way."

A DIME A THROW

"It's not so bad, really," the woman in the dirndl said. "It might even be fun."

"You can stop trying to sell it to me," her husband said. "I'm here. Period."

They stood just inside the wooden gate near the parking lot and looked at the crowd. The fairgrounds were in a vacant field to the left of the state highway, less than a quarter of a mile from the little summer town of Inniggsville.

"There's no point in being sore. Losing your temper." The woman in the dirndl did not turn her head to look at her husband. She spoke through a small smile of eager interest as she stared at the colored lights and the moving people. But there was an edge to her voice. "It wouldn't have looked nice if we hadn't come. We're summer visitors. The natives would have noticed it."

"Leave out the Emily Post angle," the man said, also keeping his eyes on the fairgrounds as he spoke. "For my money, the natives know what they can do."

"As long as you're here you might try looking as though you enjoyed it."

"Don't count on it," the man said.

He lit a cigar and they walked into the crowd side by side. The fairgrounds were laid out in the form of a square. To the right and left of the entrance gate stretched two lines of tents and flimsy booths. At the far end, facing the entrance gate, a merry-go-round and a Ferris wheel made the fourth side of the square. The space enclosed was jammed with men, women, and children from the farms and summer places for miles around. Between their heads and the evening sky hung strings of colored lights, stretched across from booth to booth. Above the laughter and the shouting and the voices of the barkers the music from the merry-go-round banged away. The woman in the dirndl smiled every now and then at someone in the crowd. Once in a while her husband followed her smile with a short nod. They stopped in front of a booth where an old man with a sad face was playing checkers with all comers at five cents a game.

"Look at that," the woman said. "He's playing four, seven, nine, ten, eleven—he's playing eleven people at once!"

"I'm looking," the man said. "How long do we have to stay here?"

"For heaven's sake. We can't just come and run. It wouldn't look nice."

They walked on, past a Bingo game, a penny-pitching contest, and a tent in which you could win a carton of cigarettes or a sack of sugar by knocking down a pyramid of blocks with three baseballs. When they reached the shooting gallery, the man stopped short. He stood with his cigar poised in the air halfway to his mouth and watched. His wife glanced at him in surprise and then she smiled.

"Why don't you try a round?" she said. "You used to be able to snuff out the candles four out of—"

She stopped and turned to follow her husband's gaze. He was not watching the shooting gallery. He was looking beyond it at a booth in which blankets were being offered as prizes at ten cents a chance. The front of the booth was a counter covered with black oilcloth, which was blocked out into numbered squares. A wheel marked with the same numerals was fastened on the wall to the left of the counter. The players put their dimes on the numbered squares and the barker spun the wheel. At the top a little leather indicator rattled as the pins of the wheel whirled by, making a sound similar to that of a pencil being drawn swiftly along a picket fence. When the wheel stopped, the barker looked to see where the leather indicator had come to rest and called out the winning number.

"Step right up, folks," the barker chanted. "A dime a throw, folks. Win a one-hundred-per-cent pure-wool blanket for only ten cents. Come on, folks. Step right up. A dime a throw."

Directly in front of the counter, facing the barker across the black oilcloth, stood an old woman. She was short and fat and dirty, and the hem of her cheap gingham house dress was ragged. Her feet were stuck into a pair of shapeless men's shoes that had no laces or tongues. Her scraggly gray hair hung over her face and down the back of her neck. With her left hand she clutched to her bosom a patent-leather purse that was flaking away at the edges. With her right hand she kept pushing the hair out of her eyes. She watched the wheel, the numbered squares, and the barker with a tight, concentrated eagerness, as though she were trying to memorize his words. Her head shook and her lips quivered with the intensity of her effort.

"Isn't that Mrs. Ratchek?" the woman in the dirndl said. "And isn't that her granddaughter Marie?"

"Yes," her husband said, without turning his head. "I want to see this."

Next to the old woman stood a thin little girl in a faded dress that was even more ragged and dirty than her grandmother's. Her bare toes were curled rigidly into the flattened turf. She clutched the old woman's dress with one hand and moved her head in tiny jerks, watching the wheel, the barker, and her grandmother with wide, almost frightened eyes.

"Come on, folks," the barker sang. "Win a blanket for only a dime. Step right up and carry it away, folks. A pure-wool blanket. Only a dime a throw."

A small crowd had gathered behind the old woman and the little girl. The old woman took a dime from her purse, moving her hands very carefully, as though the coin were fragile, and peered down at the oilcloth counter. She hesitated, put the dime on a number, took it off, put it on another number, mumbled something to herself, shifted the dime again. She seemed to be in great agony. Finally she made her choice. As soon as she took her fingers away from the dime, her agitation increased. She couldn't seem to wait for the barker to spin the wheel. She looked up at him, her face a mixture of pleading and anger and suffering, and urged him with small, impatient gestures to start the game. The barker tried to coax more players to the oilcloth counter. He was not very successful. The crowd seemed more interested in the old woman and the little girl. At last three or four people came forward and put down their dimes. The barker's voice rose triumphantly, like that of an auctioneer who has received a higher bid after a long period of inactivity, but he couldn't pull any more players out of the crowd.

"O.K., folks," he said. "Here it goes."

He spun the wheel. Everybody watched. The old woman's head stopped quivering. The little girl's face froze solid. The leather indicator clicked busily. The wheel slowed down and stopped.

"Sixty-nine," the barker sang. "Anybody got sixty-nine?" He looked down at the numbered squares on the oilcloth counter. "Nope, nobody. Sorry, folks." He swept the few dimes together and dropped them into the pocket of his leather apron. "If all the numbers are covered, there's a winner every time. Come on, folks. Step right up. You may be the lucky one. Win a pure-wool blanket for only ten cents."

The old woman's body sagged. The little girl tugged at her

skirt, but the old lady opened the battered patent-leather purse, took out another dime, and began hunting for a number on the counter. The barker pretended not to see her. He looked over her head as he harangued the crowd. The desperation with which she was playing the game seemed to make him uncomfortable.

"My God," the woman in the dirndl whispered. "She can't afford this. We've all been giving her money for food. All the summer visitors. Only this morning I went out into the kitchen and saw Marie at the back door begging the cook to give her a—"

"Let it go," her husband said, without turning his head. "This is her own business."

"But she can't afford it! They're starving. They're practically public charges in Inniggsville. If it weren't for the food and the little money the summer visitors give them, why, they'd—"

"This is her own business. Period."

The woman in the dirndl bit her lip. Her husband drew steadily on his cigar. They watched Mrs. Ratchek repeat the same performance four more times. Each time she lost she seemed to grow more desperate, and the look on the little girl's face deepened to terror.

"The old girl must want that blanket pretty bad," someone in the crowd said. "She's been at it over an hour now."

Finally, after the woman in the dirndl and her husband had seen Mrs. Ratchek put down six dimes, a middle-aged man in a panama hat won a blanket.

"There it goes," the barker chanted, as he handed the blanket to the winner. "I told you so, folks. The more numbers are covered, the better chance of winning. If every number is covered, there's a winner every time. Come on, folks. Step up and win your blanket. A dime a throw."

Mrs. Ratchek and the little girl watched the man in the panama hat walk away with the blanket. There was no envy in their eyes. They just watched him. Then the old woman turned back, opened her battered purse, and clawed around in the bottom for a dime. The little girl tugged her grandmother's dress again, but Mrs. Ratchek shook her off.

"This is ridiculous," the woman in the dirndl said. "She can't afford this and she needs that money for food and—"

"I told you to let it go," her husband said. "This is her business."

His wife gave him an angry look, turned sharply, and hurried after the man in the panama hat. She stopped him and they talked for a few moments. The man in the panama hat seemed surprised and then embarrassed. Finally he nodded and handed over the blanket. The woman in the dirndl gave him some money and came back to the booth.

41

"Listen," her husband said. "I told you to stay out of this."

She paid no attention to him. She strode up to the old woman in front of the booth.

"Here, Mrs. Ratchek," she said. "Here's a blanket. You'll never win one that way. Take this and—"

The old woman peered at her through a scowl of annoyance, her hand still groping inside the patent-leather purse. Then she seemed to realize the meaning of the offer. The annoyance on her face turned to anger. She snatched the blanket and threw it on the ground.

"Get away from me," she said harshly. "Don't you go telling me what to do. Everybody always telling me what to do. You get away from me."

The woman in the dirndl stared at Mrs. Ratchek. She put her hand up to her cheek, as if it had been slapped, and her face grew red. The little girl released her grandmother and swooped down on the blanket.

"Grandma, look!" she cried in a high, excited voice. "We got the blanket! Grandma, look! We got the blanket!"

Mrs. Ratchek turned angrily and slapped the blanket from the little girl's hand.

"You leave me be," she snarled. "All of you. Always telling me what to do. You leave me alone."

The little girl started to cry. The barker sucked his teeth and looked uncomfortable. The crowd was so silent that the music from the merry-go-round in the distance seemed to blare out with a tremendous roar. The woman in the dirndl caught her breath in a gasp, turned on her heel, and hurried away. Her husband dropped his cigar and followed.

"I told you not to mess in there," he said quietly, almost gently. "It's her business."

His wife looked at him once out of the corner of her eye, but did not answer. She continued to push her way through the crowd. He walked along after her. When they reached the booth where the old man with the sad face was playing checkers, the woman in the dirndl stopped, opened her purse, and examined her face in a pocket mirror. She did a few small things to it with lipstick and powder. Her husband lit a fresh cigar.

"What do you say?" he said. "Go?"

"No," she said, and she snapped the compact shut. "The natives would talk."

He examined the end of his cigar to make sure it was burning evenly, then followed his wife. They walked slowly past the Bingo game, the penny-pitching contest, and the booth where you could win a sack of sugar by knocking down a pyramid of blocks with three baseballs. At the far end of the fairgrounds, near the merry-go-round, a small crowd had gathered. The woman in the dirndl and her husband stopped to look.

"Well!" she said in a startled voice. "Did you ever?"

In the middle of the crowd stood Mrs. Ratchek. The little girl with the wide eyes was still clutching her grandmother's dress. Mrs. Ratchek was holding the blanket she had hurled to the ground twice a few minutes before.

"Feel it," Mrs. Ratchek said in a proud, excited voice. "Feel how soft it is. A hundred-per-cent pure wool. It's worth ten dollars easy. Maybe more. And I won it with only sixty cents. Honest. The sixth dime." Her hands quivered with her happiness. Her head shook. "Feel it," she said. "Feel how soft it is. And I won it for only sixty cents."

The people in the crowd felt the blanket good-naturedly and congratulated the old lady. Some of them stroked the little girl's head.

"After insulting me like that," the woman in the dirndl said. "In front of all those people."

Her lips grew thin and she took a step forward toward the crowd. Her husband jammed the cigar into his mouth and grabbed her wrist.

"Let it go," he said in a low voice. "Just let her alone."

His wife looked at him in the same way she had looked at Mrs. Ratchek earlier in the evening, as though her face had been slapped. Then her eyes dropped to his hand on her wrist.

"She insulted me in front of all those people!" she said, her voice rising uncontrollably. "She's lying to them and saying she won the—"

"Never mind," her husband said quietly, like a teacher explaining to a child a problem he knew it could not possibly grasp. "Just let her alone."

"But why? Why? She's telling them she—"

"I said never mind," her husband said. "Just let her alone."

EYEWITNESS

"You sit here," Major Pennon said. He pulled a straight-backed chair away from the wall and set it next to his desk. "That all right?"

"Yes, sir," Cotter said. "Sure. Any place."

"And then we can put Mrs. Maywood—well, let me see." The Major took his lower lip between thumb and forefinger

43

as he looked thoughtfully around the small, bare office. One wall was covered by that week's Army Service Forces News-map, there was an insignia chart on the wall facing it, and the glass panel of the door from the corridor was hidden by an enlarged photograph of three B-17's in flight. "I guess near the window, don't you think?"

"I guess so, sir," Cotter said. "Yes."

Major Pennon pulled another chair away from the wall and set it in the stream of sunlight that poured in from Fifth Avenue.

"It's not very comfortable, I guess, but it seemed a little better than taking her to a restaurant or a bar or something." The Major was pinching his lower lip again. "I don't want it to seem too impersonal and sort of cold, but a restaurant or a bar—you know, it makes it look like a party or something. Sort of bad taste, don't you think?"

"Yes, sir," Cotter said. "This looks fine, sir."

"Good." Major Pennon smiled suddenly, with relief, and touched Cotter's shoulder. "You sit down, then, and I'll go out and get her."

"Yes, sir."

Cotter remained standing while the Major crossed the room briskly. At the door, Major Pennon paused, his hand on the knob, and gave the small office a final, hasty glance, like a hostess surveying her dining room before going up to dress for dinner. He nodded, tapped his tie into more precise position in the V of his tunic lapels, and went out. Cotter drew a deep breath, exhaled through his open mouth, and turned to look out of the window.

He had heard in London that there was a ban on pleasure driving in New York and the London Sunday papers were full of feature articles on how the face of Manhattan had changed because there were so many uniforms on the streets, but Fifth Avenue looked just about the same as it had always looked in the late-afternoon sun from a seventeenth-story window. Cotter's forehead creased as he thought of what he was going to say, tried to figure out how he was going to begin, and he wished to God it was an hour later, or even twenty minutes later, because no matter how he began, or what he said, it couldn't possibly take longer than that, and all he wanted was to get it over with. Cotter didn't blame Mrs. May-wood for wanting to come all the way from Ohio to see him, or Major Pennon for asking him to talk to her, but he just didn't see what there was to tell her. She knew all there was to know. She knew everything he knew.

A girl in a bright-green hat stepped off the curb in front of St. Patrick's and Cotter's eyes followed with interest her darting progress, among the taxis and buses, clear across the Avenue. The door behind him opened and he turned quickly.

"This is Sergeant Cotter," Major Pennon said. "Mrs. Maywood, Sergeant."

"How do you do?" Mrs. Maywood said. "It sure is swell of you to let me come and see you like this, Sergeant. I certainly appreciate it, I really do."

Cotter nodded awkwardly as Major Pennon helped her into the chair by the window. Mrs. Maywood looked just about as Cotter had expected and probably about the same as she had always looked. There was nothing tragic or unusual about her appearance. She was short and stout, a woman of about forty, with a pleasant, broad face and a slightly unpleasant voice. She wore a black suit with a neat white collar and a small black hat with a brim that was a trifle too saucy. The cloth coat she held folded on her lap showed the label of a Cleveland department store.

"I think, if you don't mind now, I'll leave you two alone." Major Pennon smiled kindly. "Is that all right?"

"Yes, I think so," Mrs. Maywood said. "Thank you, Major."

"Yes, sir," Cotter said, even though he had a moment of annoyance. He had not counted on being left alone with Mrs. Maywood. "Sure."

"I'll be back in a little while. In the meantime, if there's anything you want, if you want me for anything, just open the door and speak to the adjutant. He'll get me. All right?"

Mrs. Maywood and Cotter nodded and the Major went out. The door, swinging shut, sent a draft across the room and for a moment the only sound in the small office was the faint crackling of the Newsmap on the wall.

"I want to thank you again for letting me come to see you," Mrs. Maywood said. "It was really nice of you to take all the trouble."

"That's all right," Cotter said. "I live right here in New York and I'm on sick leave. It's no trouble, really." Mrs. Maywood smiled politely, but it was plain that her mind was on other matters. She was looking down at her coat, tracing the stitching of the department-store label with a stubby forefinger. "How long are you staying here?" Cottter asked. "I mean in New York."

"Until tomorrow," Mrs. Maywood said. "I come on just to have this talk with you and then I've got to be back. I left the children over at my mother's house. She's wonderful with them. They love her and all that, but you know how it is, especially now." She stopped and looked up. "Tell me how it happened, Mr. Cotter. Sergeant Cotter."

"Well." Cotter took a deep breath. "There isn't much to tell, I'm afraid."

"You were with him, weren't you?"

45

"Yes. We were together. I was—well, you know what happened."

"Please tell me the whole thing, Sergeant Cotter. The way it happened. Everything."

"Well, sure. Of course," Cotter said. It was not her eagerness that embarrassed him. He could understand her wanting to know in detail, to know more than was contained in the War Department's formal notification, more than he himself had put into the letter that Major Pennon had sent her. What embarrassed Cotter was the fact that there just wasn't any more to tell. He had told it all in his letter. There were no further details. "You see, I was sent down to London from the aerodrome where I was stationed to pick up a truck and drive it back. I don't know why. Those things happen all the time in the Army." Cotter spoke slowly, keeping his eyes on the photograph of the B-17's on the door, trying to enlarge the shamefully trivial incident with irrelevancies about himself. "I got the truck all right, but it was too late to drive back that night because of the blackout, you know, so the lieutenant said I could have the night off there in London and drive back in the morning. I got myself a room at the Red Cross and had my dinner there and played some cards with a few of the men there. Pinochle. Then we went out to a pub—that's what they call a bar over there—for a couple of beers." Cotter stole a glance at Mrs. Maywood. She was leaning forward over her folded coat, her inexpertly rouged lips parted, listening eagerly, like a child hearing an old bedtime story told by a stranger, hoping that perhaps this time the familiar ending would be different. Cotter's face grew hot and he looked away. "There were quite a few American soldiers in the place and when I left a bunch of them were going out. I didn't know any of them—just met them in the pub, you see—and I found myself walking along in the blackout beside one guy—one man. I couldn't even see his face, it was so dark. It turned out later he was your husband."

Now that he was into it, now that he was reconstructing the scene for Mrs. Maywood, Cotter could see the whole thing clearly, could almost smell the odor of weak beer that came from the stranger in khaki walking along beside him in the blackout toward Hyde Park Corner. Suddenly the siren went, and Cotter could hear again the derisive laughter from the soldiers ahead of them down the street and the ribald comment by the man at his side. Cotter was chuckling at the man's remark when he heard an astonished gasp, followed by a sickening thud. Cotter stopped and spoke to the man. There was no answer. The man had simply vanished. Cotter called out nervously. The soldiers down the street came back. One of them had a flashlight. He flashed it and they found that the

46

man who had been walking beside Cotter had fallen down an areaway.

"We got him out and found a doctor right away, but it was too late. Fractured skull. He was dead by the time the doctor got there." Cotter paused and glanced at Mrs. Maywood. She was sitting back in the straight-backed, uncomfortable chair, staring at Cotter with disappointment. The story had not come out differently. The ending was the same. Cotter dropped his eyes. "A couple of months later, I received a letter from Major Pennon. He said you'd asked for details, and I wrote him that letter he sent on to you. About three months after that, I was shipped home. Last week Major Pennon got in touch with me and said you were coming to New York and, well, that's all there's to it, I'm afraid."

Mrs. Maywood shifted in her chair and leaned forward. She shook her head very quickly, as though she were brushing away an expected objection.

"That's what Major Pennon told me," she said impatiently. "And that's what you said in your letter. But there must be more. It's very important. Please tell me, Sergeant."

"I wish I could," Cotter said. "But that's all there is, really. There's no more to tell."

"Please, Sergeant Cotter." Her plain, broad face was suddenly creased into lines of anguished pleading. "There must be more. Please try to remember. It's so important."

"Well," Cotter said slowly. "Let me think a moment." He stared across her black hat, with its saucy brim, at the insignia chart on the wall, scowling hard and chewing his lower lip, pretending to be in deep thought and fighting back the exasperation that was rising in him. There was no more to tell. Why did she keep nagging him? It was a silly, a stupid, even a slightly sordid way to die in a war, falling down an areaway and cracking your skull on your way home from a saloon during a blackout. It made Cotter uncomfortable just to think about it. Six months after the event, how could Mrs. Maywood stand talking about it, begging for more details? Cotter supposed he could tell her how her husband had looked when they got him to the Army hospital, a middle-aged, lifeless man, his lips parted in an expression of hurt surprise, as though the shock of death had come like an unexpected insult from an old and trusted friend. The only other thing Cotter remembered was the dead man's hands. They were very white and seemed curiously small, like the hands of a doll, and the fingers were spread wide, as though at the moment of death their owner had been holding them out for a manicure. Cotter supposed he could tell her that, and in his exasperation he was tempted to do so, but he shoved the impulse back and shook his head. "No, I'm sorry,

47

Mrs. Maywood. I've told you everything I can remember. I can't think of anything else."

"What about shooting?" she said. "Wasn't there any shooting going on?"

"Shooting?" Cotter looked at her in puzzlement. "What do you mean, shooting?"

"You said the siren went, there was an air raid. There must have been shooting."

"Oh, that." Cotter shook his head. "No. You see, they came over regularly, and the siren used to go all the time, every time they were reported on the way, but they were usually stopped before they got to London. This was long after the blitz, you know, and the British had air superiority. Every once in a while a plane or two would get through, and then the barrage would go up or a bomb would come down, but very seldom. The siren didn't mean anything."

Mrs. Maywood shook her head, dismissing the explanation.

"There must have been shooting," she said. "Please try to remember." Cotter opened his mouth to say no again, but she wagged her hand quickly to silence him. "You must remember," she said angrily. "What am I going to tell the children? What am I going to tell my parents, the neighbors? I've got to go home tomorrow. The other men who were with you when it happened, Major Pennon says they can't be traced. You're the only one who was there, the only one I can talk to. You're the only one who can say it. Please help me, Sergeant. Please try to remember. Please."

"Well," Cotter said, feeling in his throat the slight, painful constriction he had felt during his first air raid. He looked down at his hands until the tightness eased a little. "Now that I think of it, there was quite a bit of shooting."

"There was?"

"Yes, quite a bit." Cotter continued to look at his hands so he would not have to see her leaning eagerly toward him. "A couple of them must have got through, more than a couple, probably, because the anti-aircraft batteries opened up with everything they had. It was a mess, as I remember. The papers said the next day it was the heaviest raid on London since the blitz. Many people were killed, a great many."

The door opened, sending a draft through the room that caused the Army Service Forces Newsmap to rustle on the wall, and Major Pennon entered.

"Well," he said, "everything all right?"

Cotter stood up and Mrs. Maywood began to gather her coat and purse.

"Oh, yes, Major," she said, blinking her eyes rapidly through a cheerful smile. "Everything is fine now."

The waiting room of the midtown bus terminal was lined with benches, on which perhaps a hundred people were sitting. They all looked tired and they all had some sort of luggage —cheap suitcases, parcels wrapped in paper, battered hat-boxes—resting on their laps or on the benches beside them or on the floor between their feet. Above the archway leading to the asphalt platform was a large electric clock. The clock showed twenty-five minutes after midnight. Two middle-aged men and two girls hurried in together from the street, glanced around, and stopped short.

"Well, what the hell you know?" the short, solid man said. "Damn thing's not even here yet."

"That's buses." The tall, sharp man's voice rasped. "Train says it leaves ten-twenty, it leaves ten-twenty. Leaves twelve-thirty, leaves twelve-thirty. These damn buses. Even on a Sunday night, end of a weekend, you can't depend on them."

The two girls laughed, exactly the same way, a moment too late, as though they had been reminded to do so by a sharp nudge. Then, both at the same time, they noticed that the two men were not laughing. The men looked annoyed. The girls stopped their laughter, brought it up short, as abruptly as they had started it. They exchanged a worried glance, dropped their eyes guiltily, and raised them at once to look with feigned interest past the two men into the waiting room.

It was a large, square room with a high ceiling and a great many lights. All the lights were turned on, yet they did almost nothing to dispel the atmosphere of thick, brownish gloom. The left wall was broken by a line of ticket windows. The wall at the right had two doors, on each of which was a dignified brass sign. One sign said "Ladies" and the other said "Gentlemen." In the wall at the far end of the room was a huge, wide, arched doorway that led out to the asphalt platform, empty now, on which the buses stopped to unload and pick up passengers.

"Gee, Charlie," said the girl in red. "What do we do now?"

Her voice sounded like a musical saw, whining and weak and delicately metallic. It brought the head of the short, solid man around in an arc until he was looking at her across his shoulder. He had no hair on the top of his head. His scalp was the same color as his fleshy face, a leathery, sun-tanned brown that looked unhealthy. His lips seemed too large for his mouth. They moved around too much when he talked. The coat of his single-breasted, wrinkled seersucker suit was open, making him look more slovenly than he actually was. The end of his long, washable blue-and-white tie was tucked into the belt of his trousers.

"What do you *think* we do?" he said. "We wait."

"I only meant—" the girl in red said. "I only asked—"

"Sure, Flo," the tall, sharp man said kindly. "Charlie only meant we're on time, your bus is late, what the hell, there's nothing else to do. *Nat*urally we wait. What else?"

The kindness in his voice petered out gradually with each word until, when he reached the last one, his voice sounded exactly the way Charlie's had. In appearance he was entirely different from Charlie. He was much taller and much thinner and much neater. His head was thatched with thick black hair and the stripes of his seersucker suit were wider. He wasn't sunburned. Yet somehow, at first glance, the men gave the odd impression that they looked exactly alike. A second glance showed why. It was almost as though they were imitating one another—in the expressions on their faces, the sound of their voices, and their attitude toward the two girls.

"Sure. Herbie's right," Charlie said. "That's all I meant." Some instinct of chivalry, buried deep under layers and years of neglect and misuse, fought through to the surface of his lumpy, perspiring face. He forced a smile that showed his bad teeth. He even patted the girl's arm awkwardly. "Don't be sore, Flo."

Flo laughed nervously, again a moment too late. The girl in yellow laughed, too.

"I'm not sore," Flo said. "I'm never sore. Am I ever sore, Iris? Am I?"

"Crazy," Iris said. "Flo sore?" She laughed harder, without mirth and with unconvincing nonchalance. "Flo's *never* sore. All the years I know her, I never saw Flo sore. You ever, Herbie?"

The tall, sharp man was setting his wristwatch by the electric clock over the archway. He glanced up and pushed in the watch stem with a faint click. "What?" he said. "Oh, Nah. Flo's never sore. Nobody's sore. What's with these damn buses?" He spoke directly to Charlie, as though the girls had disappeared. "What do we do?"

"Wait here," Charlie said. "You just wait, all of you." He stepped between the girls, across their two tiny suitcases, and strode toward the ticket windows. His was the only movement in the large, hot, tired room. All the people on the benches, the people who had been idly watching the two

50

middle-aged men and the two girls, turned their heads as their glances followed Charlie. When he came back to the group near the doorway, all the heads turned again.

"That Philadelphia Express, it's plenty late," he said. "Guy there says the twelve-thirty, it won't be in before one, maybe a quarter after. Anyhow, I bought the tickets." He sounded angry, trapped.

"Oh, Christ," Herbie said. "These damn buses."

"Gee whizz," Flo said in her weak, whining, metallic voice. "That means Iris and me, we won't get home before maybe four in the morning. Maybe even later."

The two men scowled at one another. The girls watched them anxiously. Charlie's oversized lips worked impatiently.

"Well, the hell with it," he said finally. "We're stuck. Might as well have a drink."

The girls brightened at once and dipped down to pick up the suitcases, which were so small they looked like boxes of candy to which handles had been attached.

"No, wait," Herbie said. "I'll tell you what." The bright looks vanished from the faces of the girls. They straightened up, holding the tiny bags in front of them. "We better see about parking the car first," Herbie went on. He smiled at the girls with exaggerated enthusiasm. "So we won't get a ticket, see?"

"That's right," Charlie said. He grinned. "We'll just go out and make sure the car is parked O.K. So we don't get a ticket. You girls sit down and wait. We be right back. All right?"

"Better give Flo and Iris the tickets," Herbie said as he took their arms and started herding the girls toward a vacant bench. "So's just in case the bus comes while we're parking the car, the girls won't be left flat and—"

"Aah, gee," Flo said. "You gonna—"

"No, no, no," Charlie said hastily. "Hell, no. Nothing like that. No, I'll hold the tickets." He scowled at Herbie and shook his head—a short, quick nod of warning. Then, with a smile, to the girls he said, "Don't you worry. We won't run out on you. We're not that kind of guy. We be right back. In a couple minutes, soon's we get the car parked right. Then we'll have a drink before the bus comes and slip you girls a piece of change. One last drink. Just a couple minutes."

The girls sat down on the bench. The two middle-aged men grinned, waved, turned sharply, and strode out of the waiting room into the street. The girls watched them with lips parted slightly, with doubt in their eyes. The moment the men crossed the threshold and disappeared, the girls turned toward each other. The doubt in their eyes was replaced with quick anger. Their thin, pinched, heavily made-up faces creased into scowls.

"Listen," Flo said. "You think they—"

"No," Iris said. "Don't be crazy."

"Them bastids," Flo said bitterly. "They try that, I'll—"

"Sh-h-h." Iris made a small motion with her head toward the people on the benches all around them. She spoke out of the corner of her mouth. "You got to expect that once in a while, kid. There's all kinds."

Flo bit her lip. Both girls straightened up. They sat very erect, keeping their backs primly from touching the bench. The tiny suitcases rested on their laps. They kept their knees together, their hands folded on the suitcases, and watched the big red second hand sweep smoothly around and around the face of the large clock on the wall. A terrible awkwardness, a frightening discomfort, had suddenly settled down on them. They were absolutely motionless, yet the eyes of all the tired people waiting for buses were turned on them with almost murderous concentration.

The two girls in their red and yellow dresses, sitting stiffly erect, seemed to shrink slightly, as though from an accusation unspoken but clear, familiar yet dreaded. They were all right so long as there was constant motion, so long as there were no gaps like this one, oases of silence and inactivity with nothing to do or say or drink to help drown out the condemnation of respectable eyes. All their brassy gaiety was gone. In these few moments of silence their only buffer against terror had been stripped away.

The door marked "Ladies" groaned open and a fat woman came out. The small sound caused the girls to jump. The people on the benches turned their heads to watch the fat woman walk self-consciously to a bench. Flo fumbled for her purse. She couldn't get it open.

"Gimme a cigarette," she said. "Huh?"

"Sure." Iris struggled with her purse. "Here."

She held the match for Flo and then brought the flame to the end of her own cigarette. The fat woman sat down. All the heads in the room swung back. Iris's hand jumped nervously. The people on the benches stared at them. The two girls sat up straight, their eyes on the clock's circling second hand, their faces set in hard little lines of unconvincing bravado, minute ridges of tiredness and misery. The freshly lighted cigarettes burned disregarded in their hands, which were folded on the tiny suitcases on their laps.

A huge Negro in dirty brown overalls came into the waiting room through the door marked "Gentlemen." He was carrying a pail and a large broom. He sprinkled water on the littered, dusty floor and began lazily to sweep up the cigarette stubs and matches and chewing-gum wrappers. All the heads in the room turned to watch him. The two girls hastily stole puffs from their cigarettes. By the time the heads turned back to them, they were again sitting primly erect. Worriedly, they watched the clock. It was now a few minutes after one o'clock. The only sound in the room was the soft scratching of the Negro's broom across the concrete floor.

All at once the silence was shattered by the noise of a bus roaring to a halt on the asphalt platform outside. A low hum of conversation and movement spread across the waiting room. The tired people started to get up, began to gather their bundles and hatboxes and suitcases. Flo and Iris looked at each other with quick, confused dismay. They stood up halfway, sat down again, turned nervously toward the row of ticket windows, swung around to look out through the arch-way. Across the front of the huge bus was an electric sign that said "Philadelphia Express."

"What do we do?" Flo said. "They got the tickets."

"Them bastids," Iris said. "I guess I better buy us a couple new ones. Otherwise we'll miss this bus and—" She stopped, and then, quickly, she stood up and laughed with relief. "Here they are!"

Charlie and Herbie strode toward the two girls. Both men looked flushed. The end of Charlie's long, blue-and-white washable tie had pulled loose from the belt of his trousers and was swirling around in front of his large, solid belly. Herbie didn't look quite so sharp and neat any more. Their eyes took in the bus outside, the people walking toward and climbing into it. They saw that the moment of departure had finally ar-rived, definitely and irrevocably. There would be no more postponements. The men started to grin. They walked faster toward the girls.

"Here we are," Charlie said boisterously. The smell of brandy was strong on his breath. "Had a little trouble getting the car started, but we got it parked all right. Got back just in time. See the bus is here. Come on, girls."

He fumbled in the pocket of his seersucker suit for the tickets and reached for the two tiny suitcases.

"No, wait," Herbie said grandly. Now that they were finally getting rid of these girls neither one of them could seem to control his exuberance. "We do this in style." He snapped his fingers in the air. "Porter!" he called. "Porter!"

The people walking out to the bus were attracted by this disturbance. They turned and looked back. The girls blushed. Iris reached up and pulled down Herbie's arm.

"Gee, don't," she said. "We don't need no porter. We'll miss the bus."

"Say, what do you think we are?" Herbie said. "A couple of pikers? We're sending you girls back in style. Right, Char-lie?"

"Sure," Charlie said. "No small-time stuff for us."

53

"Porter!" Herbie bellowed. "Porter!" The people on the asphalt platform outside and the people still in the waiting room stared at the two men and the two girls. Nobody answered Herbie's imperious call. "Wait a second," he said. "I'll get a porter." The girls tried to stop him, but he stook them off and ran over to the ticket windows. "Say, buddy," he said pompously to the man behind the grille, "you got a porter around here to carry some bags?"

The man looked out at Herbie. Then he looked across Herbie's shoulder at Charlie and the two girls. It was the look of a man who had seen situations like this before and had contempt for the actors in it. His glance came back to Herbie, and he nodded toward the large Negro who was sweeping the floor.

"That's him," he said. "The only porter around here."

Herbie turned and hurried across the room. "Here," he said as he shoved a coin into the Negro's hand. "Take these bags out to the bus, will you?"

The Negro stared with astonishment at the money in his hand, at the two tiny suitcases, then back at the money. A slow, silly grin spread across his face. "Sure thing, boss," he said. "Sure thing."

He dropped his broom and picked up the two bags. He did it with one hand. The bags were so small and so light that they did not even pull his arm down straight. He strode out through the archway to the bus, grinning widely, as though he had been let in on some tremendous private joke.

Charlie took Flo's arm and Herbie seized Iris's. The two men, smiling, propelled the girls, in the wake of the Negro, across the waiting room and out toward the bus. The people on the asphalt platform smiled. The two girls hung their heads just a trifle and tried to smile, too. They couldn't quite do it. Their lips twitched and their cheeks bunched into little, thin hills, but they were not smiling. They took small, quick, mincing steps, trying to keep up with the bouncing strides of the exuberant men. The girls kept their eyes on the ground. Their faces and necks were flushed. When they reached the bus it was almost full. The Negro went ahead of them.

"Take care of them bags, boy!" Herbie called after him. "I want you to treat them like they was your own."

"Yes, suh." The Negro laughed. Everybody in the bus watched while he put the bags on two empty seats and walked back to the door. He stepped out onto the asphalt, grinning, and touched his hand to his cap. "All safe, suh."

Herbie helped the two girls up the step into the bus. Charlie leaned in and handed the tickets to the driver.

"That's a couple of great girls you got there," he said cheerfully and loudly. "You take good care of them."

54

A few people in the bus laughed. Most of them just stared. The driver took the tickets, but he did not speak. He looked at the two men the way the man behind the grille of the ticket window had looked at them. Iris and Flo blushed a deeper red. Their lips quivered. They ducked their heads to walk down the narrow aisle toward their seats. Charlie stepped up to follow them.

"Just be for a second," he explained grandly to the driver. "Want to make sure these two girls are comfortable. A couple of great girls like these, don't want them to be—"

Flo swung around and said "Oh," a small, compressed gasp of exasperation, a whimper of anger she couldn't seem to control. Her thin, badly made-up face contracted sharply, as though with a pain that had suddenly become too much to bear. All the little tired creases stood out near the corners of her mouth. Iris turned quickly and put out her hand warningly. She was too late. Flo beat her fists against Charlie's chest.

"Get out!" she gasped. "Get out, get out, get *out!*" Her voice no longer sounded like a musical saw. All the whine and all the weakness were gone. It was desperate with accumulated suffering, with hatred too long suppressed. "Get out!" she panted, hammering at Charlie's chest. "Get out!"

The short, solid man tumbled out of the bus. He fell against Herbie. They grabbed each other and staggered about for a few seconds until they recaptured their balance. Both men stared into the bus with astonishment. Then Charlie let out a bellow of anger and started for the door. The driver closed it in his face. He hit the starter, gunned his motor, and the bus began to roll.

Flo turned to Iris and looked at her guiltily, then caught her breath in a sob. "I don't care," she said desperately. "I don't care. I don't care if we never get another party in New York again." Her voice rose higher. "I don't care. I don't care."

Iris bit her lip and stole a glance at the people around them. "Sure," she said as she guided Flo down the aisle of the swaying bus toward their seats. "Sure, kid. It's all right."

"I don't care about the money," Flo cried. "I don't care. I couldn't stand any more. A whole weekend they—they were —two whole days." Her voice broke. "It was too—they—" Then the tears came. "I don't care about the money," she wailed brokenly. "I don't care. I don't care. I don't *care!*"

"Sure," Iris said. "I know."

DEATH IN THE FAMILY

On Wednesday of the week before Easter my cousin Laura was taken sick suddenly and was rushed to the hospital. Her appendix had burst and the doctor said she had peritonitis. My mother and father were both very much upset, because Laura was their favorite niece. My father kept a small dry-goods shop in Brooklyn, and the week before Easter was the busiest of the year, but early Thursday morning, before the store became crowded, my mother hurried to the hospital. She was not permitted to see Laura. Visiting hours, they told her, were from seven to nine in the evening, which was out of the question for all of us. The store had to be kept open until ten.

Friday morning my mother tried again, but she met with the same answer. She explained the situation to the girl in the reception room at the hospital and pleaded with her, but it didn't help. Patients, the girl said, could not be disturbed during the day. If they let my mother see Laura, they'd have to let everybody have visitors. They couldn't make exceptions. However, the girl did call the doctor on the inter-hospital phone and then told Mother that there was a "fair chance" that my cousin Laura would recover.

Mother came home in a state of nervous excitement, and my father, who had been waiting anxiously for news, lost his temper and shouted at her, saying she shouldn't have let them put her off like that. My mother started to cry, and he ran out to the drugstore on the corner and called the hospital. There was no change in my cousin Laura's condition, they told him.

Business was very brisk during the afternoon, but my father and mother were so worried about Laura that when I came home from school my father told me to stay in the store and went off to the hospital. We had a hard time handling the customers, because I didn't know as much about the stock as my mother did and she was too distracted to pay much attention to what she was doing. At five o'clock my father returned, more worried than ever, and almost beside himself with anger. They hadn't let him go up to see Laura.

By seven o'clock the store was jammed and my father couldn't really spare me, but he had to know about Laura, so he sent me to the hospital to visit her, with instructions to stay as long as possible, but not too long, and then rush home.

I reached the hospital at twenty to eight and went up to the girl at a desk in the reception room. I asked her where I could find my cousin. The girl hunted through a small card index in front of her and asked me to spell the second name, which I did, and then she shuffled a thin batch of cards that had been stuck loosely into one corner of the desk pad. Finally she looked up, holding one card in her hand.

"Harrison?" she asked.

"Yes," I said.

She looked at me curiously.

"You her brother?"

"No," I said. "I'm her cousin. I'd like to go up and—"

"Well, I'm sorry," the girl said, pushing the card back into the corner of the desk pad. "She died at seven-fourteen tonight. No one can go up except the immediate family. Sorry."

"Harrison?" I said. "*Laura* Harrison?"

"Yes," she said in a softer voice. "Seven-fourteen. Sorry."

I turned away from the desk. My only emotion was bewilderment. I didn't know Laura very well, but I had been sent to bring news of her improved condition, and here she was, dead. It was like being sent to the bakery for bread and coming back with fly paper.

All the way home on the trolley car I tried to think of what to do. It wasn't so much that I was upset about Laura; in my fourteen years I had never known her very well. But I was worried about my father and mother. They were crazy about Laura and they were expecting me to say she was feeling better. I couldn't tell them she was dead. It would be too much of a shock.

As soon as I came into the store, my mother cried, "How is she? How does she look?"

"They wouldn't let me see her," I said. "They told me she was feeling a little worse."

"Worse?" My father looked startled. "When was this? What time?"

"A little before eight, I guess."

He glanced at his watch and, forgetting the customers around him, pushed me to the door.

"It's a quarter to nine now," he said. "Run to the drugstore and call up. Find out how she is."

I went to the drugstore and bought a package of gum, chewed a piece until all the flavor was gone, and then walked back to our store.

"Well?" my mother asked anxiously.

"Not so good," I said without looking at her.

"What do you mean, not so good?" my father shouted. "Talk so a person can understand you. What did they say?"

57

"They said she wasn't feeling so good." I went behind the counter and waited on a couple of customers. My mother and father went on selling dry goods, but their minds were in the hospital on Clarkson Street. Ten minutes later my father hurried over to me.

"Go and call up again," he said. "Find out how she is. Quick!"

I went out to the drugstore once more. Mr. Metzger, the proprietor, looked at me curiously when I came in.

"Hello!" he said. "Falling in love with my place, or something?"

"Pack of gum," I said.

He laughed when he handed it to me and took my nickel.

"You know what to do with gum, don't you?" he said. "You don't swallow it right away. You chew it for a while."

I laughed a little, too, embarrassed.

"I know," I said, and put the gum in my pocket and went out. The store wasn't very crowded when I got back.

"What did they say?" my mother and father asked together.

"She's getting worse," I said.

They stared at me for a moment. Then my father threw down the box of underwear he was holding and went for his hat.

"Business or no business," he said, with more fright in his voice than anger, "I'm going down to the hospital now!"

My mother started to follow him.

"There's no sense in going," I said quickly. "They won't let you in. It's after nine. No more visitors. They told me that on the phone."

He put his hat back slowly on the clothes tree and returned to the counter. We all worked for a few minutes. There were no sounds in the store except the rustle of paper and a customer's occasional question about size or price.

"I'm going out to call up," my father said suddenly.

"I'll go," I said, and before he could reply I was past him and out in the street. I didn't want to go to the drugstore again, but this time I knew my father was watching me through the front window, and I couldn't help myself.

Mr. Metzger looked at me in amazement when I came in.

"Could you let me have a couple of nickels?" I said.

"Sure," he said. "Why not? You're getting to be one of my steadiest customers."

I put a dime on the counter and he gave me two nickels. Then I went into a phone booth. I could see him staring at me through the glass door, so I dropped a coin into the slot, held the receiver to my ear, and tried to figure out what to tell them when I came back. Suddenly there was a click at the other end of the wire and the operator said, "Number, please."

58

I jumped and hung up without speaking. Then I went out and walked back. There was only one customer in the store when I came in.

"She's pretty bad," I said.

The customer, a stout woman with a faint mustache, looked at me in a puzzled way, and then she turned to discuss her purchase with my mother. While it was being wrapped, my father spoke quietly from the other end of the counter.

"You better go out and call again," he said.

This time, when I came into the drugstore, I didn't look at Mr. Metzger. Instead I walked into the phone booth, dropped the other nickel in the slot, and held the receiver away from my ear. When I had counted ten, I hung up.

"Hey!" Mr. Metzger called after me as I walked out. "Whats the matter? Something's wrong maybe?"

"No," I said, without turning back.

There were no customers in the shop when I came in. My mother and father were putting the stock in order for the night. My mother had a bolt of cloth in her hands. She held it in mid-air, halfway to the shelf she had been reaching for. My father was straightening a box of shirts. I closed the door very gently behind me. For a moment there was silence while they looked at me. I could tell that they already knew what I was going to say.

"She's—she's dead," I said finally.

The tissue paper rustled a little as my father closed the shirt box. My mother finished putting the bolt of cloth on the shelf and sat down heavily on the stool behind the counter. A single large tear hesitated on her cheekbone for a second and then went bouncing down her face quickly.

I wasn't worried about them any more. I knew now that they would be all right.

DUMMY RUN

"You hear what I hear, Clyde?" The fat man in the sheepskin coat shifted his heavy boots on the sill of the stove and looked up from his newspaper. "My ears maybe, or is that another batch?"

The young man at the desk raised his eyes from his book and listened attentively. From the street outside came the dry, crunching sound of heavy footsteps approaching on the snow.

"I'll tell them," Clyde said in a low voice as he stood up. "Too bad they have to come all this way for nothing on a night like this."

He glanced toward the door and then across the wooden railing that divided into two sections the single room of the small frame building which served as immigration depot for the crews of ships loading or unloading in this Canadian port or anchored in its harbor while waiting orders to join convoys. The door from the street opened into the office section of the room, which contained the small stove and the desk, a couple of extra chairs, and, near the door, a long, waist-high wooden counter. The other and larger part of the room, dimly lit and very cold, was an improvised waiting room with wooden benches running along its bare walls. About twenty seamen—American, British, Canadian—were asleep or dozing on the benches; each of them wore a pink slip tucked in the ribbon of his hat. They had come ashore that morning or the day before on twelve- to twenty-four-hour passes and were now waiting for the harbor launch to take them back to their ships. Clyde saw that none of them had been roused by the approaching footsteps. He walked to the counter. The door opened and he dipped his head slightly to avoid the rush of wind and swirl of snow that came hurtling into the room.

"Close it, Clyde," the fat man said irritably from the depths of his sheepskin collar. "Tell them to close that damned thing."

The door slammed shut. Six men and a woman had come in. They stamped the snow from their boots and stood in an awkward group, blinking helplessly in the weak yellow light.

"Good evening," Clyde said pleasantly. "Terrible night, isn't it?"

The newcomers nodded very quickly, as though they had been reprimanded for some unconscious act of impoliteness. Five of the men were young—under thirty. They wore heavy blue mackinaws and blue pancake hats. A line of gold print, the characters strange and foreign, ran around the bands of their hats. The sixth man was older, perhaps forty or forty-five, with a strong, lean face and very broad shoulders. He wore a thick brown overcoat and an officer's cap without insignia. The woman was completely muffled in an old raccoon coat with a huge collar that stood up around her head and hid her face. They looked as though they had just come from a shopping expedition. The five young sailors were carrying clusters of small parcels, paper sacks with packages of toothpaste and shaving cream sticking out of their tops, a string bag full of oranges, and cartons of cigarettes. The woman had a large, unwrapped box of face tissues under one arm and, clutched tightly in a mittened hand, a bouquet of gaudy artificial flowers whose stems were wrapped in the glazed tan paper peculiar to five-and-ten-cent stores. The older man carried no parcels. Clyde's greeting seemed to puzzle and embarrass them. The five young sailors and the woman looked expectantly at the older man. He took off one glove, stepped up to the counter, and held out seven pink slips of paper. They had obviously been torn from the same pad as the slips that the sleeping men in the larger section of the room were wearing in their hats.

"Tell them to scram," the fat man in the sheepskin coat said behind Clyde. "There's no boats going out tonight."

"I know what to tell them, Coombes." Clyde spoke without turning, and his high voice shook with faint annoyance, but he smiled across the counter at the older man in the officer's cap. "I'm sorry about these," Clyde said, and tapped the pink slips in the man's hand. "We can't send you out to your ship tonight. A lot of ice has formed in the harbor and a lot more has drifted down from Bedford Basin. The launch can't get through it tonight in the dark. I suggest you try to find some accommodations here in town for the night, and tomorrow morning, at eight-thirty, we'll send you all out to your ships. We should be able to get through the ice or around it in daylight. We can't try it tonight."

The older man laid the pink slips on the counter and pointed to them with a large forefinger. It was plain that he hadn't understood Clyde's explanation.

"They're a bunch of Poles from that freighter came in last night," Coombes said from his place at the stove. "That's the captain or the first mate or something with his wife and those five young guys are his gun crew. They came through on the morning launch when Drew was on duty and he gave them twelve-hour passes. They don't talk English. Tell them to beat it till tomorrow morning eight-thirty."

"How can I tell them if they don't understand English?" Clyde said in an exasperated tone. "I wish you'd let me do this in my own—"

Coombes dropped his heavy boots from the ledge of the stove with a bang that rattled the kettle steaming on top. He stood up and walked over to the wooden railing that divided the room.

"Hey!" he called loudly. "Any of you men speak Polish?" The seamen asleep or dozing on the benches stirred. Several looked up and squinted at Coombes. "Polish," he said, his voice rising. "Any of you men speak Polish? Any of you understand it?" The men looked at one another and back at Coombes. Nobody answered. Coombes took the pipe from his mouth and spat across the rail in disgust. He walked back to his chair beside the stove and sat down. "No Polish. Nobody

61

understands them and they don't understand us. Just tell them to beat it. Do it in sign language. Anything. Get them out of here."

"I'm afraid we cannot send you out tonight," Clyde said, spacing his words and enunciating with care, as though he were talking to a deaf man. "There is ice in the harbor. Do you understand? Ice? Ice in harbor? *No boats tonight.*"

The middle-aged Pole turned and spoke sharply to the group behind him. The five young sailors shifted their parcels and dug into their blue mackinaws. The woman put the bouquet of artificial flowers in her other hand and opened her fur coat to reach an inner pocket. The huge collar fell away from her face and the bulky coat dropped open, revealing an attractive, slender woman in her early thirties. She and the five young sailors handed small, square booklets to the older man. He bounced them on the wooden counter to make an even pile and pushed it across toward Clyde.

"No, no," Clyde said. "We don't want your passports. We saw your passports when you came through in the morning, when you went ashore, when our Mr. Drew gave you these twelve-hour passes." He smiled quickly, a friendly, strained grimace. "Nothing wrong with your passports." He waved his hand across the railing toward the men on the benches. "Nobody's going back tonight. These men are all staying over tonight, too." He pushed the passports back across the counter and then, remembering, began again to space his words and raise his voice. "You find place sleep tonight. Hotel or rooming house. Come back in morning." He stopped. The older man was staring at him, the lean, strong face expressionless except for his eyebrows, which were rising slowly. "You can all stay here if you like. On benches like the other men. But I think—" Clyde stopped again and all of his thin face grew as red as the tip of his thin nose. "The lady with you. I think it's too cold for her to sit up all night in there. I don't think it would be—" His uneven voice petered out.

"Lay off the lady stuff," Coombes said drily. "That's his wife and these Poles get jealous easy. He'll take a sock at you."

Clyde looked with embarrassment at the Pole; apparently the older man had not understood. He put the passports in his pocket, his face still blank. With a deliberate, dignified gesture he pointed to a line of print on one of the pink slips: "Your launch will leave Bedford Wharf at——." "10:30 P.M.," and wrote in "8:30 A.M." above it. "You see?" he said eagerly, tapping the slip with his pencil and leaning far forward across the counter as though he hoped to cross the barrier of language by bringing himself physically closer to the other man. "Not tonight. Not ten-thirty. Tomorrow morning. Tomorrow morning eight-thirty. Time is changed. Because of ice. Ice in harbor. Too dangerous. No boat tonight. No—" He stopped again and pointed desperately to the figures "8:30 A.M." on the pink slip. There was no sign of understanding from the impassive Pole. Clyde drew a deep breath and waved his hand toward the men in the other section of the room. "It's not only you. All these men—they're not going at ten-thirty tonight. All waiting for tomorrow. You better try to find a place to stay for the night. You can use the phone here to call a hotel. I'll help you if you want." Like a teacher explaining a problem with diagrams on a blackboard, he pointed to the box phone on the wall, flanked by a large Canadian Pacific calendar and a newspaper picture of Winston Churchill. "Find hotel," he said. "Or rooming house. And then tomorrow—"

The sound of laughter, low but derisive, came across the rail from the other section of the room. "How's about cutting out the jokes so we can sleep," one of the American sailors called. "If there was a room anywhere in this town, you think we'd be sitting up all night in this icebox?"

Clyde tugged hopelessly at the folds of the woollen muffler around his neck. The middle-aged Pole looked without expression across the railing at the men sprawled on the benches, shifted his glance to Clyde, to Coombes beside the stove, and then back to Clyde. Slowly he pulled off his other glove, unbuttoned his thick brown overcoat, dipped into an inside pocket, and pulled out a fat wallet. He slid open the zipper fastener and, very deliberately, began to count out a pile of bank notes on the counter. Clyde stared blankly.

"Well, I'll be a son of a gun," Coombes said. Clyde turned, his face puzzled. "He don't believe us," Coombes said slowly, getting up. "He thinks we're not sending them back because they're Poles or something." He pulled the pipe from his mouth and came up to the counter. "He wants to pay us for sending the launch out."

"We can't do that." Clyde swung back to face the Pole. "It's not a question of money. You're entitled to the launch trip free. It's the ice. Ice in harbor. No boat because of ice. *Ice. No boat. Dangerous.*"

The Pole drew several more bank notes from his wallet and added them to the pile. His face was still blank, but there was a suggestion of contempt in the movement of his wrist as he flicked the money over.

"Who says we can't?" Coombes' bilious face was creased with cold anger. He spoke to Clyde but he kept his glance on the Pole. "We can't send the launch because it might get banged around. Sure. But if this wise guy is willing to put up the dough for any damage, O.K." He grinned unpleasantly as he pulled the sheepskin collar up higher around his ears and buttoned it across his chin. "Stamp up those passes. I'll take them out."

"Listen, Coombes. That's—"

"Stamp them up," Coombes said, his cold glance fixed on the Pole. "I'll take them out, the wise guy."

Clyde hesitated, then picked up the rubber stamp, punched it down on an ink pad, and began hitting the pink slips. He stamped six and stopped.

"I'm not going to stamp the woman's," he said. "The men, all right, if they insist. But I'm not going to stamp the woman's."

"Stop being a damn fool," Coombes snapped. "It's their funeral. They're asking for it."

"I don't care," Clyde said stubbornly. His voice quivered. "The men, all right, if they insist. But not the woman. It's too cold and it might be dangerous. I'm not going to—" Coombes snatched angrily at the rubber stamp. Clyde swung it out of reach. "No," the younger man said in a shaking voice. "If you stamp the woman's, if you take the woman, I'll report you, Coombes. The others, all right. They're insisting. But not the woman."

Coombes glared at him. "All right," he said finally. He came around from behind the counter and poked his finger at the five sailors and the middle-aged man. "You and you and you and you three. Not the woman. Come on." The middle-aged Pole said something sharply. Coombes shook his head. "I don't know what you're saying, brother, but if it's about the woman, no soap. Here." He thrust the pink slips at the six men. "You coming or not?"

The Pole turned to Clyde and spoke again, a stream of short, sharp words.

"No," Clyde said, his face white. "I'm sorry. It's too cold and it might be dangerous. I won't let the lady run the risk."

All the control seemed to go out of the Pole's face. He hit the counter with his big fist and spoke angrily, in a furious roar. The upper part of Clyde's body bent backward, away from the angry man, but the front button of his jacket still touched the edge of the wooden counter. He shoved the seventh pink slip behind his back and shook his head again.

"No," he said. "I'm sorry. She can't go. It's too dangerous."

The Pole drew a deep breath, turned to the five young men, and spoke in a low voice. The young men nodded. The middle-aged Pole placed his own pink slip on top of the bank notes, moving his wrist with the small, contemptuous gesture.

"O.K., he's staying behind, too," Coombes said brusquely. "Come on, you guys." He pushed through the swinging gate in the wooden railing. The five young Poles followed him across the room toward another door, which led to the dock.

There was a flurry of movement among the men on the benches. "Don't get excited," Coombes said to them. "This is only a dummy run. There's no launch in the harbor can get through that ice tonight, but these birds are willing to pay for taking a chance. Relax, you guys. You got till eight-thirty tomorrow morning."

He pulled open the door, ducked his head into the wind and the snow, and the five young men followed him out onto the dock. The men on the benches sank back. In the other section of the room the young woman and the Pole remained erect, staring at the closed door. From the dock outside came the sputter of a motor. The sound became a roar, rose higher and higher, and began to fade. Soon it was gone and the only sound in the room was the gentle hissing of the kettle on the stove. Clyde's hand shook as he brought it out from behind his back to place the woman's pink slip next to the rubber stamp.

"Would you care to come in here?" he said awkwardly, with a gesture toward the stove. "The lady, she might be warmer near the stove? In here? Warmer for the lady?"

The middle-aged man gave him a long glance, full of hatred and contempt, stalked to the benches, and sat down on a vacant seat. The young woman followed timidly, clutching the box of face tissues and the bouquet of artificial flowers, and sat down next to the man. She placed the box on the seat beside her but still held the artificial flowers. The other men in the room stared at them curiously for a while, then relaxed into their former postures. The Pole and the young woman sat erect and stared straight ahead, across the heads of the reclining men. Clyde sat down at the desk and picked up his book. During the hour that followed he did not turn a single page.

At last, muffled by the snow and the wind, came the purring roar of the motor. The men who were not asleep sat up straight. Clyde put down his book. The middle-aged Pole and the young woman turned their heads slightly. The purring roar grew louder and then it stopped. Clyde looked at the alarm clock. It showed twenty minutes to midnight. Feet tramped heavily across the snow-covered dock. The door opened and Coombes came in, followed by the five young sailors. Everybody watched as they crossed the room. Coombes walked with a firm, fast, purposeful stride, slapping fresh snow from his coat. The young Poles moved more slowly, uncertainly. They all looked tired and very cold. Coombes snatched the pile of bank notes from the counter, pushed through the wooden gate, and strode to the bench where the Polish officer and his wife were sitting.

"Here." Coombes dropped the money contemptuously into the man's lap. "We don't want your dough."

He shoved his way back through the gate, went behind the counter, and flung himself into the chair beside the stove.

"What happened?" Clyde said. "Did you—"

"What did you expect to happen?" Combes barked the words as he filled his pipe, tamping the tobacco in with fierce thrusts of his thumb. "We couldn't get through. The ice is too damn thick and you can't see where the hell you're going in all that damn snow." He jerked his head toward the other section of the room, where the five young sailors were talking rapidly to the older man, explaining in Polish what had happened. "We used up a little gas, but at least we'll have some peace around here. Damn near froze their ears off, but now they can tell that wise guy when I say a launch can't get through, it can't get through." He lit his pipe, taking huge, angry sucks on the stem, and buried his head in the newspaper.

Almost immediately the door from the street opened and a man wearing a heavy coat sweater and a peaked cap came in. "Hello, Clyde," he said, brushing the snow from his sweater as he walked behind the counter. "Hello, Coombes."

Coombes grunted without raising his head from the newspaper.

"Hello, Drew," Clyde said. "You're early."

"The hell I am." The newcomer blocked out half of Winston Churchill's face by hanging his peaked cap on one of the nails that held the picture to the wall. "That alarm clock is slow. It's after midnight. You been off duty five minutes already, Clyde, only you don't know it." He laughed, walked over to the counter, glanced idly at the papers there, and looked across to the benches. "This whole bunch waiting for the eight-thirty?"

"Yes," Clyde said. He stood up, took his neatly folded overcoat from the back of his chair, and slipped into it. "Their passes are all stamped. All except one." He finished buttoning his coat, picked up the unstamped pink slip from the counter, and marked it with the rubber stamp. "Those seven over there," he said in a low voice, keeping his glance on the man who was relieving him, "they're Poles. They don't understand English. You might make the lady a cup of tea later if you get a chance." He nodded toward the kettle on the stove. "She'll be pretty cold by morning."

"Sure," Drew said cheerfully. "I remember them going through this morning." He looked across the railing at the woman and winked at Clyde. "Not bad, huh?"

"You, too?" Coombes said from behind the newspaper. "Why don't you two guys keep your mind on your work?"

66

"What's up?" Drew said with a sly grin. "Clyde been—?"

"Quit it," Clyde said, his face bright red. "It's just she'll probably be cold and it's a long wait till eight-thirty." He walked out from behind the counter, pushed through the wooden gate, and stopped in front of the group of Poles. His hand shook as he put the pink slip on the middle-aged man's lap. "This the pass for the lady." He spoke slowly and clearly, his voice quivering, like a convicted prisoner who knows the jury will not believe him but makes his final, hopeless protest of innocence for the record. He looked directly at the man and carefully avoided looking at the woman. "You'll all get through to your ship in the morning, when it's light. I hope the wait isn't too uncomfortable for you. Good night."

He swung around abruptly, pushed through the gate, and pulled his coat collar up around his narrow head as he walked stiffly toward the door, like a man who knows he may be shot in the back but is determined not to give way to his terror by turning or running.

"So long," Drew said. "See you tomorrow."

"So long," Clyde said, pulling the door open. "Good night, Coombes."

"Good night," Coombes grunted from behind the newspaper. "Close that damn door, will you? It's—"

He stopped and lowered the newspaper. Clyde was hesitating at the door. The middle-aged Pole had jumped up. Everybody watched as he took the young woman by the hand and helped her to her feet. He led her through the swinging gate, toward the door, his lean face expressionless. The young woman walked trustingly beside him. Clyde stood there, his hand on the knob of the open door, his head bent slightly against the wind and the snow that poured in and seemed to freeze him in his tracks. His frightened face grew white and he stepped back slightly when the Pole reached him, as though he expected to be struck. The Pole stopped and bowed stiffly. He took the bouquet of artificial flowers from the young woman and held it out. Clyde stared at the older man, at the flowers, at the young woman, and then back at the man. The Pole bowed again and held the flowers out further. The young woman curtseyed. Drew started to laugh. Clyde flushed scarlet.

"It's for you," Drew said. "He's making you a present."

Clyde reached out hesitantly, his hand shaking, and took the flowers. His fingers slipped on the glazed tan paper and he almost dropped them.

"Thank you," he mumbled. Then he cleared his throat and spoke louder. "Thank you very much."

The Pole bowed once more and said something in his own language. The young woman nodded gravely. Clyde stared at the flowers, which he held gingerly, as though he expected them to explode, and then his thin, scared face broke into a small smile of gratitude and understanding. He bowed stiffly, awkwardly, to the Pole. He whipped off his old felt hat and bowed to the young woman. Both of them bowed to him.

"Listen," Coombes called. "You going to close that damn door or you going to let the—" The door slammed shut and Clyde was gone. For a few moments the sound of his steps on the snow could be heard and then it faded out in the windy night. The Pole and the young woman walked back to their bench. The kettle hissed gently in the silent room. "What do you say, Drew?" Coombes said from behind his newspaper. "You going to make that lady that cup of tea now?"

THE THIRD ALPHABET

The room that housed the typists' pool was at the foot of the long corridor, on what was considered the least desirable end of the building, the south end, facing Pennslyvania Avenue and Eleventh Street Northwest. The building was shaped like a flatiron at that end, so that the room was almost completely surrounded by traffic noises and, because there were tall, wide windows on both sides, the sun poured in all day. This was not really an inconvenience, because the sun helped keep the room warm in winter, and the building was air-cooled in the summer.

When the agency was created, two weeks after Pearl Harbor, and it took over the entire second floor from the overflow staff of one of the old-line agencies whose new marble and sandstone structure on the Mall had just been completed, the Space Committee had assigned the room to the typists' pool because it was so oddly shaped that there was no way of cutting it up sensibly into smaller offices, no matter how the partitions were arranged. Besides, even though half the girls used noiseless machines, the other half pounded away on vintage L. C. Smiths and Remingtons and Underwoods, anything at all that could be dug up and put into some sort of working order, and when all the typewriters were going the racket could be heard forty feet down the corridor. It made sense to keep the typists at the south end, as far away from the executive offices, at the north end, as possible.

Miss Keating, coming out of her office near the north end,

four doors from the mahogany arch that led to the executive offices, looked up from the memorandum in her hand. Something had plucked at her mind. After a moment she dropped her eyes back to the half sheet of pale blue paper with the name of the agency printed across the top in a rich, darker blue ink. Miss Keating went through the arch, reading as she walked, turned left, and stopped in front of a door on which was lettered "Office of the Associate Director." Miss Keating finished reading, opened the door without knocking, went in, and put the sheet of pale blue paper in the middle of the desk that almost filled the small room.

"Be with you in a minute," a girl called from the inner office. "Who is it?"

"Miss Keating," Miss Keating said. "Don't bother. Mr. Jowett wanted the lower echelon personnel estimate for the budget hearings." The memorandum would have reached Mr. Jowett just as quickly if she had put it into the box on the desk in her own room. The inter-office messenger system, which was one of Miss Keating's responsibilities, was fast and efficient. When Miss Keating was dealing with something she considered important to herself, however, she did not trust it even to a system she had herself created. "I'm leaving it on your desk," she said. From the pile of letters at one side of the desk Miss Keating took a paperweight, a round thick piece of magnifying glass with a picture of the Lincoln Memorial pasted to the flat bottom, and put it on the memorandum she had just brought in. "There's no rush," she said.

"Mr. Jowett is out to lunch," his secretary called from the inner office. "Just leave it on my desk."

Miss Keating went out and returned to her own room. It was not large, perhaps twice as big as Mr. Jowett's secretary's room, but it had a thermos water jug on a small table behind the desk, a nontipping smoking stand next to the visitors' chair, and the desk itself had a glass top. Miss Keating opened her black suède purse with the lucite ball on the thong of the zipper, took out her large silver compact, and made a few small adjustments to her face. She was a tall, cool, pretty girl with a long, pointed chin and very black hair parted in the middle and wound into two severe buns at the base of her skull. Miss Keating, who was twenty-eight, looked a year or two past thirty and would probably look exactly the same age for another six or seven years. She had that kind of face.

Miss Keating snapped the compact shut, plucked a loose hair from the shoulder of her good, neat, well-cut, single-button black suit, adjusted the collar of her pin-tucked white silk blouse, slipped the purse up under her arm, and looked at her wristwatch. It was twelve-thirty. The heavy silver bracelet, which matched her heavy silver earrings, both purchased during her summer in Mexico after she graduated from Wellesley, tinkled dully as Miss Keating walked out of her room and down the long corridor to the south end of the building.

As she put her hand on the knob and pushed in the door of the room that housed the typists' pool, Miss Keating knew what it was that had plucked at her mind a few minutes earlier. The clatter of typewriters that could usually be heard forty feet down the corridor was missing. A dozen girls looked up when Miss Keating came in. They were standing around the desk of Nancy Hull, the little girl from Vermont with the cute figure and the round face. A box from the Statler Flower Shoppe, in which a corsage of gardenias lay in a bed of crinkled green wax paper, stood on Nancy's typewriter and an open box of candy sat on her desk calendar. Nancy was holding a smaller box, about two inches square, and her lips were pursed in a small circle of awed delight. All the girls looked up at Miss Keating in the doorway and then stepped back a little, as though to clear a path between her and Nancy.

"Hello," Miss Keating said with a smile. "It's twelve-thirty, Nancy. Ready?"

"Yes, I'm ready," Nancy said. "Look, Miss Keating. The girls gave them to me. Aren't they pretty?"

Miss Keating came forward and took the box from Nancy and looked at the silver earrings in their small square nest of white cotton.

"Yes, they are," Miss Keating said, and she handed the box back. "They're lovely."

"They're just the most beautiful things I ever had," Nancy said. "And look, flowers, too, and a box of candy. Honestly, I'm so, gosh, I don't know what to say." Nancy smiled at the girls around her and they smiled back happily, but none of them spoke. "Would you like a piece of candy, Miss Keating?" Nancy said, picking up the box from the desk calendar. "They're delicious."

"Thanks, Nancy, not before lunch, I don't think," Miss Keating said. "Perhaps later. Hadn't we better go along?"

"Oh, yes," Nancy said, and she giggled. "I'm so excited, honestly, I don't know if I'm coming or going." She put the cover on the box of earrings and she put the box into her purse, a large white bag made of imitation leather that matched the belt around the waist of her flowered organdy dress and her white high-heeled shoes. " 'Bye, now," she said to the girls. "I'll see you later. Meantime, thanks a million again."

The girls murmured in a happy group, but none of them said anything distinguishable, and Miss Keating and Nancy Hull went out.

"They're so sweet, honestly, Miss Keating," Nancy said as they walked down the corridor. "It makes me feel terrible to be leaving."

"Why don't you reconsider, then?" Miss Keating said. "And stay?" Nancy looked startled, as though a completely revolutionary idea for which she was wholly unprepared had been tossed into her mind, and her shoulder bumped the jamb of the doorway into which she was turning, the doorway that led to the hall that led to the cafeteria. Miss Keating took Nancy's elbow and pulled her back gently into the corridor. "No," Miss Keating said. "We're eating upstairs."

"Upstairs?" Nancy said and then, when she understood, she said, "Oh, upstairs."

They walked on to the elevator and Nancy stood there quietly, playing with the snap fastener of her white imitation leather purse, while Miss Keating pressed the button. Neither of them spoke. The elevator came and they stepped in and Miss Keating said, "Five, please," and they got out on the fifth floor. Here Miss Keating went on ahead and Nancy followed a foot or two behind. The executives' dining room was not crowded, because the rush didn't start until one, but half the tables were taken.

"Two today," Miss Keating said to the white-haired woman with the armful of menus who was standing near the cashier's desk. "A side table if you have it, please?"

The woman nodded and gave Nancy a short glance before she led the way across the room. Everybody in the room looked up and several men smiled and nodded to Miss Keating, who smiled and nodded back. Aside from the white-haired woman, Miss Keating and Nancy were the only girls in the room. They sat down at a wall table, facing each other, and Nancy didn't know what to do with her bag until she saw Miss Keating put her black suède purse on the table, leaning it against the wall next to the sugar bowl. Nancy did the same, and she waited until Miss Keating took the folded paper napkin from the plate in front of her and opened it and spread it on her lap, before she picked up her own napkin. The white-haired woman handed Miss Keating a mimeographed menu and then gave one to Nancy.

"I thought I'd be able to put my hands on a leg of lamb for today, but no luck," the white-haired woman said, speaking to Miss Keating. "The meat loaf is good, though, and we have real hot fudge to go with the chocolate ice cream."

"I'll have the apricot salad," Miss Keating said, handing back the menu. "And a hot fudge sundae. No beverage. You, Nancy?"

"I'll have the same," Nancy said. "With a glass of milk?"

"Wouldn't you rather have the meat loaf?" Miss Keating said. "It's so hard to get these days?"

"No, I'll have the salad," Nancy said. "And a glass of milk, please?"

The white-haired woman wrote the order, took back the mimeographed menus, and went away. Nancy looked around the room quickly, as though memorizing her surroundings for the future, and she saw the white-haired woman give their order slips to a Negro waiter before she brought her glance back to the maple table top in front of her.

"I was quite serious," Miss Keating said. "Why don't you reconsider and stay?"

"Gosh, I'd like to," Nancy said. "But I just can't, Miss Keating."

"Why?" Miss Keating said with a smile. "Someone you're interested in back home in Vermont?"

Nancy looked up, as though she had been punched, and then she started to blush. She shook her head quickly.

"Oh, no, Miss Keating," she said. "It's not that."

"What is it, then?" Miss Keating said. "You can tell me, Nancy."

"Gosh, there isn't anything to tell," Nancy said uncomfortably. "Honest, Miss Keating. It's just I feel I've got to get back home."

"I see," Miss Keating said, and she leaned back to let the waiter set down the salads. She waited until he went away before she leaned forward again. "How old are you, Nancy?"

"How old?" Nancy said. "Twenty-one," she said. "Last April."

"Twenty-one," Miss Keating said. "And how long have you been in Washington?"

"A little over ten months," Nancy said. "Be eleven months next week."

"Oh, then you worked for somebody else before you came with us?" Miss Keating said.

"I was with Agriculture for two months when I first came," Nancy said. "And then I switched to OSS for four months before I got this job."

"First time away from home?" Miss Keating said with a small, kind smile. Nancy nodded. "Where do you live here in Washington?"

"I've got a room in a house up on Holly Street, near Silver Spring," Nancy said. "They're very nice people; her two sons are in the army and she has the space."

"Holly Street," Miss Keating said. "That's all the way out in the third alphabet, isn't it?"

"Yes," Nancy said. "But it's not so bad, Miss Keating. I take the Georgia and Alaska bus down Sixteenth, and then I transfer to the Number Thirty trolley at Pennsylvania and Fifteenth. It's only about forty-five, fifty minutes. Sometimes less."

Miss Keating put down her fork, wiped a dab of cottage cheese and apricot delicately from the corner of her mouth with the paper napkin, and looked down at her heavy silver bracelet. She moved it back and forth on her wrist for several moments, chinking the thick links dully against each other, her wide, smooth forehead, from which the black hair was so neatly combed away, creased in thought. Finally, she looked up and leaned forward again.

"Look, Nancy," Miss Keating said. "I don't want you to think I'm prying into your personal affairs, but there is something I'd like to say to you and it has nothing to do with the office. I'm speaking of you, Nancy. You personally. You understand that, don't you?"

"Yes," Nancy said, because there was nothing else to say, and she stared across the table at the cool, tall, pretty girl wearing the sort of suit it had never occurred to Nancy Hull to buy, the girl playing with the sort of heavy silver bracelet Nancy Hull had never dreamed of wanting, and even though she didn't understand at all, Nancy nodded again. "Yes," she said. "I understand."

"I'm so glad you do, Nancy," Miss Keating said. "Because this is so important to you, so much more important than you can imagine at the moment, Nancy. This is the first time you've ever been away from home, the first time you've been out of Vermont, the first time you've been in a large, metropolitan city. I know how difficult it is, how much you can miss your home and how lonely you can be in a large, strange city, even when you work all day with a group of nice, friendly girls, and how strong the temptation is to pack up and leave and go back. That's just the thing you mustn't do, Nancy. Because if you do that you admit defeat, you admit to yourself that the big city, the outside world has beaten you. And once you take a beating like that, you never really recover. You never again have the nerve to take a second chance. You're stuck up there for the rest of your life, you're locked away forever in a prison of your own making, in Vermont or Minnesota or Arkansas or wherever it is. You must fight it, Nancy. You mustn't give in. You mustn't crawl back, beaten."

Miss Keating stopped and leaned back, and the younger girl with the round face, wearing the cheap organdy dress, stared down at the table as the waiter took away her half-eaten apricot salad and replaced it with a hot fudge sundae.

"Thank you, Miss Keating," she said in a low voice. "You're

73

very nice to me and I think you're right in what you say, but I don't know, it isn't exactly that."

"Waiter, we get one glass of milk here," Miss Keating said. The waiter nodded and went away and Miss Keating said, "What is it, Nancy?"

"It's, oh, I don't know how to say it," Nancy said and then, to her own surprise, it seemed all right to say it. "I came here because my three brothers are in the army and I wanted to do something in the war effort and Miss Lauchlin, she's our high school principal in Battle Forks, she said they needed girls who could type and take shorthand in Washington, and my mother and father said it was right to go. But they didn't have much for me to do in Agriculture, I don't know why, so I switched to OSS, but it wasn't much better there, so I came here. I don't mean that I haven't been given enough to do here," Nancy said quickly. "It's just that when you're in the pool you don't feel you're working for anybody in particular, you just do whatever comes along and you take dictation from anybody that happens to need a stenographer that minute. What I mean is, you don't belong to anybody, you don't see your part of it piling up, sort of. You don't get the feeling you're helping with the war effort. It's just bits and pieces. But it's not only that," Nancy said, talking faster, rushing the words now, to get it all out before she was interrupted. "It's also I can't make out on my salary. I just can't, no matter how hard I try. Everything is so expensive here, by the time I pay my rent and buy my trolley pass and my lunches and suppers and my laundry and all those things, gosh, Miss Keating, there's nothing left. Last month I went to the dentist and I had to write my mother to send me the money to pay him. It makes a person feel terrible to do that, Miss Keating, write home for money when you're working and earning. I bought only three dresses in the whole ten months, nearly eleven, the whole eleven months I been here, and my mother and father, every month they have to send me something to I won't have to borrow from the other girls. That's not right, Miss Keating. They shouldn't be sending me money. I should be sending them something every month. That's the way it should be."

She stopped and looked up with a frightened little start, then she saw who it was and she leaned back to make room for the waiter. He set down the glass of milk and looked inquiringly at Miss Keating.

"That's all, thank you," Miss Keating said. "Nothing else."

The waiter took from his outer breast pocket the checks the white-haired woman had written. He added the figures, scribbled the totals, and put the checks on the table face down. Miss Keating pulled the two slips of paper toward her and tucked the corners under the edge of her purse.

"I'm glad you told me all this, Nancy," she said. "It's partly my fault that you haven't had an opportunity to tell me sooner, but that's how it is in Washington. You don't get to know a person until the day that person is leaving, when you take her to lunch for the first time to say goodbye." Miss Keating folded her long, slender fingers on the table and leaned forward. "If we could find you a place to live nearer the center of things, Nancy? Near Dupont Circle, for instance, where I live, and not all the way out there in the third alphabet? And if I talked to the administrative office about getting you upgraded, say to CAF 5, or even a six, perhaps? And if we could do something about not letting you grow so lonely, have lunch together once in a while, or something like that? I might even talk to Supply and get you a noiseless instead of that rattletrap old L. C. Smith? Nancy, if I could do all that, would you reconsider and—?" Miss Keating stopped, and the look of intense seriousness disappeared as her long, pointed chin tilted upward in a sudden, eager smile. "Hello, Mr. Jowett," she said. "I recommend the meat loaf. It's very good."

Nancy turned quickly. The Associate Director had stopped behind her chair.

"Thanks, I've just finished," Mr. Jowett said. "Sorry to bother you at lunch," he said across Nancy's head. "But I saw you on my way out and I thought I'd ask about that memorandum?"

"It's on your secretary's desk," Miss Keating said. "I left it there half an hour ago."

"I should have known better than to ask," Mr. Jowett said, laughing. "If the rest of my staff was as efficient as you are, I'd be the happiest bureaucrat in the war effort. We can't afford to lose any more of our stenographic help. If these kids keep on going home we'll have to close up shop. How does it look?"

"Not so bad," Miss Keating said, and her voice, suddenly edged with warning, went up slightly. "I think I can guarantee that your lower echelons won't be decimated."

Mr. Jowett's eyebrows went up, and he made a circle with his lips, and he looked down quickly at the top of Nancy's head, and then he winked across the younger girl at Miss Keating.

"Check," Mr. Jowett said. "Keep up the good work," he said, and he waved as he moved off toward the cashier's desk. "See you later," Mr. Jowett said.

Miss Keating followed him with her smile for a moment and then the smile disappeared as she brought her intense, serious glance back to Nancy and leaned forward again.

"If I did all those things, Nancy," she said. "Or tried, any-

way? Would you reconsider and stay?" Nancy didn't answer.
"For your own good?" Miss Keating said. "Will you not admit
defeat and give yourself another chance?"

Nancy Hull's round little face was set so hard that, for the
first time in her life, she looked older than her years and then,
as she caught her lower lip in her teeth and bit hard, she
looked young again. Young and something else, something
new that was not part of her youth.

"Perhaps I could even get you out of that awful crowded
room at the south end?" Miss Keating said. "And have you
attached to one of the executives?"

Nancy reached across the table and took one of the two
checks from under the edge of Miss Keating's purse and she
looked at it. Salad twenty-three cents, sundae eighteen cents,
milk six cents, total forty-seven cents. It was the right one.
She'd had the milk.

"Oh, now, look," Miss Keating said, reaching out. "I'm taking that. I invited you."

"No," Nancy said, and she picked up her white imitation
leather purse and she leaned back, as far as she could get,
pressing the luncheon check against the purse so hard that
she could feel the small box inside. "I'll pay my own," Nancy
said.

"But how silly," Miss Keating said. "Let me have it, Nancy.
You're my guest."

Nancy shook her head, trying not to think of the things she
had said, trying to think it was only that she would never be
able to wear the earrings in the little box because she would
always remember that Miss Keating had been wearing a pair
exactly like them when she had trapped Nancy into saying
those things.

"I'll pay my own check," Nancy Hull said, getting up. "I'm
not your guest."

JOUST

For some reason, perhaps because of the congestion of people and houses, Fourth Street between Avenue D and Lewis
was either bitterly cold or stiflingly hot. Spring and autumn
were unknown on the block. One day in June, or so it seemed,
the sun would suddenly become unbearable, the heat intense,
breathing difficult. Then winter was over for Fourth Street

and the older boys were free to go swimming from the dock.

The water was the only practical escape from the heat of Fourth Street. Trips to Coney Island involved too much time and preparation and were always in the nature of an event. The East River was a commonplace. You grew up with it and accepted it, like school and the inevitability of occasional illness.

Every boy on the block knew how to swim and used the river regularly. Periodically some parent would get a first clear glimpse of the oily filth in the water and forbid his offspring to swim from the Fourth Street dock. Such injunctions, however, always proved temporary and were regarded by the rest of the block as an unwarranted display of a finicky and undesirable trait known as being "high tone."

As a matter of fact, most parents on the block, not being swimmers themselves, were rather proud of their sons' prowess in the water. Mrs. Gordon, for instance, whose most prominent characteristics were her incredible obesity, her candy stand on the Lewis Street corner, and her son Mozzick, was particularly outspoken. Mozzick was the block's champion swimmer, but his mother had never seen him in action because she was so fat that the task of shifting her bulk from the candy stand to the dock in the hot sun was beyond her.

"That's how life is," she said philosophically. "You raise them up, you slave, you suffer, and then, when they're old enough already they should do something you can be proud of, so then you can't see them do it! You gotta be fat! It's a lucky thing he isn't a singer. Otherwise, with the luck I got, I'd probably all of a sudden get deaf!"

Nor was Mozzick's ability as a swimmer overrated. He was not only the undisputed champion of Fourth Street, but he had successfully vanquished pretenders from other blocks who had come in summers past to wrest the title from him. Fifth Streeters in particular couldn't stand his supremacy. They were practically all Litvaks, while we on Fourth Street were almost exclusively Galician, and the traditional rivalry between the two had been carried over from Middle Europe to America and was kept alive from generation to generation.

Once, in fact, the Litvaks made such a concerted drive for Mozzick's crown that the entire neighborhood was in an uproar for weeks.

The Fifth Streeters' campaign was a subtle one. They didn't come forward with their customary annual challenge, which would have been followed by Fourth Street's customary acceptance and should have ended in Fifth Street's customary defeat. They started rumors of a mysterious swimming marvel who had been discovered in their midst and they made certain that these stories seeped into Fourth Street. When the time came for their annual challenge, in its stead Fourth Street received a set of new rumors, to the effect that the mysterious swimmer was being carefully groomed and wasn't quite ready for public appearance. And finally there were the tales of the unknown's astonishing physique: shadowy phrases, which defied substantiation, about his strange background, his appearance, his ability.

Many people on Fourth Street were upset by the vague yet persistent stories, but Mrs. Gordon was laughingly indignant at the mere thought of anyone's questioning her son's supremacy.

"What has that Litvak got?" she demanded of Fourth Street in general and of her customer at the moment in particular. "Four hands? A dozen feet? Maybe he's got a steam engine in his behind, it makes him swim faster? Don't listen to those dopes from Fifth Street."

The rest of the block shared her convictions, but not her placidity. It was difficult for a street of Galicians to listen to the smug assumption of Litvaks that they could win whenever they chose and only refrained from so doing because they weren't quite in the mood for it yet. So difficult was it, in fact, that Fourth Street, somewhat incredibly, finally broke down and challenged Fifth Street to produce its swimming marvel and enter him in a race with Mozzick Gordon.

The offer was accepted and the cleverness of the Fifth Street Litvaks became apparent at once. As possessor of the champion, Fourth Street should have received the invitation. But instead of waiting patiently it had lost its head and issued the summons. The result was that Fifth Street, having been challenged, had the right to state terms and conditions. The race, they said firmly, would be from the Fourth Street dock across the East River to Brooklyn and back; no pause on the Brooklyn side for rest; both swimmers to be accompanied by rowboats. Galicians are traditionally too proud to protest, especially to Litvaks, and the terms were agreed to. But Fourth Street knew it had been tricked and dealt a blow.

It was a fact well known that Mozzick Gordon could move through dirty water quickly. His endurance was an unknown quantity. And the distance that Fifth Street had insisted upon, to Brooklyn and back, made two things perfectly plain: endurance, not speed, would be the deciding factor in the race, and Fifth Street was especially confident of its candidate's staying powers.

There was a good deal of comment on Fourth Street about the stupidity of certain unnamed people in permitting themselves to be trapped in such fashion, and on the day of the race there were probably only three people on the block who felt utterly confident that Fourth Street would retain its East

Side swimming supremacy. They were Mrs. Gordon, her son Mozzick, and Srul Honig, whose father was a professional gambler and ran a poker game in their fifth-floor apartment on Fourth Street. Srul was taking bets on the contest, basing his confidence on some mysterious version of what he called the "lawvaverages."

On the day decided on for the race a large crowd assembled on the dock and spread over onto the huge, flat coal barges that were moored alongside. Srul Honig moved through it quickly, jotting down bets and loudly giving his opinion of the outcome. A small knot of Fifth Streeters was gathered at one side, completely surrounding and hiding from view their contestant. A similar group of Fourth Streeters surrounded Mozzick Gordon at the other side of the dock. Somebody blew a whistle and the noises on the dock stopped. The Fourth Street group parted and Mozzick Gordon stepped jauntily to the edge of the dock. He wore a pair of trunks and a wide grin, and he bounced up and down on his toes as he waited.

Then the Fifth Street group parted and three people stepped out. Two were fully dressed and between them walked a grotesque-looking young man of uncertain age. A murmur of amazement crossed the dock quietly. He was short and thin and stooped. He had only one arm and his face bore the blank, childish look of the mental defective. The two men brought him to the edge of the dock. Mozzick, a few feet away, stared at them with his mouth open. Before he could speak, however, the whistle blew again.

"Ready?" the starter called.

Mozzick nodded, crouching on the edge of the dock.

"Ready," said one of the men with the Fifth Street swimmer.

There was the crack of a gun. Mozzick dived gracefully outward. The two Fifth Streeters seized their man firmly and pushed him off the dock. He fell without a cry and struck the water with a loud slap. Everybody craned to see him as he rose to the surface and began to move. The helplessness he had displayed on the dock was suddenly gone. He glided through the water smoothly and evenly, lying on one side so that only his one arm was visible as it rose and fell to pull him forward. There was grace in the rhythmic rise and fall of his single arm and there must have been power, too, because Mozzick did not appear to be increasing the lead he had gained by his dive. The two rowboats pulled out after them and the crowd on the dock settled itself for a long wait.

As the bobbing heads and the accompanying rowboats grew smaller many people left the dock. It was estimated that the swimmers would not be back for several hours. A few small groups, consisting of those who had placed bets on the event and those whose allegiance to one or the other of the contestants was deeper than the discomfort of the hot sun, lay about on the coal barges, shielding their eyes, listening to the slap of the water and the creaking of the ropes as the barges strained at their moorings.

Gradually, as the hours went by, people began to drift back onto the dock, until it was almost dangerously crowded.

"There's one of them!"

Everybody followed a pointing finger. A rowboat was coming toward the dock, growing larger with each pull of the oars.

"There's the other one, too!"

The second rowboat seemed just slightly behind the first one, a little to one side. It was hard to tell how much space separated them. And it was still impossible to identify the swimmers.

"Who's in the lead?"

"Can't tell yet!"

But soon they were close enough for the crowd to see that one of them rolled from side to side as he swam, while the other glided evenly, swinging one arm in a tireless circular motion, and that the latter was in the lead.

"Fifth Street's ahead!"

And he was, by quite a distance. The Litvaks cheered wildly, but nobody even bothered to urge Mozzick on. He was too far behind and he seemed too tired for a spurt. The Galicians watched glumly while the Fifth Streeters began to call instructions to their swimmer.

"Over here, dope! There's a ladder here!"

They were pointing to a ladder that was nailed to the end of the dock. But he paid no attention to them. He continued his easy, powerful strokes without raising his head from the water, heading straight for a huge coal barge which was moored loosely to the dock, so that it swung to and fro, bumping against the dock with soft, deadly force at regular intervals.

"Head him off!" the Fifth Streeters cried to the men in the rowboat. "Steer him around to the ladder!"

The men in the rowboat, who had stopped rowing as their swimmer neared the dock, suddenly realized that he was about to enter the narrow strip of water which had just opened between the barge and the dock. One of them bent to the oars while the other began to scream. "Over to the left! Stay out of there! Get over to the ladder!"

The swimmer did not change his course or seem to hear the shouting.

"He don't understand anything!" the Fifth Streeters on the dock cried. "All he knows is how to swim! Hurry up! Grab him!"

But there was too much distance between the rowboat and the swimmer. Before they could reach him, he had glided into the dangerous opening. The screaming and the shouting stopped suddenly. A long line of heads peered over the edge of the coal barge at the swimmer below, watching in terrified silence. Every face twisted with the same tense thought. It was a long barge, but he was swimming strongly, rapidly. He might get through.

The barge completed its outward swing and was brought up with a shudder as it reached the end of its ropes. It hung hesitant for a moment and then began its backward swing. The space of water narrowed slowly, inexorably. He was two-thirds of the way along its side when one man on the barge pulled back his head and turned away quickly. Everybody did the same.

There was a single, weird scream, and the barge touched the dock gently and began to swing away again.

MY AUNT FROM TWELFTH STREET

When I was a child, the strangest thing to me about my Aunt Tessie from Twelfth Street was that she lived on Fifteenth Street. I liked her and she liked me, but I was not permitted to visit her very often because the rest of our family always considered her something of a renegade. She was a large woman, with a quick laugh, a generous purse, and a small tailor shop that her husband had left in her hands when he died, and she baked the largest and best sugar-covered cookies that I have ever eaten. But these virtues were impressive only to me. It was hard for my mother and father and our other relatives to forget that she did not live, by choice, among us.

We were Galicians and lived, quite properly, on East Fourth Street. Sixth Street was almost exclusively Hungarian, Fifth Street was full of Litvaks, Seventh and Eighth Streets were reserved for Russians, and so on. Nobody lived on Twelfth Street.

We all knew Aunt Tessie's explanation for not living with her own people—she said furnished rooms had been cheaper on Twelfth Street than in any other place in the city when she landed in America—but it was disregarded. The difference in rent between Twelfth and Fourth Streets was not enough to excuse such a lapse in nationalistic loyalty. There-fore, in our family she was always referred to, with an un-complimentary twist of the lips, as Tessie from Twelfth Street.

Later, when she married the small tailor on Fifteenth Street and moved three blocks uptown to live in a tiny apart-ment behind the shop, she was still called that. Even after her husband died, Aunt Tessie showed no signs of capitulation. "You know Tessie," my father said with a shrug. "You say black, she says white. As long as she knows you want her to move to Fourth Street, where she belongs, she'll spend her life on Fifteenth Street, there, with the Italians and the Irish. That's Tessie from Twelfth Street for you."

It was hard to understand her loyalty to Fifteenth Street. From the few glimpses that I had had of her section of it, be-tween Avenue A and First Avenue, the family accusation of stubbornness seemed justified. In fact, the street was so cold and dreary-looking, so shabby and lifeless, that I still don't know why I liked to go there. Fourth Street, where we lived, between Avenue D and Lewis, was no Coney Island, but at least it was cheerful and friendly, with plenty of movement and noise, if nothing else. But on Fifteenth Street the houses were dirty and old; no children played in the gutter; nobody yelled or laughed; no groups stood on the sidewalks and gossiped. Fifteenth Street was dead. But I liked it and never seemed to be able to visit it often enough.

Just after my tenth birthday, however, I was treated to what I considered a windfall. My mother, I was told, was about to "go away for a while." This puzzling phrase was delivered with a benevolent smile and later, in translation, proved to mean the addition of a baby sister to the household. The problem of getting rid of me for a few days became a choice between a Fourth Street neighbor and a Fifteenth Street aunt. Finally, and with reluctance, my parents decided on the latter.

Arrangements were made several weeks in advance, and one hot July evening my father delivered me at the small tailor shop with final instructions to be a good boy.

"Don't worry so much," Aunt Tessie told my father. "We're people here the same as you are on Fourth Street, not wild animals. I'll take care of him."

She started me off with a handful of her huge cookies and told me I could stand near the window of the shop and look out into the street while she prepared dinner.

"Can I go outside and sit on the stoop, Aunt Tess?" I asked.

"No," she said. "We'll be ready to eat soon. You can stand by the window and look out."

I was puzzled by her refusal. It was too hot to be indoors. But I couldn't disobey her, so I went to the front window and looked out into Fifteenth Street as I munched cookies. There wasn't much to see. The intense July heat had driven more people than usual out into the street, but they seemed curiously listless and disinterested. Occasionally an automobile drove through and once an ice wagon went by, but they did not stop. The only change that the heat seemed to have made in Fifteenth Street was that all the windows were open. I could tell by the way the curtains fluttered in and out whenever a faint breeze found its way into the block. On Fourth Street you could tell when a window was open because someone was almost always framed in it, leaning on a small pillow and usually yelling into the street or to a neighbor a floor or two above or below. But nobody leaned out of the windows on Fifteenth Street. The heat and the inactivity were depressing. I began to wonder why I had looked forward to this visit and by the time my aunt called me to dinner I was wishing I was back on Fourth Street.

After dinner I asked my aunt if I could go outside.

"No," she said.

"But it's so hot, Aunt Tess!" I protested.

"Well," she said, hesitating; then, "All right. Wait till I finish the dishes and I'll go out with you."

When she was ready we carried two folding chairs out onto the stoop and I helped her set them up. She settled herself with her knitting in one of them and I took the other. The dinner hour was apparently over for most of the block, because a surprising number of people were sitting on the stoops of the houses, the men in shirtsleeves and the women in house dresses, fanning themselves with folded newspapers. There was only one sign of activity on the block. A car was parked at the curb directly across the street from us. A handsome young man, with a tight, dark face and beautifully combed hair, was sitting in the front seat, leaning on the door and talking to three girls who stood on the sidewalk beside the car. The girls were quite pretty, or, rather, they seemed so without hats and in their light summer dresses. And the young man must have been very witty, because every few minutes they would all throw back their heads and laugh loudly at something he had said. Nobody on the block was paying any attention to them. I glanced quickly at my aunt once or twice. But she was engrossed in her knitting. She didn't seem to hear the loud laughter or see the bright little group on the other side of the street. I turned back to watch them.

Just as the sun was disappearing behind the "L" on First Avenue, another young man turned the corner and came down the block. He was carrying his hat and his hair was as thick and handsome and perfectly combed as that of the young man in the car. In fact, he looked almost exactly like the first young man, except that he seemed a little older and he wasn't smiling. He walked up to the car with an insolent swagger and put his foot on the running board and leaned his elbow on the door. The young man in the car smiled up at him and said something and everybody laughed. They talked for another minute or so and then the girls joined in a farewell burst of laughter and walked away, waving once or twice, leaving the two young men with the gleaming hair alone together.

They talked earnestly for a while in friendly fashion. Occasionally the first young man, still seated in the car, would shake his head vigorously or smile. Finally he got out of the car and the two of them started to walk off together toward First Avenue. The first young man continued to shake his head as the other talked and a few times a snatch of his quick laughter came back to me on my aunt's stoop.

Then suddenly, as I watched them, an amazing thing happened. The second young man pulled something from his pocket, pointed it quickly at the first young man, and there was the single snapping crack of a gun. The first young man jerked himself erect, as though someone had taken him by surprise and poked him sharply in the small of the back, and then he crumpled quickly and fell into the gutter. The murderer ran the few steps to First Avenue, turned the corner, and disappeared.

"Aunt Tess!" I cried, jumping up.

In an instant the motionless block was full of a quivering, voiceless activity. Every stoop was bobbing with silent, swiftly moving people. Nobody yelled; nobody screamed; nobody ran toward the young man in the gutter. My aunt clutched my arm. "Come on," she said sharply. "But Aunt Tess!" "Come on," she repeated, and dragged me toward the door. Windows were being slammed shut all along the block. Both sidewalks were empty and in a moment every stoop was cleared. As my aunt pulled me through the door I had a last glimpse of Fifteenth Street. Except for the crumpled young man in the gutter, it was deserted and quiet.

My aunt hurried into the kitchen, dropped her knitting, and ran back into the store, where I was standing at the window.

"Get away from there," my aunt said.

She pushed me aside roughly and I watched her in amazement as she closed the windows and hauled down the long green shades.

"Aunt Tess, what——?"

"Keep quiet," she said.

She seized my arm again and dragged me into the kitchen,

pushed me into a chair beside the kitchen table, and sat down at the other side, facing me. Then she picked up her knitting and began to work quickly. With all the windows shut, the heat was almost unbearable in the small room. The sweat gathered on my forehead and I could feel a thin trickle of it begin to work its way down my spine.

"Aunt Tess," I said, "what—?"

"Don't talk so much," she said.

Her voice was hard and frightened. She had never spoken like that to me before. She continued to knit determinedly, scowling at her nervously working fingers, without looking up and without wiping the sweat from her face.

"But Aunt Tess," I cried, "what happened? They—"

"Shut up," she said.

Not a sound came through to us from the street outside. The sweat was running into my eyes.

"It's hot in here!" I cried. "What—"

My aunt did not look at me. "Just shut up!" she said.

GALLANTRY IN ACTION

"Look, Dad, this one here, with the blue band in the middle and the wide gold stripes on both sides," the small boy said in his high-pitched, eager voice. "That's the Air Medal." He stood up on his toes and pointed to the ribbon over the second lieutenant's pocket. "For meritorious achievement," he recited, stumbling slightly over the long words, "while participating in aerial flight."

"Bobby, stop." The middle-aged man smiled at the young officer and pulled the boy back gently to his side. "That's not very nice, you know, pointing."

The lieutenant, his shoulder bumping back and forth on the foyer wall at the end of the dining car, looked up from his magazine. He grinned good-naturedly at the boy, nodded to the father, and returned to his reading. About a dozen people, most of them service men, were jammed into the foyer, waiting for seats in the crowded diner. They looked down with amusement at the boy. He was small and thin, about ten or eleven years old, with a narrow, intense face and thick-lensed glasses sitting a bit crookedly on his snub nose. His face and hands were freshly tanned and his dark hair was closely cropped. The lapels of his expensive camel's hair jacket were covered with army and navy insignia, including two sets of a captain's silver bars. He sucked nervously on the gold brace across his upper teeth as he peered about at the uniforms around him.

"The Purple Heart, Dad, look," he said, leaning far over to point at the ribbon on a sergeant's tunic. "All purple with the narrow white stripes at the ends." He tugged at his father's hand. "For wounds received in action against an enemy or as a direct result of an act of the enemy," he recited. "The Purple Heart."

The sergeant grinned self-consciously, dropped his freshly lighted cigarette, and ground it out with his toe. The soldiers around him laughed in a friendly way and peered into the dining car, where a second group of people could be seen waiting at the other end.

"Bobby, don't. It's not nice to point." The father hauled the boy back to his side. He was a heavy man in the late forties, with a strong, pleasant face, and an air of authority that made his somewhat awkward affection for the boy seem oddly attractive. None of the men in the foyer looked directly at the boy or his father, yet all were watching them with obvious pleasure. The father smiled at the soldiers around him as he drew contentedly on his excellent cigar. "He knows all the insignia, every decoration, every ribbon," he explained, speaking to the entire group but to no one person in particular. His rich, well-modulated voice contained a note of pride as well as apology. "The colors, what it's for, how it should be worn and when, everything. Memorized them from a book, every one of them."

The steward came bustling down the aisle between the tables, ducked under the tray a waiter was holding aloft, and bobbed up in front of the group in the foyer. His forehead was damp with perspiration.

"Two singles," he said, breathing hard, fanning himself with a batch of menus, and smiling automatically. "Two singles, please?" Nobody moved for several moments. Finally a couple of soldiers squeezed through the group. They looked about questioningly, at the waiting men, and then at each other. "Two, thank you," the steward said impatiently, backing away. "This way, please." The soldiers followed him self-consciously into the dining car. "A few more minutes, gentlemen, please," he called back to the people in the foyer. "Just a few more minutes, please."

"Few more minutes," captain said. "That's pretty good. We've been waiting damn close to an hour now."

"And there's a gang big as this one up the other end," the first lieutenant next to him said. "What do you say we say the hell with it, Don? By the time we get seats, there won't be any food left, anyway."

"You're probably right," the captain said, turning around. He was a young man, very handsome in his tailored uniform, with blond hair clipped in a crew cut. "We lay over in Cleveland for twenty minutes or so to change engines, I hear. We'll be able to get a sandwich or something in the station. Let's go."

The enlisted men pressed back against the walls to make room. The small boy's face brightened. He pulled his father's hand as though it were a bell rope and he pointed up at the young captain's chest.

"Look, Dad," he said. "The Silver Star. Just like Marvin."

"Now, Bobby, please," his father said, trying to pull him out of the way. "I told you that's not nice."

"It *is* the Silver Star, Dad," the boy said. "The red stripe in the middle, and then the white on either side, with the blue outside that. I know it, Dad." The glasses started to slip down his tiny nose and he pushed them back excitedly. "For gallantry in action," he recited. "Just like Marvin."

"I'm sorry, Captain," the father said. "He's a little excited. His brother's got the Silver Star, too. My oldest boy."

"That's all right," the captain said. He smiled and rubbed his hand through the boy's closely cropped hair. The gesture swung the boy's attention from the decoration to the man. He blushed through his tan and stepped away quickly. "What outfit's your brother, son?"

The boy, suddenly speechless with awe and embarrassment, dropped his eyes and hid behind his father.

"Eighth Air Force," the middle-aged man said. "Somewhere in England."

"He is?" The captain's eyes spread with interest. "That's our outfit, too." He nodded toward the first lieutenant at his side. "Mine and Hap's, here."

"Really?" the father said. "The Eighth?" The captain nodded. "Well, now, that's quite something, isn't it?" The middle-aged man looked into the crowded dining car and then he turned back to the two young officers. He took the cigar from his mouth and snapped his fingers. "I've got an idea," he said. "Come with me a minute, gentlemen, will you?"

He led the way through the group jammed in the foyer, across the platform between the dining car and the Pullman beyond, and he pushed the door shut behind the two young officers and his son.

"What's up?" the captain said. "Anything wrong?"

"Not a thing," the middle-aged man said with a smile. "But I couldn't help hearing what you and the lieutenant said.

About the chances of getting any dinner out there, I mean, and it gave me an idea. Bobby and I, we've been waiting almost an hour, too, and it doesn't look very hopeful. Here's what I thought." He raised his voice a bit to make himself heard above the clacking of the train wheels. "We've got a drawing room all to ourselves at the end of this car, Bobby and I, and I've got a couple of bottles of good scotch in my bag. How about you and your friend, the lieutenant, here, how about having a few drinks in comfort while I take a crack at bribing our porter to bring us something to eat in our drawing room? Sandwiches or something, whatever he can get out of the galley, there, before the food runs out? How does that sound?"

"Why, it sounds swell to me, thanks," the captain said. "Hap?"

"You bet," the lieutenant said. "Thank you, sir."

"Then it's settled," the man said cheerfully. "Bobby, you take these gentlemen to our drawing room while I round up the ice and some glasses. All right?" The boy nodded eagerly. "Go right along, gentlemen. I'll join you in a moment."

The boy turned and walked down the shaking car, steadying himself against the berths on either side. His small back was arched with excitement and he breathed rapidly, his mouth open, as he peered ahead through his thick glasses. At the end of the car the boy pushed in the heavy drawing room door and held it open with both hands, standing aside shyly for the captain and the lieutenant to enter.

"After you, Bobby," the captain said. The boy blushed and shook his head, clutching the door knob hard. The captain laughed and ran his hand through the boy's hair again. "Okay, Hap," he said to the lieutenant. "Bobby after us."

They went in and sat down on the settee. The berths were closed and the table was set up between the facing seats. Four beautiful pigskin bags were stacked on the floor against the wall. The boy went to the top one, opened it, and pulled out a bottle of scotch.

"That's the stuff to give the troops," the lieutenant said. "Right, Bobby?"

"Yes, sir," the boy said and his voice cracked with happiness. He cleared his throat and set the bottle on the table and then he stood there awkwardly, blushing and trying to get rid of his hands. "My father will be here in a minute," he said. "Would you care to have a drink before he comes back? There are paper cups in the bathroom."

He was halfway across the room before the captain stopped him by placing his foot up against the door.

"No, we'll wait," the captain said, leaning back on the

couch and lighting a cigarette. "Where did you get the sun tan?"

"In California, sir," the boy said. The ease with which the lounging young men talked seemed to relax him. "I have been staying with my uncle for my health," he said, speaking neatly and precisely, as though he were reciting a lesson for a teacher. "My father came out two weeks ago to take me home to New York." He stopped, as though he had come to the end of his recitation, and he sucked the brace on his teeth. Suddenly he drew a deep breath, gathering his strength for a special effort, and he said, "What did you get the Silver Star for, sir?"

"Nothing very important," the captain said through his easy smile. "Where did you get the bars?"

The boy touched the two sets of captain's insignia on his lapels.

"They're my brother's, sir," he said. "He sent them to me in California. He said in his last letter he's going to send me his Silver Star, too."

The door opened and the middle-aged man came in, carrying a tray with glasses, ice, and soda. The lieutenant stood up.

"Here, let me take that, sir," he said. "No porters, eh?"

"Thanks," the man said. "On the table, I think, don't you? That's fine. No, I found one, all right, but I sent him after the food. He said he wasn't sure, but he thought he might be able to get us something if he got back to the galley fast enough. If not, we'll be pulling into Cleveland within the hour, he told me, and they'll put more stuff on board while they're changing engines. He'll try to get us something then. I made it worth his while." The middle-aged man laughed. "I see Bobby got the bottle out. Thanks, Bobby." He poured the drinks and handed them around. "You all right there, or would you prefer to sit at the table?"

"No, we're fine," the captain said. "Anyway, I am. You, Hap?"

"I'm fine," the lieutenant said. "Swell."

"Well, here's to a happy meeting," the middle-aged man said, holding his glass high. "To our side, to a speedy victory, and to the Eighth."

"Our side, a speedy victory, and the Eighth," the captain said.

"Our side, a speedy victory, and the Eighth," the lieutenant said. They drank. The lieutenant sighed and smacked his lips. "Boy, that's good," he said. "I didn't know there was scotch like this around any more."

"There isn't," the middle-aged man said. "My brother put a couple of bottles in my bag before we left California. He makes airplanes out there and he gets a case every now and

89

then, don't ask me how." He laughed again and sat down at the table, turning sideways to face the young officers sprawled comfortably on the settee. "Bobby's been out visiting him for a while, getting his health back."

"Yes," the lieutenant said. "He told us."

"Here, sit down and be comfortable, Bobby, and take this," his father said. The boy slid into the seat at the other side of the table and took the glass of plain soda. "Feel all right?" his father said.

"Yes, Dad," the boy said. "Thank you."

He sipped the soda slowly as he watched and listened to the young officer and his father. As the train sped through the night, everybody in the drawing room on that particular Pullman was having a good time, but it was plain that the small boy, who didn't say a word, was having the best time of all. His father explained that he was in the silk business, that his plant had been converted completely to war production, that he felt guilty about taking the time off to go to California but he'd been worried about Bobby and, anyway, the moment he got back to New York he'd be in that office seven days a week for the duration to make up for it. The officers said they were back from England on a training mission, had wangled a ten-day leave, which they'd just spent with the captain's family in Chicago, and were now returning to their assignments in New York. The young men drank steadily, two or three highballs to the middle-aged man's one, without much visible effect. They laughed and told funny anecdotes about their experiences with the British and in the air over Germany. Twice the subject of the young captain's Silver Star came up, and the small boy leaned far forward, but both times the captain dismissed it with a laugh and said Hap, who had been flying on his left wing, should have received the decoration. Hap grinned and said nuts and reached for the bowl of ice. It was empty.

"I'll get some more," the middle-aged man said, getting up. "You might open that other bottle while I'm out."

"Let me get the ice," the lieutenant said. "You went the first time."

"You're my guests," the middle-aged man said, pushing the lieutenant back onto the settee. "Besides, I want to find that porter and see about the food he promised."

"Bobby, here's to your father," the lieutenant said, raising his glass. "A swell host. Your health, Mr.—" He paused and blinked. "My God, we haven't even introduced ourselves," he said. "Here, sir." He put his hand on the captain's shoulder. "This is my pal, Don Babcock, and me, my name is Wilde, Hap Wilde."

"A very great pleasure, gentlemen," the middle-aged man

said. "My name is Loewenstein, Frank Loewenstein. And this is my son Robert."

"Glad to know you, sir," the lieutenant said, smiling and touching his glass to Mr. Loewenstein's. "And you, too, Bobby."

The boy blushed with pleasure and touched his glass of soda to the lieutenant's highball.

"How do you spell that?" the captain said. "Your name?"

"L,o,e,w,e,n,s,t,e,i,n," Mr. Loewenstein said. "My oldest son's name is Marvin. You know him, perhaps?"

"No," Captain Babcock said. "I never heard of him."

"Well, I'll get the ice and see about the food," Mr. Loewenstein said. "Be back in a minute, gentlemen."

He went out. Captain Babcock looked around the drawing room, examining each corner as though he had not seen it before. His eyes came to rest, finally, on the four pigskin suitcases. He sat up on the settee, leaned over, and placed his highball on the top suitcase. The train lurched and the glass slid several inches, leaving a wet streak across the leather.

"Hey," Lieutenant Wilde said. "You're messing up that bag."

"It's only water," Captain Babcock said. "Doesn't stain." He sucked in his cheeks, pursed his lips, and narrowed his eyes, as though he was in deep thought. Lieutenant Wilde splashed some whiskey into his own glass and reached over to freshen the one on the suitcase, but Captain Babcock stopped him. "No more for me," he said. "I've had enough." He leaned forward, his elbows on his knees, and he smiled at the small boy. "You really want to hear how I got the Silver Star, Bobby?"

The boy's face grew crimson with pleasure.

"Yes, sir," he said.

"Val, I'll tal you," Captain Babcock said, and his handsome face contracted into a complicated grimace and he twisted his shoulders in what was apparently his version of a dialect comedian's routine. "In de whole skvodron dere vass oney fun plane vid a pilot a lootenint, und dot vass me."

Lieutenant Wilde stared at his friend in quick surprise and, after a short glance at the small boy, he said, "Hey, Don, look." Captain Babcock shook off the interruption with a wave of his hand and swung into an account of a flight over Germany that, from the details he described, could only end in disaster. It was a thrilling story, in spite of the odd manner in which the young captain had elected to tell it. The suspense mounted even though Captain Babcock was an embarrassingly bad performer. Lieutenant Wilde sat slumped down on the settee, behind his friend, and hugged his highball glass in both hands. He kept moving his head from the talking captain beside him to the listening boy at the table, and his lips were spread slightly, as though his gums hurt. The boy listened with his whole body. He stared straight at Captain Babcock, his eyes unblinking behind the thick glasses, and his tongue ran back and forth across the gold brace on his upper teeth. His small tanned hands were clasped tightly together in his lap, and his narrow shoulders were hunched forward in the camel's hair coat, as though he was cold. Occasionally, when the movement of the train swung his rigid little body off balance, he seemed to be shivering.

"So I gafe heem two boists vid da guns," Captain Babcock said, "und den I peeled off."

The door opened. Mr. Loewenstein came in, carrying a fresh bowl of ice and three bottles of soda. Captain Babcock didn't glance up. He continued talking. Mr. Loewenstein stopped in the doorway, holding the ice and the bottles. The boy, oblivious to everything but the story, did not seem to be aware of his father's presence. Lieutenant Wilde looked at the middle-aged man in the doorway, set down his glass, and started to get up, his hands outstretched for the bowl and the bottles. Mr. Loewenstein smiled and shook his head. The lieutenant sank back on the settee. Mr. Loewenstein remained standing, his hands full, and listened attentively while the cigar went cold in his mouth.

"De next ting I knew, de two Jerries dey vass boining und falling," Captain Babcock said, leaning back in conclusion. "Und me? I opened up de trottle vide, I headed for mine base, und ven I came down safe dey vent und dey giff me da Silver Star."

He grinned at the boy. There was a long moment of silence. The only sound in the drawing room was the rhythmic clack of the train wheels. Finally, the boy's intent, expressionless face cracked, like a piece of shatterproof glass on which a stone has been dropped, and tiny wrinkles of confusion spread from his mouth to his eyes. He unclasped his small hands and looked timidly around the room, at the grinning young captain, at the sober-faced lieutenant, at his father in the doorway, as though waiting for the word of explanation to something he knew he should have understood but which, because of his inexperience or stupidity, had escaped him.

"I'm sorry I missed the first part of that," Mr. Loewenstein said. "Judging from the end, it must be an exciting story."

He moved into the room, dropped his dead cigar into the waste basket, and dipped down to place the bowl and the bottles on the table. As he straightened up, he let his hand rest for a moment on his son's shoulder. The boy swung

92

around to face him. His father smiled as he squeezed the camel's hair gently.

"I'd be glad to repeat it," Captain Babcock said. "It's no trouble."

"Will you?" Mr. Loewenstein said. "Thanks. But would you wait just a little while? I've got that porter started on the food, and I want to make sure it gets here. Have another drink. I won't be but a minute, and when I come back we can eat." He turned the smile down on his son and it seemed to change slightly. "Don't you be afraid, Bobby," he said. "I'll be right back."

He went out and walked down the car. At the far end he met a porter carrying a tray piled high with sandwiches.

"All set, sir," the porter said. "Turkey, ham, cheese, and a couple of tongue, on rye and white. I got a big pot of coffee coming along in a minute, too."

"That's fine," Mr. Loewenstein said. "Don't take it in yet, will you?" He drew the porter into the men's washroom, which was empty, and he pulled a five-dollar bill from his wallet. "How soon before we get into Cleveland?"

The porter shifted the tray to one hand and looked at his watch.

"About five minutes, sir. Maybe six or seven."

"All right," Mr. Loewenstein said. "Here's what I want you to do. Go back to my drawing room and leave these sandwiches for the two officers you'll find in there. Then tell the little boy, that's my son, tell him I want to see him. I'll wait for him in here. Then I want you to get our bags out of there. Four of them. My hat and coat, too. And bring them in here." He put the five-dollar bill into the porter's hand. "That all clear?"

"Yes, sir." The porter looked at the five-dollar bill and then at the tray of sandwiches. "But don't you want these?"

"No, they're for the officers," Mr. Loewenstein said. "My son and I, we'll get something to eat in Cleveland."

"In Cleveland?" the porter said. "Ain't you booked through to New York, sir?"

"I was, but I find my plans have changed and we'll have to lay over in Cleveland for one night." Mr. Loewenstein stared through the washroom window, at the night smashing by outside, and he fingered the side of his strong face delicately, like a man probing for an old, forgotten bruise that has unexpectedly become painful again. "And porter, a little later," he said without turning, "you won't forget to bring the officers their coffee, will you?"

"Who?" Pearson said. "No, I don't," he said, and then he listened, his head tipped to one side, cradling the phone between his shoulder and his ear, while his eyes ran along the lines of the neatly typed letter on top of the pile in front of him and, for the first time in three and a half years, he wondered idly why government typewriters were equipped with blue ribbons. "Oh," Pearson said, and his left hand came up fast to keep the phone against his ear as he straightened in the chair. "Sure, yes, of course," he said. "Give me a couple of minutes to sign these letters, Miss Mead. Then you bring him in when you come for them."

He put down the phone and took one of the two pens from the brown and black onyx base with the small brass plaque that said "To Raymond B. Pearson From The Staff V-E Day May 8, 1945." Pearson started to read the top letter, stopped as though he had suddenly remembered something important, raised his head, and looked around the room.

It was a rectangular room, about twenty-five feet long by fifteen feet wide, with the large, glass-topped desk at the far end. The single window was behind the desk. At the other end of the room, near the door, there was a heavy library table on which were piled neat stacks of FCC reports, copies of the Congressional Record, and a set of thick looseleaf Prentice-Hall Tax Service binders. On the wall above the table, facing the window and the desk, hung a large production chart framed in black wood. A heavy line zigzagged boldly up the face of the chart, from a point in the lower left-hand corner marked "Dec. 7, 1941" in red, to a point near the upper right-hand corner marked, also in red, "May 8, 1945." The rest of the line, which was dotted and drawn with lighter ink, disappeared under the frame at the top of the chart. To the right of the desk, fastened to the wall with scotch tape, was a reproduction of the Atlantic Charter. Under it, also fastened with scotch tape, was a glossy print of a group of men with briefcases photographed standing around a jeep in which Franklin Delano Roosevelt sat in front of a C-54 on an airstrip with palm trees in the background. Pearson, looking at least twenty years younger than anybody else in the picture, and three or four years younger than his actual age, which was thirty-six, was at the extreme right, blinking against the sunlight reflected from the windshield. On the floor of the office, which was several shades darker than the pale gray walls, there was a wine-colored carpet with one ragged edge. The carpet seemed too small for the room. A low-slung red leather chair with brass nail heads stood next to the desk. It matched the chair behind the desk except that Pearson's chair swivelled and had a higher back. On the desk, flanking the onyx fountain-pen set, were two imitation mahogany trays, one marked *In* and the other *Out*. A black DDT bomb was holding down the papers in the *Out* tray. All the furniture in the room had small stencil code numbers stamped in yellow on the edges.

It was an impressive room by war agency standards, but a person who didn't know much about those standards, a person accustomed to private business offices, for example, or a naval officer who had never been inside a war agency office, might not have thought it was impressive. Pearson stopped scowling, put the pen between his teeth, turned around, and adjusted the Venetian blind so that the morning sun fell more brightly into the room. Through the slats the Capitol dome and the square bulk of the House Office Building could be seen a quarter of a mile away. The phone rang again.

"Yes?" Pearson said around the fountain pen. "All right, yes." He took the pen out of his mouth. "I'm ready now, Miss Mead."

He signed the letters quickly, without reading them, and he was pushing the pen back into the desk set when the door opened and Miss Mead came in with the young man in naval uniform.

"Mr. Pearson," she said. "This is Lieutenant Lomas."

"How are you, Lieutenant?" Pearson said, coming out from behind the desk with his hand outstretched. "My God," he said, thinking how much wiser he would be if he were not saying it, "you look like a Christmas tree."

Lieutenant Lomas looked startled, glanced down at the ribbons on his chest, and then, as he took Pearson's hand, a slow pink flush of embarrassment came through his tan. He was a tall, good-looking young man of about thirty, with black hair and square white teeth, who looked so well in uniform that it was difficult to imagine him wearing anything else.

"Oh, hell," he said. "You know how it is, sir. Every time you stop at a place to take on water they slap another area ribbon on you. I'm very glad to meet you, sir."

"I'm glad to meet you, too," Pearson said. He nodded to the letters on his desk. "All right, Miss Mead."

She picked up the letters, walked back to the door, and stood there for a moment, holding it open and looking at Lieutenant Lomas. The two lines of neat black lettering on the ground glass of the open door that said "Raymond B. Pearson, Chief, Hard Fuels Branch" were just over her head. Lieutenant Lomas became aware of her glance and turned. Miss Mead smiled and stepped quickly out of the room and pulled the door shut.

"Miss Mead is partial to the navy," Pearson said. "Her brother is somewhere with Halsey. Sit down, Lieutenant. When did you get in? How is Clyde?"

"Thank you, sir." Lieutenant Lomas waited politely, until Pearson got back into his own chair behind the desk, before he dropped into the red chair next to it. "Clyde's fine," he said. "Just dandy. About two hours ago," Lieutenant Lomas said. "Few minutes before nine."

"All the way from Guam?" Pearson said.

"Yes, sir," Lieutenant Lomas said with a grin. "All the way from Guam. You sure move fast these days, once you get going. It's damned nice of you to see me like this, sir, just walking in on you, without an appointment or anything."

"Don't be silly," Pearson said. "Any friend of Clyde's is welcome to anything I've got, certainly my time, and I think the war effort can spare a few minutes of that for a friend of Clyde's. We grew up together. Everything all right with him?"

"Yes, he told me you grew up together," Lieutenant Lomas said. "Everything's fine with him. He'd like to get home for a while, everybody does after two years, and I guess he will, pretty soon, although those things are never definite, but aside from that he's great. He's been promoted, you know."

"Lieutenant commander?" Pearson said, his voice rising. "When?"

"Yes, sir, lieutenant commander," Lieutenant Lomas said. "It came through about two weeks ago. No, wait, let's see. I left Guam Thursday and today's Monday, that's four days, and it happened just a week before I left. Eleven days ago."

"That's wonderful," Pearson said, and then, because it didn't sound quite right, he said, "That really is terrific. Eleven days. I guess that's why we haven't heard yet. I imagine it'll be in his next letter, except he's so damned modest."

"He sure is," Lieutenant Lomas said. "A real swell guy, sir."

"Tell me more about the old son of a gun," Pearson said. "No, wait." He picked up the phone. "I'll call my wife and you come to dinner tonight. We're in Arlington, but I'll drive you out and see that you get a taxi back. She'll want to hear, too. She's known Clyde since we were both kids."

"No, I'm sorry," Lieutenant Lomas said, half rising in the chair. "I wish I could, sir, and it's damned nice of you to ask me, but I'm afraid I can't make it. I've got a seat on the one o'clock plane to New York. My family's up there. I won't be in Washington but another two hours."

"That's a shame," Pearson said, and then, into the phone, "Never mind, Miss Mead." He dropped the phone back onto the hook. "Mrs. Pearson will be disappointed. Well, you tell me and I'll tell her. By the way, what's the one on the left, with the blue and white in the middle?"

Lieutenant Lomas looked down at his chest and then he started to fumble awkwardly in his pocket.

"Philippines Liberation," he said, pulling out a pack of cigarettes. "Will you have one, sir?"

"Thanks, I don't smoke," Pearson said. "But you go ahead."

Lieutenant Lomas twisted his head to get his eye away from the smoke as he blew out the match, and his glance stopped on the glossy print under the Atlantic Charter. Pearson began to feel a little better.

"Is that you, sir?" Lieutenant Lomas said. "On the right, near the windshield?"

"Yes," Pearson said. "I was with him at Casablanca in January of '43."

Lieutenant Lomas leaned over to examine the picture more closely. "He sure was a wonderful guy, sir," he said. "Wasn't he?"

"A wonderful guy and a great man," Pearson said, and he could feel himself growing tense with anticipation but, from the speed with which Lieutenant Lomas' glance swung around the room, it was clear that neither the chart on the wall at the far end, nor the reversed black lettering on the ground glass of the door, held any significance for him. His glance stopped on the ragged edge of the carpet on the floor and he started to rub the two gold stripes on his sleeve absently. "Well," Pearson said. "I guess there isn't really much more to tell, is there? Except that he's well and doing fine and been promoted."

"Yes, sir, that's about all, really," Lieutenant Lomas said, looking up from the carpet. "Clyde's well and he's doing fine and he's been promoted."

"I know how it is," Pearson said, beginning to rub the sleeve of his tweed coat. "Every time I go over on a trip, people here in Washington always give me a long list of friends and relatives to look up, and I always do, even though it means running yourself ragged, but when I get back all I can really tell them is their friends and relatives are well, and doing fine and, once in a while, that they've been promoted. They're always disappointed and want to hear more, but there never seems to be any more to tell. I was almost glad when I had to turn down the trip to Yalta and send my assistant, because we had a big battle coming up on the Hill and I had to be here for the hearings." Pearson waited a moment, but Lieutenant Lomas had either never heard of Yalta, or he was not listening.

97

He was drumming his fingers on the brass nail heads of his chair and looking for an ash tray. "Here," Pearson said, wishing he had not talked so much and wishing he did not feel the way he felt, as he pulled an ash tray out of his desk drawer and pushed it forward. "Not being a smoker myself, I always forget that other people use them."

"Thank you, sir," Lieutenant Lomas said. He punched out his cigarette and lit a fresh one. "Yes, that's how it is, I guess," he said.

"Well, now, Lieutenant," Pearson said, making a final effort, knowing it was foolish to feel the way he felt. "Is there anything I can do for you during the two hours you've got here in Washington?"

Lieutenant Lomas looked up from his examination of the end of his cigarette. "As a matter of fact, sir, there is," he said. "But I'm sort of embarrassed to ask."

"Nonsense," Pearson said. He stopped rubbing his tweed sleeve and he sat up straighter. "Anything I can do, it will be a pleasure to do it, I assure you."

Sitting far forward in the low chair, his elbows on his knees, and scowling down at the cigarette which he twirled between the fingers of both hands as though it were a swizzle stick, Lieutenant Lomas explained what he wanted. His wife's brother, a kid of twenty, was a corporal in the army. They knew he was in China but they were not sure just where in China. He had been there for a year and a half and had written home regularly, but, several months ago, his letters had stopped. Two parcels that his sister, Lieutenant Lomas' wife, had sent him months ago had been returned last week without any explanation, and only yesterday a batch of her most recent letters had come back. Lieutenant Lomas' wife had not written her husband about this because she didn't want to worry him but, an hour or so before, when he got off the plane here in Washington, he had called her long distance from the airport to say he had a seat on the one o'clock plane and would be in New York that night, and she had told him about the problem and asked if he could try, during his few hours in Washington, to get some information about her brother. She and the rest of the family were worried sick. They had written to the War Department several times, but the replies had not been very helpful or reassuring. All the War Department would say was that the corporal was not listed as injured or missing. The War Department would not, or could not, explain why the boy had stopped writing or why his letters and parcels were being returned.

"I haven't seen the kid for two years," Lieutenant Lomas said. "Before I went overseas. He wasn't quite eighteen then, and he wasn't in the army yet, but he was kind of a

98

wild one, I guess. Sort of irresponsible and reckless, the way kids that age are, you know, and frankly my wife is afraid that he may have got himself into some kind of jam." Lieutenant Lomas raised his head from the cigarette, dusted the long ash carefully into the ash tray, and smiled apologetically. "Frankly, sir, I thought of you right away, not only because Clyde had told me to look you up, and I was coming to see you anyway, to give you his regards and all, but also because Clyde has told me a lot about you and how much weight you pull in this town. I know it's a hell of a thing to ask a man you've just met to do for you, but I just can't think of anything else. I don't know anybody in Washington."

Pearson made a small gesture with his forefinger, as though he was rubbing away the mist on a train window so he could look out to read the sign on a station platform, and he smiled back at Lieutenant Lomas. There was genuine pleasure in the smile. For the first time since the younger man, and he couldn't be so very much younger, had come into the room, Pearson felt like himself again.

"Don't apologize," he said, picking up the phone. "I'm delighted to be able to help." He was telling the truth. "Miss Mead," he said into the mouthpiece. "Get me General Wheeler at the Pentagon, will you? I'll hold on. It's important."

He tipped his head to one side, tucking the instrument into the bend of his shoulder, and he watched Lieutenant Lomas' forehead begin to crease.

"Is that *General* Wheeler you're calling, sir?"

Pearson nodded and hoped, as he put his free hand over the mouthpiece, that the small, exultant skip of his heart was not reflected in his face.

"The General and I work very closely," he said. "We were at Casablanca together and actually, although this is off the record, of course, I briefed him for Yalta when I found I couldn't get away myself. We're very good friends. He just sent this thing over to me this morning." Pearson reached across the desk and lifted the DDT bomb from the papers in the *Out* tray. "We've been having some trouble with mosquitoes at our house out in Arlington, and you can't buy this stuff commercially, you know." Pearson bounced the black metal container in his hand several times and set it back in the *Out* tray. "Yes, that's all right, Miss Mead," he said into the mouthpiece. "I'll hold on. It's important." Pearson put the mouthpiece back against his chest. "Too bad you can't stay overnight," he said. "The General and Mrs. Wheeler are coming to dinner."

"I guess Clyde wasn't kidding when he said you were big stuff in this town," Lieutenant Lomas said with a grin. "Wait till I write him about this."

"What's that?" Pearson said into the phone. "Oh. Well, look. Will you leave word for the General to call me as soon as he gets back to his office? It's important. Yes." Pearson hung up. "He's at a meeting, but they expect him back within the hour. I'll tell you what, Lieutenant." Pearson pulled a pad from his drawer and took one of the pens from the onyx set and held them out to Lieutenant Lomas. "Why don't you put the kid's name and serial number and his APO down on this pad, and write your own address in New York under it, and when the general calls me back I'll get the dope from him and send you a wire or write you a note. You'll be in New York for a while, won't you?"

"Yes," Lieutenant Lomas said, taking the pen and the pad. "I've got thirty days."

"Well, fine, then," Pearson said. "You'll get this tomorrow or the day after, at the latest."

"That's damned swell of you, sir," Lieutenant Lomas said. Pearson made the motion in the air with his forefinger again. The lieutenant put the pad on his knee and hunched himself over it to write. Pearson noticed how much smaller the lieutenant was than he had looked leaning back in the low-slung chair. Even the uniform, which had seemed so smart and well cut when he was standing up, was now bunched up around his chest and the collar stood away from his neck. "There it is, sir," Lieutenant Lomas said, standing up and putting the pad and the pen on the desk. "That other name, that's my mother-in-law. We gave up our apartment when I went in, and my wife's been staying with her."

"Right," Pearson said, glancing at the pad as he pressed the buzzer under the ledge of his desk and stood up. "Don't you worry about this any more, Lieutenant. I'll see that you get the information."

"I don't know how to thank you, sir," Lieutenant Lomas said. "My wife and her family will be very grateful to you. I know I am, right now."

"Not at all," Pearson said, and he smiled as he put out his hand. "It's been great fun meeting you, Lieutenant. Good luck, and if you write to Clyde, give him my regards."

"I sure will, sir," Lieutenant Lomas said, shaking Pearson's hand. "And thanks again."

The door opened and Miss Mead came in.

"Oh, Miss Mead," Pearson said. "After General Wheeler calls me, will you be sure to remind me to wire or write to Lieutenant Lomas in New York?"

"I certainly will," Miss Mead said.

Pearson nodded and waved, and Lieutenant Lomas waved back as he went to the door. Miss Mead held it open for him and, when he reached her, she smiled.

"I beg your pardon," Miss Mead said. "But could you tell me what that one is? I've seen it several times before, but I never found out what it's for?"

"This?" Lieutenant Lomas said, looking down at his chest. "Oh, heck, that's just the Presidential Citation. Everybody and his brother has that. So long, sir," he said, across his shoulder. "And thanks again."

Pearson didn't answer. The smile slid from his face as they went out, and he sat down abruptly in the red leather chair with the high back and the brass nail heads. Pearson took his lower lip in his teeth and he swivelled himself around and he stared out through the slats of the Venetian blind at the Capitol dome, trying hard to bring back the good feeling, to erase the sudden irritation by cutting from his mind the few moments after Miss Mead had come in, fighting with himself to leave only what had been there before she opened her big mough, but he couldn't do it. He wasn't that good. When the phone rang he reached for it and brought it to his ear without turning.

"Yes?" Pearson said.

"General Wheeler returning your call," Miss Mead said.

"I'm not in," Pearson said, letting just enough of his irritation come through in his voice so she would know it was meant for her and not for the General. "The call wasn't important," he said. "Just thank him for sending over the DDT and tell him I'll talk to him tonight."

MOVABLE FEAST

"Perhaps I can explain it this way," Miss Holcomb said, keeping one eye on her wristwatch. "Let me give you an example, children. Let's take Washington's Birthday. That always comes on February twenty-second. It has to, because that's the day the father of our country was born. Washington's Birthday is always on February twenty-second. It never changes. It can't. Do we understand that?"

She looked anxiously down into the faces of the forty little boys. It was the last day of school before the Christmas vacation, and in a corner to the right of Miss Holcomb's desk was a Christmas tree. The forty little faces looked back up at Miss Holcomb. Some of them were fat and some were thin. Some were dark and some were pale. Some looked as though they belonged at the scarred, once honey-colored desks, and some looked as outrageously misplaced as they would have been on a silver platter in a performance of "Salome." Yet in one way all the little faces in Miss Holcomb's 1A class looked curiously alike. It was quite clear that they didn't understand what was going on. Miss Holcomb turned quickly to look at David Sternshus, the boy who had asked the question. Usually she felt in him a depth of understanding and sympathy, inarticulate but definite, for what she was trying to do. But now the lean, wide-eyed face of little David Sternshus looked exactly like the thirty-nine others in the classroom.

"Good," Miss Holcomb said without conviction. Her glance strayed for a moment to the windows, plastered with silver stars and prancing reindeer and small, fat cut-outs of Santa Claus. Through the glass she could see the city snow, piled in dirty mounds along the curbs of Houston Street. "Let's take —well, let's take Labor Day. Labor Day doesn't come on a particular date. It comes the first Monday in September. Now, if the month of September begins on Monday, why then Labor Day comes on September first. But if the month of September begins on any other day, let's say on a Thursday, then Labor Day that year comes on—let me see now, Thursday is the first, Friday the second, Saturday the third, Sunday the fourth—Labor Day that year comes on September fifth. Is that clear, children?"

She stole another look at David Sternshus. The little boy's face had not changed.

"That's not the way it is with Christmas," Miss Holcomb said. "Christmas Day is like Washington's Birthday. It always comes on December twenty-fifth. Do you understand that, children?"

Most of the really bad waterfront tenements have now given way to a beautiful and somewhat implausible East River drive, and no cold-water flat, however small or mean or poor, is without a radio or a daily newspaper. But in those days, shortly before the first World War, when Miss Holcomb passed her examinations and received her certificate and was assigned to teach the first grade at P.S. 188, on New York's lower East Side, there were no radios and the only newspapers that were sold in the vicinity of Houston Street were read from right to left. The Lewis Street streetcars that ran in front of the school were still drawn by horses, and the East Side world Miss Holcomb came down to every day from Morningside Heights was far removed from the world she was used to.

That was what had excited Miss Holcomb about her job. It was her first job and she was young—twenty-three—and she wanted desperately to do good things for the under-privileged. She felt there was so much she could bring into the narrow, drab lives of these six-year-old sons of Polish and Austrian and Russian immigrants. She disliked the older members of the faculty—callous, middle-aged women who had been teaching children like these for fifteen and twenty years and called them kids. The older teachers had tried to tell her about the necessity for a calm, reasonable, even cautious approach to minds that were at once infantile and aged, fragile and tough. Miss Holcomb attributed these warnings to the jealousy these older teachers must feel toward her, the youngest teacher in the school, and refused to be discouraged by what they said. But she had to admit that she had not accomplished as much as she had hoped to. Four months was such a short time, yet at least in little David Sternshus her efforts had been crowned with some success. He had learned from her the right words for asking to leave the room. He drank his milk at recess without gulping noises. He even whipped off his cap when he met her on the street. Miss Holcomb had high hopes for little David Sternshus and, through him, for the rest of her 1A class, for her future as a teacher.

Miss Holcomb's young man, whose name was Alfred Orcutt, approved of her zeal. They were going to be married as soon as he finished his internship at Bellevue and set himself up in practice. He listened with interest to her tales of life below Fourteenth Street and at first he had shared her indignation when, the second week in December, she came home with the amazing information that she was the only teacher in the first grade who planned to give her children a Christmas party.

"When I mentioned it at lunch in the teachers' rest room today," she said, "they told me to forget it. They said it had been done before several times and the children hadn't appreciated it. Can you imagine that, Alfred? Can you imagine children of six not appreciating a Christmas party? They're lying to me."

"I guess they are," Alfred Orcutt said. "But I don't see why they should. Come to think of it, if you gave the children a Christmas party, you'd have to pay for it yourself, wouldn't you?"

"Of course," Miss Holcomb said impatiently. "But you don't think I'd let that stop me, do you? After all, it's just a few dollars for candy and favors and decorations, things like that, but to those poor children it would mean—" She waved her delicate, manicured hand to indicate the entrance of loveliness, sunshine, and joy into lives now darkened by the absence of all three.

Miss Holcomb and Alfred Orcutt made a list of things

103

needed for a Christmas party, and they shopped in the evenings, when he could steal an hour or two from his duties at the hospital. During the day, Miss Holcomb had the children paste decorations on the classroom windows and copy Christmas scenes out of picture books onto the rear blackboard with colored chalk. The party was to be held in the classroom the last day of school, right after lunch, from one o'clock to the three-o'clock dismissal bell. Alfred had got permission at the hospital for time off and was to drop in at P.S. 188 about two o'clock. He would have a hired Santa Claus suit with him and the plan was that he would appear in the classroom while the festivities were at their height and distribute the stuffed gauze stockings under the Christmas tree.

The day before the party, Miss Holcomb had a feeling that all was not well. She didn't know why. She just felt it in her bones. But in the late afternoon, snow began to fall and her spirits soared again. It would be a white Christmas on Houston and Lewis Streets. The following morning, as Miss Holcomb approached the school, she saw that snow on Lewis Street was not quite the same as snow on Morningside Heights. Once she entered the gaily decorated classroom, however, she forgot about the dirty-gray snow outside.

All morning she found it difficult to keep her mind on the arithmetic and spelling lessons she was giving her children. She was thinking of the moment when Alfred would come in dressed as Santa Claus.

A small Christmas tree stood in the corner to the right of her desk, and it was all twinkly with slivers of tinfoil and bright balls of red and blue and yellow glass. Under the tree were forty red gauze stockings, stuffed with cookies, raisins, nuts, and inexpensive gifts, such as whistles, toy soldiers, pencil boxes, and mechanical tops. On Miss Holcomb's desk stood the purchase that had given her and Alfred Orcutt the most pleasure—a huge box of bright little hard candies, each with a tiny Christmas scene or a colored design all the way through the sugar, so that the pictures would not disappear until the candy itself disappeared. It was the sort of candy that Miss Holcomb and her young man remembered having at Christmas parties all through their childhood.

During her lunch hour, Miss Holcomb scarcely spoke to the teachers in the faculty rest room. At one o'clock, when the forty little boys streamed back into the classroom, she met them with a happy smile and fingered the sprig of holly she had tucked into her hair. They took their seats sedately and looked up at her. Miss Holcomb's heart skipped a beat. It occurred to her suddenly that she didn't know how to begin a Christmas party like this.

She looked desperately around the room. She couldn't start by distributing the stockings under the tree. That was reserved for Alfred. She couldn't begin by asking the boys to come up and take scoops of candy out of the large wooden box on her desk. That was too abrupt. Her discomfort was not helped by the growing realization that there was more curiosity, more bewilderment, on the faces of the children than anticipation. Miss Holcomb took one look at David Sternshus, her favorite and her barometer, and at once she was convinced she knew what was wrong. Why hadn't she thought of it before?"

In all the excitement of preparing for the party she had neglected to tell these children the significance of the various preparations. They had to be explained to these children in the same way that they had had to be explained to her and to Alfred Orcutt when *they* were children. Miss Holcomb glanced at her wristwatch. It was a quarter after one. She had three-quarters of an hour before Alfred would arrive. Smiling brightly, she launched into a history of the Yuletide celebration.

As the minute hand of her watch passed the one-thirty mark and began to crawl toward two o'clock, she became aware of the stillness in the room. None of the little boys had moved. Miss Holcomb stumbled over a word or two, managed to finish her sentence, and looked at her pupils.

"Are there any questions, children?" she asked. "Is there anything you want to know before we begin our party?" Not a sound came from the forty boys. Miss Holcomb's heart seemed to drop out of her body. What was wrong with these children? The watch on her wrist said quarter of two. If only Alfred would be early. If only he would come bursting in through the door now. Miss Holcomb turned to her favorite pupil. "Is there something you don't understand, David?"

The little boy moved uncomfortably in his seat. He tried to lower his eyes, but couldn't. He stared back at the beautiful, clean, rich, puzzling young woman from uptown. She wanted him to do something. He didn't know what it was. Then her voice came to him, louder this time. He took the words apart and put them together again so they made sense.

"Why is it Christmas now?" little David Sternshus asked. "Why does it come this week?"

When Miss Holcomb had finished her explanation, it was seven minutes after two, and still no sign of Alfred Orcutt.

"That's why Christmas Day always comes on December twenty-fifth," she said. "Because it doesn't move, like Labor Day. It's always the same day, like Washington's Birthday. Is

105

that clear, children? Now, do we all know why Christmas always comes on—"

The door burst open. Miss Holcomb hurried to meet the tall young man with a badly pasted-on white beard and a bulging red flannel coat.

"Alfred! I thought you were never—" she whispered.

"Sorry to be late, darling," he said out of the corner of his mouth. "Got stuck." And then, in a loud, booming voice more false than his beard, "Let's see what Santa Claus has for all these good boys. Let's see what old Santa brought in his pack. Ah, here we are. A present for every little boy."

Miss Holcomb, smiling and nervous with happiness, called the boys up by name, one at a time. Alfred Orcutt adjusted his awkward disguise and handed out the red gauze stockings under the Christmas tree. As the pile of stuffed stockings grew smaller, Miss Holcomb's nervousness disappeared. When all the boys were seated behind their desks again, the Santa Claus and Miss Holcomb turned to face the classroom. They beamed happily on the forty little boys and, at that moment, they seemed to realize that the forty little boys were not beaming back at them. The dismissal bell rang. Forty pairs of small feet began to shuffle under the desks. Miss Holcomb glanced at her wristwatch. It was three o'clock.

"The candy!" she said. "We've forgotten the candy!" She hurried to her desk and picked up the tin scoop from the box. "The party isn't over yet, children. There's a scoop of candy here for everyone. Alfred, the paper bags, please!"

From out in the hallway came the sound of children hurrying by on their way home. Their voices poured in through the open transom above the door.

"Here we are," Alfred Orcutt said, opening a paper bag. Miss Holcomb poured a scoopful of the little hard candies into it and he twisted the top of the bag closed. "Come on, boys," he said. "One at a time."

He held the bag out to the boy behind the first desk in the first row. The boy didn't reach for it. Alfred Orcutt shook the bag and held it out again, a trifle further. The boy remained motionless.

"Come along, Abraham," Miss Holcomb said. "Take the candy from Santa Claus." The boy didn't move. "Abraham! I'm talking to you!"

Alfred Orcutt touched Miss Holcomb's arm. She looked at him and he shook his head. Then he turned with a smile to the second little boy in the row.

"Here we are, son," he said heartily. "A bag of nice candy from Santa Claus."

The second little boy didn't reach for the bag. Alfred Orcutt bit his lip and got a mouthful of false beard with it. The sounds of feet and voices in the hallway grew louder. Now the sounds were coming in from the street, too, but Miss Holcomb's classroom was quiet. The young intern shrugged help-lessly. The expression on Miss Holcomb's face changed to anger. She snatched the bag of candy from Alfred's hand and stalked down the aisle between the desks until she reached the seat of her favorite pupil.

"I don't know what's got into the other children," she said. "Here, David. Take this. It's perfectly all right. It's another present. There's a bag for everybody."

The little boy looked up at her. His small body bent back in the seat, stiffly, as though he were trying to escape from her. He shook his head.

"Will you stop this nonsense?" Miss Holcomb snapped. "Take this!"

"Look," Alfred Orcutt said uncomfortably. "Maybe they don't want—"

The door opened. Miss Holcomb whirled around. In the doorway stood a group of the older teachers. Boys streaming by on their way home stopped to gather behind the teachers. Soon there was a large group in the doorway. They all stared into the room.

"Oh," one of the teachers said. "We were just wondering how the party was going. We thought we'd drop in and—"

The forty boys in Miss Holcomb's class rose halfway in their seats, their faces puckered with relief.

"Close that door!" Miss Holcomb said. "Sit down! All of you!" The little boys sank back in their seats. "Nobody is going to leave this room!" She rushed to the door. "Get out! All of you! Get *out!*" She pushed the teachers and the staring boys out into the hallway and slammed the door shut. Then she turned back to the class, her hands clasped on the door-knob behind her. "Nobody is leaving this room until I find out what's wrong."

Alfred Orcutt snatched off his false beard, flung it aside, and came toward her. "Listen," he said. "They just don't want it, darling. Let them—"

She shook her head. "I don't care what they want or don't want. I've gone to all this trouble. I've spent good money to give them a party. They've been difficult all day. Now they won't take the candy. It's good candy. It's Christmas candy. It's the kind of candy I had at Christmas parties when I was a little girl in school. I want to know why they won't take it." She strode down the aisle again until she reached David Sternshus. She held the paper bag out to him. "Are you going to take this, David, or aren't you?" The boy didn't answer.

"Listen, darling," Alfred Orcutt said. "Don't—"

"Keep quiet!" Miss Holcomb said to him. "David, I'm talking to you! Why won't you take this candy?"

The little boy's lips began to quiver. He didn't hear Miss Holcomb's words. Fright was blocking everything out. All he could see was the bag of bright, hard candies. The same sort of candies he and the other boys had been tricked into taking the year before at the party in the kindergarten class, the party that had been called by the same name, the party that had come at the same time of year, when there was snow on the ground. His brain froze with terror. The temptress from uptown was holding out a paper bag filled with sweet little pellets of treachery, bits of bright hardness that would crawl into the holes in his teeth, into the cavities that a dentist could have fixed for him and for the other boys if the father of David Sternshus and the fathers of the other boys had been in America long enough to have learned about dentists or could afford to send their children to one. In the small boy's fevered mind was stamped only the blinding horror, the pain of last year's toothache.

"Answer me!" Miss Holcomb said. "Why won't you take the candy?"

The door opened. Everybody turned. The school janitor, white-haired and bent, wearing brown overalls and carrying a broom, stared into the room.

"Excuse me," he said in surprise. "Didn't know anybody was still here. Everybody's gone home."

"Get out!" Miss Holcomb screamed. "Get out of here! I don't want—"

She stopped. David Sternshus had slipped out of his seat, stumbled against her, and was running down the aisle. Before Miss Holcomb could recapture her balance, the other boys had leaped up. The janitor gaped and moved hastily out of the way. The forty little boys poured past him, out of the classroom and into the hallway. Their feet pounded down the corridor toward the exit. The janitor blinked stupidly, scratched his head, and dragged his broom out into the hallway after him. Very gently he pulled the door shut on the classroom.

Alfred Orcutt slipped out of his Santa Claus suit. "Listen, darling. Don't let it—"

Miss Holcomb's rigid body folded. She dropped into one of the little seats and stared around the silent room, at the colored chalk pictures on the rear blackboard, at the scarred desks, on which were lying forty stuffed red gauze stockings, at the Christmas tree up front, at the decorated windows, in which were framed the mounds of dirty snow on Houston Street. She ran her hand through her hair. The sprig of holly

tumbled to the floor. Her clenched fist pounded the desk noiselessly.

"Those kids," she said. "Those horrible kids."

HOUDINI

It was Sunday morning and the sun on the river was bright
without too much heat, the crowd of hikers on the ferryboat
noisy and large. The girls wore ribbons in their hair and when
they stood against the rail of the boat the wind whipped at
their slacks. The young men chewed the stems of pipes with
initials cut into the bowls, and they carried shoe boxes full of
lunch, which were fitted with tricky little arrangements of
rope or string, so that they hung over the shoulder or on the
chest like a nightclub cigarette girl's tray. Some of them
played kazoos or harmonicas or ukuleles, and they all sang.
They sang loudly and steadily, and at times it seemed that the
whole boat was singing the same song.

There was also a troop of Boy Scouts on board, who
were very busy chasing back and forth across the deck and
through the lounge, shouting, shoving, tossing their bulging
knapsacks around, and tripping each other. There were sixteen of them and they were making so much noise that they
could easily have been mistaken for twice that number, but the
other hikers didn't pay attention to them. Neither did the
three scoutmasters. They leaned against the rail and watched
the girl hikers with a deep interest. Two of the men were thin
and dark haired, with small mustaches, and it was obvious
they hadn't shaved that morning. The third scoutmaster was
taller and much broader, with stiff, blond hair and a pink,
clean-shaven face. As the boat began to bump its way into the
ferry slip on the Jersey side, he turned to the other two. "We
better get them all together, huh?" he said. "Before we get
off the boat, I mean."

The two dark-haired scoutmasters shrugged. "Yeah, sure,"
one of them said. "Might as well. Go ahead."

The blond scoutmaster left the rail and moved across the
crowded deck toward the Boy Scouts. As soon as they saw him
coming, they surged toward him, laughing as they pulled at his
uniform and dodged his good-natured shoves. When he ordered
them into line, they did not obey promptly, but there was no
disrespect in their voices or their actions and gradually they

formed two columns. He kept them in some sort of order and joked with them as he marched them toward the front of the boat. When the two other scoutmasters fell in behind, the joking and the horseplay stopped immediately and the boys became quiet and subdued. They called these scoutmasters Mr. Bowen and Mr. Fuller, very respectfully. They didn't speak to the blond scoutmaster at all when the other two were within earshot. When they weren't, the boys called him Johnny.

On the shore, outside the ferryhouse, Bowen and Fuller conducted a brief inspection of the boys and of their equipment, and then gave the order to march north.

"We always go north toward Alpine," Johnny said. "I promised the kids today we'd take them south."

"Who are you to go around promising?" Bowen demanded. "Fuller and me, we got something to say in this troop too, you know. In case you're forgetting."

Johnny flushed and drew them aside.

"Sure you have," he said earnestly. "I didn't mean that. It's just that the kids pestered me at the last meeting we should go south and—well, as long as that's what the kids want, I don't see that it makes any difference where we—"

"It's a matter of discipline," Fuller said.

"You let them ride all over you roughshod," Bowen said, walking toward the boys and speaking over his shoulder. "Come on. We're going north, up toward Alpine." The boys hesitated.

"You heard what he said," Fuller said, following Bowen. "North to Alpine. I said it, also. That makes it two to one."

The procession started slowly and in sullen silence. Johnny led the way, several yards in front of the first two boys. Bowen and Fuller brought up the rear, several yards behind the last boys. For a while they maintained that formation, walking along without speaking. Gradually, however, the first two boys quickened their pace to catch up with Johnny. The others followed and it was plain that he was glad to have them. In a few minutes they were all bouncing along noisily in a formless snarl, with the big blond head and the pink-faced grin sticking up in the middle. Bowen and Fuller maintained their distance in the rear. Once, while the formation was breaking, Bowen started to step forward. Fuller stopped him.

"Aah, what can you do?" he said in a low voice. "You can't teach him nothing about discipline. It takes brains. Of which he's got you know how much. Let him alone."

As they walked, Johnny kept the boys' minds off the heat and the weight of their knapsacks by testing them on the names of trees, cloud formations, and birds. He reached up to pluck leaves from overhanging branches and he called for volunteers to name them. When he pointed out a piece of rock at the river's edge that he wanted them to notice for its color, they raced to it and fought to bring it back to him. At two o'clock they left the river path and made camp in a cleared space in the woods. The incident at the ferryhouse had been forgotten.

The boys paired off to do their cooking and Johnny went from group to group supervising the fires and the meals. Nobody would begin to eat until Johnny had tasted the first bite of blackened steak and pronounced it done. Bowen and Fuller busied themselves with their own meal.

After lunch the boys wanted to go swimming. Fuller said they would have to wait a full hour before going into the water. Johnny agreed and filled in the time by teaching them tricks with knots. His fingers were broad and clumsy-looking, but they curled with surprising deftness in and out of the twists and loops of the rope. After he tied a knot he would open it and do it over again several times, very slowly, until the boys watching him could repeat it. Then he would go on to a new one. Bowen and Fuller stood on the outskirts of the group for a while.

"Lemme take a look at that rope," Fuller said finally. "I got a little trick here I'd like to show you."

"Sure." Johnny handed over the rope. It was a seven- or eight-foot length, of the kind that is used for clotheslines. Fuller took it and turned to Bowen. "Come on," he said, "we'll show the boys something."

"Right," Bowen said, turning around and clasping his hands behind him. He did it without hesitation, as though he knew what was expected of him. Fuller tied Bowen's wrists together, then had him lie on the ground while he tied his ankles. A short piece of rope was dangling. Fuller twisted this through both knots and hauled on them hard. Bowen's bound ankles came up to touch his bound wrists behind his back. Fuller tucked in the loose end of rope and stood up. "O.K., boys," he said, dusting his hands. "Take a good look."

Johnny and the boys came close and inspected the knots. One boy reached out and tested them. They were solid and tight. Bowen grinned up at them from the ground and shook his head comically. "He's got meh, boys," he said. "He's got meh."

"All right," Fuller said, waving them back. "You satisfied the knots are O.K.? You satisfied it's on the level?" Everybody nodded. "O.K.," he said to Bowen. "Do your stuff."

Bowen twisted himself over on his back, so that the knots were hidden behind him. In a few moments he jumped up. His hands and legs were free and he was waving the rope. Johnny and the boys looked at him in astonishment. Bowen

111

bowed elaborately, like a vaudeville performer, and walked up to Fuller. "Now you," he said.

"Right," Fuller said. When his wrists and ankles were tied together, he twisted over on his back exactly as Bowen had done. He writhed gently for a few moments and then jumped up, holding the rope in his hand and grinning. Bowen took the rope from him and turned to the puzzled group.

"What do you say? Anybody else want to try it?" The boys glanced at each other and at Johnny. Nobody spoke. "What do you say? Any volunteers?" Bowen looked directly at Johnny. "How about you? You're such a shark with the rope, teaching the kids knots and all, what do you say? Like to try it?"

Johnny smiled slowly. "Well, sure, I don't mind," he said. "It's just that—let me ask you. Those knots. They're all on the level?"

"What then?" Bowen said. "You just got through looking at them, didn't you?"

"Yeah, sure," Johnny said. "I tested them."

"Of course, if you're afraid," Bowen said, "why, just skip the whole business."

"I'm not afraid," Johnny said quickly. "I just wanted to know if—"

"Sure, Johnny, go ahead," one of the smaller boys cried suddenly. "You can do anything they can do! You can do it better!"

Bowen and Fuller swung around sharply. The boy who had spoken looked frightened. He backed away and tried to hide behind the others.

"All right," Johnny said. "I'll try that rope trick, too."

The sixteen boys crowded around Bowen, watching intently. He appeared to be doing the identical job he had done on Fuller and that Fuller had done on him. The only difference was that he worked more slowly over the knots this time. When he finished, Johnny was lying on the ground, his wrists and ankles trussed tightly behind his back. Bowen stepped away and dusted his hands. "O.K., Houdini," he said. "Go to it."

For several seconds Johnny lay still. Only his fingers moved. He couldn't reach all of the knots, and those he could reach didn't have the loose ends of the rope in them. The boys gathered closer.

"I'll give you a tip," Bowen said. "That's not the way."

"Hey, now, wait a minute," Fuller said. "No coaching from the sidelines, there."

"A little tip like that is coaching?" Bowen asked.

"It doesn't matter," Fuller said. "A great woodsman like Johnny, he doesn't need any tips. He knows leaves and clouds.

112

He knows birds and rocks. He knows knots. He knows everything. If you and I can do it, he can do it, too."

"He can do it better," Bowen said.

"That's right," Fuller said. "I forgot. It's a cinch for Johnny. He's a regular Dan Beard."

Johnny twisted over on his shoulder. He was very red in the face and he started to smile halfheartedly.

"What's the matter?" Bowen asked. "You licked?"

Johnny dug his teeth into his lower lip and tugged at the knots. The veins on his forehead stuck out. Three or four of the boys turned and walked away. They looked at each other guiltily as they went, but they did not speak. Bowen suddenly sat down on the ground beside Johnny. "O.K.?" he said. "Had enough?"

Johnny's left cheek was touching the grass. He didn't raise it from the ground, but he could see the circle of shoes around him. And he could see the legs of the boys who were walking away. He shook his head.

"Well, well, well," Bowen said, falling back on his haunches. "On top of everything else, he's one of these strong, silent guys, too." He pulled out a package of cigarettes, took one, and passed the package to Fuller. "Something for your nerves?"

"Thanks," Fuller said; then, with a nod toward Johnny, "Maybe the smoke'll bother him?"

Bowen leaned down close to Johnny. "What do you say, Houdini? Should we take it off?"

Johnny didn't answer. He was breathing heavily and his blond hair was tumbled forward on his face. His lower lip was bleeding from the pressure of his teeth.

"If that's the way he wants it," Fuller said with a shrug, "so all right, that's the way he wants it."

Bowen shook his head and scowled. Suddenly the expression on his face changed. He dropped his cigarette and leaned forward. "Come on, Johnny," he said. "Stop acting like a jackass." He reached over for the knots. "You'll never get out of that. It's a trick and you don't know how to work it. Lemme open the—"

Johnny writhed violently and swung himself out of Bowen's reach.

"Go on, let him alone," Fuller said, his voice full of disgust. "If he wantsa be stubborn about it, O.K., lettim be stubborn. Come on, we'll take the kids swimming. We'll—hey!" He jumped up and looked around. The boys had all disappeared. "Well, of all the—hey, the kids! They—"

Bowen stood up and dusted his breeches slowly. "Aah, they're all right. They're around somewhere. Don't worry about them." He leaned over Johnny and spoke quietly. "Listen, Johnny, cut it out, will you? A gag's a gag, but this is gone too far. I'm telling you it's a trick. You'll never make it unless—" He reached for the knots. Again Johnny moved away from him.

"If he wantsa do it, he thinks he's so smart he can do it, let him do it," Fuller said. "Let's go find those kids."

"With you in a second." Bowen took out his pocketknife, opened the blade, and placed it behind Johnny within reach of his hands. "Don't be a dope," he said in a low voice.

Johnny looked at him. Then deliberately he swung himself over and rolled away from the knife. He lay there, panting with the effort. Bowen stared at the knife and stooped to pick it up. But he stopped halfway, straightened without touching the knife, and walked toward Fuller.

"Come on," he said. "Let's find the kids."

When they returned with the boys an hour later, Johnny was lying in much the same position. The boys huddled together, looking at him.

"Break camp," Bowen snapped.

He bent down for his knife and cut the rope from Johnny's wrists and ankles. Johnny sat up and began to rub his hands, looking down at them with scowling concentration, as though he had never seen them before. The boys kept their heads carefully averted as they dismantled the fireplaces, scattered the ashes, and strapped on their packs.

"Get up to the road and wait for us," Bowen said.

Without a word they began to clamber hastily out of the clearing that had served them as a camp.

"You all right?" Bowen asked awkwardly when the boys were gone.

"Uh, yeah," Johnny said. "I'm all right."

"Then come on," Fuller climbed through the gap in the bushes that the boys had taken. Johnny got up slowly and followed. It was late, almost five o'clock, and the heat had gone out of the sun. On the path, which was crowded with noisy hikers going to the ferry, the sixteen boys stood in a silent, ragged group. Bowen and Fuller walked out of the bushes and approached the boys. Johnny came last and stood a bit to one side, rubbing his wrists. The boys watched him furtively. All the confidence was gone from their eyes and all the affection.

"O.K., Johnny," Bowen said. "Let's get started."

Johnny hesitated. Then he raised his head.

"Uh, all right, kids," he said with unconvincing heartiness. "Maybe we'd better—uh—maybe you'd better fall in."

The boys snapped briskly into line. A moment before they had been a ragged, awkward group. Now they were two rigid, soldierly columns. Johnny's mouth opened in astonishment. Then he swung on his heel and began to walk down the path toward the ferry. He did not turn his head to either side or look back.

"Come on, come on," Fuller said irritably. "What's the matter with you kids? Start walking, will you? It's getting late."

But the boys waited until Johnny had gone about ten yards before the two silent columns moved forward. They walked in perfect formation. Carefully, as though by agreement, they matched their pace to his. They were very precise about this. They did not seem to want to close the large gap that now separated them.

THE NEAT MEXICANS

The wide asphalt square behind the Pershing Building was marked off by painted white lines into numbered parking spaces, all slanting away from the narrow grassy island that ran down the middle of the square, and all reserved for division chiefs and bureau heads: CAF 14s and above, sixty-five hundred a year or better. This was the side of the building that Crossett liked, not only because it faced the river and on clear days you could see the Potomac from the fifth-floor Conference Room, but also because it was quiet. For Crossett this was the one place in the city where, even in the morning when the car pools from Chevy Chase and Alexandria and Silver Spring were unloading, you could sit and think for a few minutes.

Crossett was not a division chief or a bureau head, but he was a CAF 15: economist and planner, senior grade. Even in Washington they had enough sense to realize that you couldn't do much economic planning if you were running a bureau or were saddled with responsibility for the work of a division staff. All Crossett had asked for, back in 1941 when he was invited to take a leave of absence from Harvard and come down for the duration, was a room with an outside window and a secretary who didn't chew gum. They had given him both and then, after V-E Day, when things eased up a little, they had thrown in the parking space. Crossett had no complaints and that, he told himself as he swung his 1936 Chevrolet into number 168, was the trouble.

He cut the wheel sharply and leaned out of the window to

look, breathing hard because the lunch had been a dandy and two martinis at twelve-thirty were getting to be heavy going for a man of fifty who seldom drank at noon and hated exercise. The Chevrolet's left front wheel was well over the line, a foot or more into parking space number 167, and Crossett grunted as he put the car into reverse and backed out for a new try. One martini would have been enough.

"Hey!" somebody yelled. "Watch out!"

Crossett kicked the brake and turned to look. A shiny pale blue Oldsmobile, a 1941 or 1942 model, was circling away from the back of the Chevrolet in a wary arc. A young army officer with a thin black mustache was at the wheel.

"Sorry," Crossett called.

"To hell with being sorry," the officer said. "Just try being careful."

The Oldsmobile shot off down the square, toward the public parking lot at the end, before Crossett could rap back a reply, and he treated the Chevvy a little roughly as he parked it properly. He switched off the ignition and flipped the keys back into the worn leather pouch with the snap fastener and shoved the pouch into his pocket. He sat back, his right arm resting on the steering wheel, the heel of his hand pumping delicately up and down on the broken horn button and, even though he knew he was late, Crossett took advantage of the one place in the city where you could sit and think. He knew he wasn't thinking well because the offer, made across a corner table in the Hay-Adams dining room, was still so fresh and new and exciting that it looked larger in any calculation he was likely to make, with two martinis not quite dead inside him, than it had a right to look. Just the same it was damned pleasant, and Crossett figured the war effort and his role in it had both reached a stage where he could afford to let the Planning Committee wait a few minutes.

Until two hours before, at exactly twelve-thirty when he walked into the Hay-Adams to meet the president of the Ohio college whose name he would probably learn to pronounce some day, Crossett had been in as good a position as several thousand other men in Washington who had answered the call just before December 7, 1941, when things were beginning to cook, or after Pearl Harbor, when they were boiling. He had an assistant professorship waiting for him in Cambridge any time he was ready to go back and take it. Now, two hours later, he was in a far better position than most. All he had to do was call the room number at the Raleigh that was written down neatly in the small looseleaf notebook he carried in the outer breast pocket of his coat, behind the folded handkerchief, or, if he preferred to take the

116

month he had been given in which to make his decision, all he had to do was write to the unpronounceable address on the same page of the same notebook, and he was a dean, not at Harvard, true, but at twice the salary Harvard had been and would be paying him. That was all there was to it, but, as he got out of the car and closed the door without slamming it because the hinge was loose, Crossett knew he was kidding himself. There was a hell of a lot more to it. There was what Crossett called his trouble.

He crossed the square and went into the Pershing Building through the back entrance. The guard in the swivel chair near the revolving door looked up from his copy of the *Times-Herald,* recognized Crossett, and nodded. Crossett nodded back, and walked down the black and gray marble hallway to the elevator, and punched the gold button. The elevator came and the handsome, stout Negro woman, in the neat blue uniform with PB embroidered in silver over her left pocket, smiled and pressed the number five button without waiting for Crossett to call his floor. She smiled again when he got out on the fifth floor, and Crossett knew there wouldn't be anything like this in Ohio, dean or no dean.

"You're late," Miss Gough said as he walked into his office. "They started at two-thirty sharp, when Captain Iverson arrived."

"They'll wait," Crossett said, crossing to the door of his own room. "I got stuck."

Miss Gough shook her head at him with a half smile, as though he were a little boy, and it occurred to Crossett that one of the advantages of Ohio would be that there would be no Miss Gough. He closed the door behind him and went into his private washroom. There were only three offices with private washrooms on the fifth floor of the Pershing Building and, as he dried his hands on the small towel with the initials PB stamped in blue in one corner, it seemed to Crossett that here was his trouble in a nutshell: Miss Gough and the private washroom.

If he had not insisted on a room with an outside window before he came down from Harvard in 1941, he would not have drawn one of the three private washrooms, they would have thought of him as just another professor and, after the shooting war was over, they would have let him go quietly, the way they were letting other professors go. Instead, they had looked around, noticed the private washroom, decided anyone who rated one of them was obviously too important to be let go, and he had been saddled with reconversion. Anybody who knew the score knew that the shooting war had been a picnic by comparison with the mess of reconversion, and Crossett knew the score.

117

If he had not insisted on a secretary who didn't chew gum, he might have drawn any one of the hundreds of nice little girls, from Arkansas or New Hampshire or Kentucky, who wagged their jaws while they typed and pasted picture postcards from vacationing friends on the wall over their desks and let their bosses alone. But Crossett had insisted on a non-gum chewer and he had drawn Miss Gough, who had gone to Smith and spelled beautifully and wore tailored suits and was so damned efficient and devoted to her job that she would cut her own lunch hour, and hang on to a phone for ten minutes, while he was paged at the Hay-Adams, to remind him that he was due at a two-thirty meeting of the Planning Committee. A man with a desk in one of the crowded offices down the hall and a girl with nothing more on her mind than tomorrow's blind date could pack up when the shooting war was over and go back to whatever he had been doing before Pearl Harbor or take an attractive, better offer. A man with a private washroom and Miss Gough had a conscience. Crossett rinsed his mouth and he was drinking a glass of water when Miss Gough came in.

"They just called from the Conference Room to ask if you were back," she said. "It's two-forty, Mr. Crossett. Is that cold enough? I could get you a glass from the cooler?"

"No, this is all right," Crossett said. It wasn't cold enough but all at once, with the alcohol dying inside him, he was so sick of Washington and the war effort and reconversion and Miss Gough's bright devotion, that he could scarcely swallow. Why couldn't they let him alone? He had done his job. Four years were enough. Why couldn't they get along with the bright young men, with this Captain Iverson and his prize-winning plans and the scores of others like him? Crossett put the glass down on the edge of the black marble basin, came out into the office, and kicked the washroom door shut. "What's on the agenda?" he said.

"Final approval of the master memorandum for the President," Miss Gough said. "And the preamble you wrote. That's all."

"All right, I'll go in now," Crossett said. "Oh, say, look. The left front door of my car is going to fall off any minute unless I do something about that hinge. Do you think you could?"

"Why didn't you tell me?" Miss Gough said. "Of course I can. I know the man at the filling station on Wisconsin and Q. He'll do anything for me. You go on ahead to the meeting, Mr. Crossett. I'll call him right away."

"Thanks," Crossett said and went out, wishing he hadn't asked her, yet knowing it was the only way the car would ever be fixed. He went down the hall to the conference room

118

and turned the knob quietly, but not quietly enough. The Director was at the head of the long table, reading from the thick memorandum, and he stopped to look across his glasses at the door. He smiled at Crossett and nodded and waited while Crossett came into the room and closed the door. Crossett started for his usual chair, halfway down the table, facing the window, and then he saw that it was occupied by a man in uniform. Crossett went around the table, to the other side, and he slipped into the vacant chair facing his regular seat, his back to the window. The Director resumed reading and Crossett looked around.

All the deputies were there, as well as the liaison boys from FEA and WPB and WMC, and Crossett remembered, now that he was here, how important the meeting was and how much he had wanted to be on time. His head ached slightly and his mouth felt furry, the way it always did in the afternoon if he drank at lunch, and now he really regretted that second martini. His glance came down the long table and stopped on the man in uniform, the man in Crossett's chair, and Crossett sat up straighter.

The man had two silver bars on his shoulder, and his face was dark and thin, and there was a narrow, black, very new mustache, so narrow and so new that it looked as though it had been drawn on with an eyebrow pencil, running in a straight line across the middle of the wide space between his nose and his upper lip. Crossett knew very little about medicine but he was willing to bet, from the shape of the young man's head, that Captain Iverson had suffered from rickets or some other disease of malnutrition when he was a boy. Crossett turned and looked out the window, down the long double line of cars parked along the grassy island, to the public parking lot at the end, and there it was, the shiny pale blue Oldsmobile, the 1941 or 1942 model. It was parked arrogantly, facing Seventh Street, taking up more room than one car was entitled to, but ready for getting away without turning. Crossett swung back and looked at Captain Iverson with interest.

A month before, Iverson had won the fifteen-thousand-dollar first prize in a national contest, sponsored by a breakfast food company, for the best manuscript plan on the problems of the postwar world. The newspapers, in which his picture had appeared in the news columns as well as in full-page advertisements paid for by the breakfast food company, had said he was twenty-seven years old. He looked older, though, with his gaunt face and his thick black hair falling forward over his eyes. Crossett wondered how he had found the time, while on active duty, to prepare a book-length manuscript on such a subject. Crossett examined Captain

Iverson's uniform. There were no campaign or area ribbons over his left pocket and, on the shoulder of his left sleeve, he wore the red, white, and blue patch of the Service Forces. That, Crossett said to himself, explained that. After four years in the nation's capital, much of that time spent at meetings in the Pentagon and Navy buildings, it was Crossett's belief that, if Tolstoy had served at a desk in the Service Forces in Washington, he could have written *War and Peace* without turning down a single cocktail invitation.

Crossett had not read the prize-winning plan, nobody but the contest judges had read it yet because the rumor around town in agency circles was that no trade publisher was interested, but the Director of Crossett's outfit had been impressed by the newspaper accounts, and he had asked the army to allow Captain Iverson to sit in on the meetings of the agency's Planning Committee. This was Captain Iverson's first visit, and it looked as though he was not impressed, but Crossett had seen too many men look like that at too many meetings to feel that his appearance was conclusive. The young captain sat slouched down in Crossett's chair, his thin little body hunched over, his lips twisted in what might not have been a contemptuous sneer, his eyes half closed, and his nervous fingers played with a beautiful gold fountain pen, obviously purchased quite recently, like the pale blue 1941 or 1942 Oldsmobile, out of the prize money.

"We've all read copies of the memorandum itself prior to this meeting," the Director said. "And before you arrived, we found that we're all in substantial agreement on the main points, so there's not much to be gained by rehashing the document itself here." Crossett realized with a start that the Director was talking to him, and he swung his glance down the table. "The plan itself, then, with all our main recommendations, goes to the President's desk as is. Is that correct, gentlemen?" Everybody nodded and Crossett noticed that the Director's glance remained on Captain Iverson. Everybody, including Crossett, turned and looked at the young man. He pursed his lips and, after a pause that seemed to Crossett just a little too long even for a much older man, Captain Iverson nodded grudgingly, without straightening in the chair. "Very well," the Director said. "The only thing about which there seems to be some disagreement, then, is the preamble you wrote, Crossett."

"The preamble?" Crossett said. "Why?"

"The point has been raised that it is, well—" The Director hesitated. "That it is needlessly belligerent, shall we say," the Director said. "I don't say that I agree with the objection, Crossett, but it has been raised, and I think we ought to get it

120

settled at this meeting. The memorandum must go to the printer tomorrow."

"Would you read it aloud, sir?" Crossett said.

"I just did," the Director said. "Weren't you listening?"

"It didn't sound belligerent when I wrote it," Crossett said, evading the question. "I didn't intend it to be belligerent. I don't know what that word means in this connection. I'd like to hear it read again and see where there's anything in it that anybody can object to."

The Director cleared his throat and started to read again. He didn't read particularly well, but it seemed to Crossett that you couldn't read that sort of thing badly. Half of it was direct quotation from Roosevelt's speeches. The rest was practically a restatement of President Truman's affirmation, in his first address to Congress, of his administration's objectives. The artless words and phrases, about education, work for all, a decent standard of living, came through the Director's bad reading voice with all the old simplicity and power. The Director finished and looked up. Crossett looked around the table. Nobody met his glance. He turned back to the Director. Their eyes met and then the Director looked away quickly. He cleared his throat.

"Captain Iverson?" the Director said.

"It's pointless," Captain Iverson said, talking to his gold fountain pen. "I think it will do more harm than good."

"Why?" Crossett said, leaning forward slightly, talking directly across the table at the younger man. "How can it do harm?"

"The President presents it to Congress," Captain Iverson said, still addressing the gorgeous fountain pen. "They're fed up with that Utopia stuff. It'll get their backs up."

"I don't think it's our job to worry about the backs of Congress," Crossett said. "Those few paragraphs, that's what this agency was created for. That's the whole point of the document itself. Let's do our job, and let's let the President worry about getting it through Congress."

"It's not practical," Captain Iverson said. "It's like looking for a neat Mexican. There ain't no such animal." Half the people around the table laughed, and Captain Iverson's eyelids lifted for a moment as his lips and his mustache twisted a little more to the left in what was apparently a modest smile. "I say nuts to the high-flown words and the fancy preambles," he said, his attention fixed once more on the gold fountain pen. "There's too much of that around. Let's show the President and Congress that we're not a bunch of long-haired dreamers," Captain Iverson said. "Let's show them we're as good businessmen as they are," he said. "That way we don't get their backs up, and we've got a chance to really sell a program."

Crossett opened his mouth, but the words wouldn't come, and he closed his lips without speaking. It was just as well. They would have been the wrong words. He leaned back in the chair, which was exactly like the chair in which he always sat at these meetings, but this one didn't feel comfortable or right because his back was to the window and he couldn't see the Potomac, and he realized that it wasn't the martinis at all. It was the accumulation, the four years, that was all. He had been at it too long. Crossett remembered a phrase the sportswriters used about a pitcher who began to walk too many men and allowed too many hits: he has lost the zip on his fast one.

"I'll tell you what," the Director said, gathering the loose pages and jogging them into an even pile on the glass table top. "I'll think this over and make the decision myself before I send the memorandum to the printer. Thank you, gentlemen."

The chairs scraped and the men broke up into small groups as they moved toward the door. The WPB man, who was on loan from Yale, fell in beside Crossett and said something humorous about the reconversion job the universities would have to do on themselves but, before Crossett could reply, one of the deputies pulled the WPB man aside and, as he went through the door, Crossett found himself next to Captain Iverson. Crossett was surprised by how short the younger man was. He had seemed taller behind the wheel of the Oldsmobile.

"Quite seriously," Crossett said. "What was your real objection to the preamble?"

Captain Iverson looked up and, as his lips twisted, he glanced quickly to his right and then to his left, as though to see if anybody was listening. Half a dozen men were.

"All that stuff about milk for babies, hell," Captain Iverson said through his thin smile. "I don't want everybody to be the same size."

Crossett was off balance when he hit him, so he recoiled with the impact and his own shoulder hit the marble wall, spoiling his view. But he must have connected in a good place because, when he turned around, all he could see, sticking out from the group of excited executives bending over the younger man, was a pair of brown strap shoes and six or seven inches of cuffless pinks. Captain Iverson was out cold. Cold enough, anyway. Crossett stepped on something, saw it was the gold fountain pen, and he paused just long enough to kick the damned thing back toward the jabbering group. Then he walked on down the hall to his own office and went in.

"I talked to my man at the filling station on Wisconsin and Q," Miss Gough said. "He said if you drive by there tonight on your way home he thinks he'll be able to fix that door for you, but you'd better not work late tonight because he closes at seven. What's all that excitement out in the hall?"

"A top executive just resigned," Crossett said. He crossed the room and opened the door of his private office. "Get me the Raleigh, will you, Miss Gough?" he said across his shoulder.

Crossett closed the door and sat down at his desk, still breathing irregularly, and he pulled the small looseleaf leather notebook from behind the folded handkerchief in his outer breast pocket. He flipped it to the page with the room number on it, and he set the open book flat in the middle of the green blotter, and he waited for his breathing to become regular again. When the phone rang Crossett was sucking his knuckles. They burned slightly.

"I've got the Raleigh," Miss Gough said. "Who did you want there, Mr. Crossett?"

"Just put me on," Crossett said and she did and then, as he read off the room number to the girl at the Raleigh switchboard, he remembered another phone call. Crossett had made that one almost four years ago, from the faculty lounge, between classes, to the man at the Copley-Plaza who had come up to Boston from Washington for a few days and had taken Crossett out and fed him two martinis before lunch.

"Five oh nine is busy," the girl at the Raleigh switchboard said. "Will you wait, sir?"

"Yes, I'll wait," Crossett said and he waited, for the man from Ohio who two hours before had pointed the way out that Crossett had just taken with his bruised knuckles, and he waited also for the suddenly remembered feeling that was four years old but still as fresh and hard and exciting as it had been then, that day in the faculty lounge, when martinis before lunch did not die until late afternoon, when he was forty-six.

"Here's five oh nine now, sir," the girl at the Raleigh switchboard said. "Thanks for waiting."

There was a click at the other end and Crossett looked around the room quickly, in a sudden panic of regret, not for the private washroom, or the guard in the swivel chair at the back door, or the stout woman in the gilded elevator who knew his floor without asking, or even for parking place number 168, but for something else, for the endless foolish meetings, and for the few quiet minutes every morning while the car pools from Chevy Chase and Alexandria were unloading, and even for Miss Gough's relentless efficiency, for

123

something he had been part of for four years. He would never have that again. Not in Ohio.

"Hello," Crossett said in a tired voice, and he turned with the phone to look out the window. It was a clear day and you could see the Potomac.

A LODGING FOR THE NIGHT

"Is that far out?" Lieutenant Driscoll said, reading the address from the canvas-backed pocket notebook that had his initials burned into the small leather square saddle-stitched to the cover. His mother had sent it to him from Mark Cross for Christmas in 1942 when he was still in OCS at Fort Sill. "Twenty-three sixteen Forty-first Street Northwest?"

"Not too far," the taxi driver said without turning. "It's in the third zone. Place called Glover Park."

Driscoll looked at the rate schedule pasted to the window near his ear, suddenly surprised and not quite pleased by a twinge of loneliness, a loneliness he must have been feeling for some time without knowing it, and he read the numbers backward: third zone, single passenger rate, seventy cents; group passenger rate, forty cents.

"Well, take it easy," Driscoll said, not meaning it, feeling the slow, mounting excitement begin to wash away the loneliness, feeling it in spite of the knowledge, buried deep down in his mind where he could keep it separate and under control that he was not entitled to the excitement, this excitement that he nevertheless wanted, wanted very badly, to feel. "But not too easy," Driscoll said. "I promised I'd be there about ten."

He put his feet up on the Val-Pak, doing it self-consciously, even though there was nobody to watch him, doing it as an exercise in self-control, telling himself to take it easy, and he humped his back into a comfortable spot in the lumpy, scuffed leather upholstery. He slipped the canvas-backed notebook into his right-hand breast pocket, under the Presidential Citation, and his fingers, reflecting the churning in his stomach, slipped once or twice as he slid the button through the buttonhole and clicked the two snap fasteners, at the pointed ends of the pocket flap, into place.

"It's twenty to ten now, and it's about a fifteen-twenty-minute ride," the taxi driver said. "You'll make it."

124

"I made it," Driscoll said, watching the lights on Pennsylvania Avenue shoot by, and he hoped the implication of his remark was not lost on the taxi driver. "Is that the White House?"

"No, that's State," the taxi driver said. "We passed the White House a block back. You getting out?"

"I'm out," Lieutenant Driscoll said. "Tomorrow, when I get to New York where my mother's been keeping my clothes, you can call me mister."

Tomorrow was the time, not now, he told himself, but he didn't really believe it, and he grinned at himself in the darkness. Tomorrow was the time, but this was the way he felt now, and it wasn't his fault. He had been told to do it, he had been urged, and he was doing what he had been told. If the feeling that was mounting in him was part of doing what he had been urged, that wasn't his fault. Driscoll relaxed and allowed the sense of anticipation to encircle him, and take him, and carry him forward twenty minutes, to Glover Park, whatever that was.

"Okay, mister," the taxi driver said. "Where were you when they quit?"

"In a C-54 out of Guam heading for Pearl," Driscoll said. "Where were you?"

"In this cab at Fourteenth and G, and I didn't move for three hours," the driver said. "The city went nuts. That's the Carlton, over there up ahead, where Anthony Eden and all them diplomats stay when they come."

"The sort of white and tan one?" Driscoll said to be polite. "With the lights?"

"No, that's the Statler," the driver said. "This side of the street, the dark gray one. What happened then?"

"The pilot dipped his wings a couple of times," Driscoll said, wishing the taxi driver would shut up. Driscoll didn't want to talk. He wanted to be alone with his anticipation, to roll it around on his tongue like good liquor. "That woke up the guys who were sleeping and then everybody brought out the bottle he was saving. Damnedest plane ride I ever had, but we made it," Driscoll said and then, as though he were repeating the tag line of a joke or the refrain of a song that had captured his fancy, he said, "I made it."

"Well, good luck, Lieutenant," the taxi driver said and, as though the song had become infectious but there was another line that he preferred, the taxi driver added, "I mean mister."

"Thanks," Driscoll said. "You, too."

He lit a cigarette and tried to put the match into the nickel ash tray set in the back of the front seat, but now he was so nervous that he missed, and then, when he tried again, he found that the thing was jammed, so Driscoll dropped the

125

match on the floor. They'd be putting new cabs on the street soon, with snap ash trays that worked, and he'd be riding in them, night after night, whenever he wanted to, feeling again this slow, mounting, wonderful tension that was part of going to pick up a strange girl, a new girl, a girl he had never seen. Driscoll dropped his feet from the Val-Pak and sat up on the flaking seat. He was getting his taxi rides mixed up. He had no right to that tension. Not on this ride.

Driscoll moved all the way over to the side of the cab and stretched the leg out straight on the seat to ease the slight, almost delicious, pain in his knee, and then he looked around quickly in the semi-darkness, moving his head back and forth several times, very fast, before he realized what was wrong. There was no meter. Driscoll grinned and looked out the window. In all the taxi rides he had taken in his mind by day and in his dreams at night during the past two years, there had always been a meter. Well, this wasn't his city. Not yet. And this wasn't that kind of taxi ride, either. Not yet. The clustered lights had disappeared and now the cab was rolling up a wide, dim thoroughfare with tall trees and large, imposing stone houses on both sides, mansions set back from the street in landscaped grounds and guarded by gates, and the street lights were widely spaced.

"Massachusetts Avenue," the taxi driver said without turning. "That's the British Embassy on your right. All the big ones are along here."

Driscoll didn't answer, although he continued to look out the window. The anticipation to which he was not entitled had given way to a more practical consideration. He was suddenly worried about the Val-Pak. Probably it would have been better if he had gone to the hotel first. Not that he was afraid he would lose the room. They had said, on the phone from the airport, that they would hold the room for him no matter how late he came in. Driscoll was worried because now the taxi was beyond Massachusetts Avenue, obviously beyond the heart of the city, riding through quiet tree-shaded streets of small, neat, nest-like houses that reminded him of Scarsdale and Bronxville, streets so quiet that he could hear the low tearing hum of the taxi's tires, and it occurred to Driscoll that on streets like these at ten in the evening, a reasonable hour downtown but clearly quite late out here, a Val-Pak might look funny, even a Val-Pak accompanied by a man who had just stepped out of a plane. Driscoll snapped the cigarette out the window and he saw it shatter on the pavement in a shower of tiny sparks as the taxi turned a corner and stopped in the middle of a block of two-story frame houses that stretched from corner to corner. They were all alike, with party walls and mansard roofs and small scraps of lawn that led into each other, like the houses themselves, and narrow flagstone walks running from the sidewalk to the doors on which the metal house numbers were nailed at an angle, all slanting up toward the identical wrought-iron mail boxes.

"Twenty-three sixteen?" Driscoll said.

"I thought you said twenty-three twenty-six," the taxi driver said. He started the motor again and pulled up five doors and stopped in front of the only house on the street that showed a light. "Twenty-three sixteen," he said.

Driscoll got out and swung the Val-Pak to the sidewalk and looked up and down the silent street as he put his hand into his pocket. "What do you do for transportation around here?" he said and then, when he saw the look on the taxi driver's face, "I mean around about midnight?"

"Not much chance of getting a cab," the driver said, taking the dollar bill and pressing the plunger of the coin machine tied to the side of his steering wheel shaft three times. "They don't cruise out here that late, but there's a bus stop around the corner, around that one, there, on the far side. It runs twice an hour on the half hour till one in the morning. You take that D-2 bus and it'll get you downtown, pretty near any place you want to go, or some place where you can get a cab, anyway."

"Thanks," Driscoll said. "That's all right."

"Thank you, Lieutenant," the driver said and he nodded as he slid the three dimes back into the coin machine. "I mean mister," the driver said.

The taxi rolled off down the street and around the corner, and Driscoll picked up the Val-Pak and started up the flagstone walk toward the door with the numbers 2316 nailed to it. The door opened and a girl, in a flowered dirndl and a white blouse with a V-neck and flat-heeled saddle shoes, came down the walk.

"You're Herb," she said, laughing as she shook his free hand and, without any sign of surprise, reached for the Val-Pak. "Hello," she said. "Let me help you with that."

"No, that's all right," Driscoll said, swinging it out of her reach. "You're Betsy. Hello," She made another try for the Val-Pak, but he held it away, and she laughed again and went on ahead and held the door for him. Driscoll dumped the Val-Pak next to the umbrella stand and she closed the door. "Sorry to mess up your place with a thing like this," he said. "But I thought if I went to the hotel first and left it and started washing up and all that, why, it might be too late to come out, and then I wouldn't have another chance, because I've got a seat on the nine o'clock train to New York tomorrow morning, and I promised Roger I'd stop by to say hello on my way through. Whew," Driscoll said. "How's that for an explanation?"

"One of the nicest I ever heard," Betsy Parker said. "And you can see for yourself that it's impossible to mess up this place any worse than it is. I've been trying to do a frantic tidying job since you called, but it was too much, so I just gave up and left it as is. Do you mind?"

"Not at all," Driscoll said. "It looks swell."

"Why don't you give me your hat, and what will you drink?" Betsy Parker said. "I've got blended whiskey and that's all, but I have tons of that. One of our girls got married last week and we sneaked three bottles from under the noses of the very drunken guests."

"I am the world's champion devotee of blended whiskey, whatever that is," Driscoll said, and he handed her his hat. "I will take two inches, with the same amount of plain water, and a lump of ice if you have it. Who's the lucky girl?"

"You wouldn't know her," Betsy Parker said, putting his hat on the keyboard of the upright piano, next to a blue bowl the bottom of which was covered with the stale dust of pretzel sticks eaten long ago. "She's one we got after I stopped writing Roger about the inmates of this asylum. There were just too many to keep track of. Can I get you a hassock or a chair for your leg? Roger wrote—"

"Your brother Roger is one of the sweetest guys currently in the Pacific Ocean," Driscoll said, sitting down on the couch. "But he is the greatest little worrier between here and Nagasaki, especially about his friends. There is nothing wrong with my leg that two inches of blended whiskey, plus the same amount of water, plus a lump of ice, will not cure. If there is ice?"

"There is plenty of ice," Besty Parker said. "Now you just wait. I won't be a second, and I want to hear everything."

She went out through an archway that led into what looked like a dining alcove and she disappeared to the left, presumably into the kitchen, and Driscoll looked around the room. It was not very large, although it ran the entire width of the house, and Betsy Parker had spoken no less than the truth. The room was not very neat. The fireplace was choked by stacks of newspapers that may have been waiting for the salvage collector, but somehow did not look it, and bits of potato chips and salted soy beans were imbedded in the multi-colored rag rug. Somebody had started to paint a mural across the front of the upright piano, but had stopped in the middle of a tree with pink branches. The dust covers on the chairs were wrinkled and some of the seams had parted. There were two Chinese prints on the wall above the couch, and half a dozen tarnished brass candlesticks on the mantelpiece over the fireplace. None of the ash trays matched and most of them were chipped and all of them were full. A dozen or more wedding invitations were pasted in a line all around the woodwork of the archway that led to the dining alcove. Driscoll counted eighteen of them. A large wardrobe trunk, slightly open, stood in the center of the room. Betsy Parker came back with the drinks in two glasses of different size that had obviously once been jelly jars.

"Thanks," Driscoll said. They toasted Roger in the Pacific and drank, and she sat down at his feet on the hassock he had spurned, and Driscoll, reflecting that you certainly could not tell from the appearance of a friend what his sister would look like, was suddenly very glad he had come. Betsy Parker was a damned pretty girl. "What's that?" Driscoll said, pointing to the trunk. "You going somewhere?"

"No, that's Elsa's," Betsy Parker said. "One of the inmates. She's going to Canada for a couple of weeks and she went to the drug store around the corner to get some Kleenex before she locks it."

"Oh," Driscoll said. "She coming back soon?"

"In a few minutes, probably," Betsy Parker said. "But then she has to run. She's taking the midnight to New York, and the express people are calling for the trunk in the morning."

"Canada?" Driscoll said.

"Elsa's Austrian," Betsy Parker said. "She has some sort of relatives up there who escaped in 1938, I think, and got as far as Montreal, but they haven't been able to get their entry visas into this country yet. Elsa's got sixteen days of annual leave coming to her from FCC where she's a research analyst, so she's going up to see them for a while. She was a year behind me at Bennington. Now about Roger."

Driscoll told her about Roger, who was fine, and Driscoll said Roger should be coming home soon, which was a lie because Roger did not have nearly enough points, but excusable because she was Roger's sister. Then Betsy Parker asked where he had been when the Japs quit, so he told her about the crazy plane trip, and then she wanted to know about his leg, so Driscoll told her about the piece of flak and his knee and the wonderfully troublesome water that kept accumulating under the cartilage, not enough to bother him but enough to get him out, and Driscoll kissed his finger tips and tapped the knee reverently and they both laughed.

"Now about you," Driscoll said, and he pointed to the string of wedding invitations pasted around the archway that led to the dining room. "Begin with those things," he said.

"Let's have another one of these before I start on me," Betsy Parker said. "Same?"

"Same," Driscoll said, handing her his glass. "But maybe

three inches this time and two lumps of ice and a little less water. If you have a little less water?"

"I have tons of less water," Betsy Parker said. "Now, don't you move."

She came back with the drinks, and she sat down on the hassock, and she explained that the wedding invitations were from all the girls who had lived in the house and been married out of it since Betsy had rented the place in the summer of 1942, when she came down, after graduating from Bennington, to work for the Office of Censorship. The rent was sixty-five a month, unfurnished, and there were three bedrooms upstairs, two doubles and a single, so they could sleep five, although there had been times when six girls had lived in the house all at once, the sixth sleeping on the couch Driscoll was sitting on at this very moment. It had been pretty hectic at times, especially since there was only one bathroom and that was upstairs, but Betsy Parker had kept the lease in her own name and she'd been pretty careful about the girls she chose to live in the house, so there had never been any real trouble and most of the time it had been fun, in spite of the problems of communal cooking and shopping and dividing up the dusting and dish washing, although in a way that had been the most fun of all. That was all finished now, of course, because the war was over and the sort of girls that Betsy Parker wanted to have in her house were all leaving Washington, although she herself liked the city and she had switched over to Agriculture when the Office of Censorship folded after V-J Day and she intended to stay on indefinitely, although she'd probably have to give up the house and find a small apartment somewhere, much as she loathed apartments with all their stupid formality, because she and Elsa were the only two left and, when Elsa went off to Canada in a few minutes, Betsy would be all alone in the place. Driscoll took a long swallow and, for a moment, he felt slightly troubled about sitting so high up and looking down on a girl at his feet in a low-cut V-neck blouse who was Roger's sister, so he took another swallow and asked about the furniture.

"Yours is empty," Betsy Parker said, and she finished her own drink. "I'll make a couple of fresh ones before I go into *that*. A little more less water this time?"

"Well, maybe not so much less water," Driscoll said, wondering why they were drinking so fast. "I've got a nine o'clock train to catch in the morning, and I've still got to get to my hotel with that Val-Pak."

While she was out in the kitchen, he looked around for another place to sit, a place not so high up, but the only thing in the room that met this particular specification was the hassock, and Besty Parker was back with the fresh drinks before he could decide to do anything about that.

"The furniture was the most wonderful part of it," she said, dropping onto the hassock and folding her legs under her skirt. "We just made it a rule that before a girl could come and live in the house she had to donate one piece of furniture, second-hand or new, it didn't matter, and she couldn't take it away with her when she left. I started with this couch and two frying pans and now look at the place."

Driscoll turned to look and the leg, which had gone slightly stiff, didn't move with him, so he slid halfway off the couch before he could catch himself, and his drink spilled.

"Oh, say, look," he said, feeling foolish as he hiked himself back up on the couch. "I'm sorry."

"Don't give it a thought," Betsy Parker said. "I've got tons of the stuff. Let me replace what you lost."

"No, thanks, this will do," Driscoll said, holding the glass away from her. "I mean the mess."

"On *this* rug?" Betsy Parker said. "In *this* house? Look at that piano. The girl who was painting that little number got married eight months ago, when she was halfway into the tree, and it's been that way ever since, and you're worrying about a little spilled blended whiskey. My, my, you fliers. Here, let me freshen that."

She captured the glass and went out with it, and Driscoll, relaxing quite suddenly and completely on the couch, said what the hell to himself.

"I just had an idea," Betsy Parker said when she came back, and he could see from the color of her glass that she had freshened her own drink, too. "It's almost eleven now, and I think it's foolish for you to go all the way across the city to a hotel at this hour. The house is empty and there are two extra bedrooms, so why don't you stay the night here, and you can go direct to the train in the morning, when I go to work."

"Oh, hell, now, wait a minute," Driscoll said. "I couldn't do that."

Betsy Parker laughed and handed him his refilled glass.

"Now, don't tell me we're getting modest," she said, sitting down on the hassock and looking at him across the rim of her glass as she took a long sip. "A great big warrior like you." Betsy Parker nudged his shoe playfully. "If it will make you feel any better, it's happened here dozens of times and my reputation on this street hasn't suffered one bit," she said. "All these girls we've married out of here, their men came in from all over when they were courting, in all kinds of uniforms, and we always put them up on the couch or in one of the spare bedrooms, when there was a spare."

Driscoll took another long swallow, half wishing he were

not, and looked down at Betsy Parker. Then he said what the hell to himself again and he grinned at her. He certainly had got his taxi rides mixed up. He started to say what the hell to himself once more, realized he must look quite foolish, and he made an effort to control his slackly grinning face. There was a knock on the front door and he turned to look.

"Come in, Elsa," Betsy Parker said. "The door's not locked."

A girl in a dark suit came in and stopped just inside the door, clutching a large square parcel wrapped in tan glazed paper.

"Oh," she said, and Driscoll could detect the slight accent even in the single syllable. "I am so sorry."

"There's nothing to be sorry about," Betsy Parker said. "This is a friend of my brother's. Lieutenant Driscoll, Elsa Miehler."

"Hello," Driscoll said, and he started to get up but Betsy Parker put her hand on his knee and pressed him back. "Sorry to butt in on you this way when you're packing," he said.

"You are not butting in," Elsa Miehler said with a smile. "My aunt said in her letter they still cannot obtain face tissue in Canada and I thought it would be nice to bring her some. I must hurry to catch the eleven o'clock bus."

She went to the trunk and dropped to one knee and started poking the glazed paper parcel into it. Driscoll made an effort and slid off the couch and stood up.

"This famous bathroom," he said. "May I?"

"Upstairs," Betsy Parker said. "First door on your left at the top of the landing."

Driscoll excused himself and went through the archway and up the stairs and into the first door on the left at the top of the landing. It was easily the most crowded bathroom he had ever seen, and when he realized, with considerable surprise, that he had brought his glass with him, he had several moments of indecision about where to put it. He looked around. There were seven towel racks nailed to different parts of the wall and, over each rack, was pasted a humorous cartoon with a hand-lettered legend that said, "This is Elsa's towel" and "This is Betsy's towel" and so on, through a list of names that were new to Driscoll. He decided, finally, to set the glass in the middle of the bathtub and, when he reached for it later, his hand misjudged the distance and he struck the glass with his fingers. It fell with a clatter but did not break and Driscoll, whose breathing was quite heavy now, was glad the drink was gone. When he came back downstairs Betsy Parker was lying on the couch, supporting her drink on her chest, and her saddle shoes were on the floor. The trunk was locked and Elsa Miehler was gone.

132

"I thought something happened to you," Betsy Parker said, getting up. "Now it's my turn. While I'm upstairs, I might as well get you a pillow and some blankets. Unless you'd rather sleep in one of the spare bedrooms upstairs?"

"No, thanks," Driscoll said. "The couch will be fine."

"You're perfectly safe," Betsy Parker said, and she laughed quite suddenly. "I hope," she said.

"Well, suit yourself," Driscoll said, and he laughed, too. "Wherever you'd rather have me. What happened to Miss Miehler?"

"She had to catch that bus to Union Station," Betsy Parker said. "She asked me to say goodbye to you."

"Thanks," Driscoll said. "Seemed like quite a nice girl. If you hadn't told me, I don't think I would have taken her for a refugee."

"You would if you had to live with her," Betsy Parker said. "But thank God that's over."

"Thank God what's over?" Driscoll said.

"I'm not going to take her back when she comes back from Canada," Betsy Parker said.

"Why not?" Driscoll said. "I thought you were friends?"

"Oh, we're friends all right," Betsy Parker said. "But she's just too difficult to live with. She's always locking closets and doors and looking under things, and she insists on having bread with every meal, and she makes me show her all the food bills, and she adds them up seventeen times, as though I were cheating her or something. She's just too damned terrified and European, I guess, if you know what I mean."

"Does she know this?" Driscoll said, not quite understanding why he was feeling slightly dizzy but certain that the blended whiskey, taken too rapidly, had a lot to do with it. "That you're not going to take her back?"

"No, but I'll write to her tomorrow in Canada," Betsy Parker said. "Fix yourself a drink while I turn down your bed and go to the little girls' room. And here, make one for me, too, while you're at it. Yes?"

Driscoll took her glass and she smiled at him across her shoulder as she went out through the archway and up the stairs, making surprisingly heavy sounds for a girl with a good figure in bare feet. Driscoll stood there for a long moment, looking around quickly at the tarnished brass candlesticks and the Chinese prints and the fireplace stuffed with newspapers, like a man hunting desperately for a likely place in which to be sick. Then he went swiftly to the piano and picked up his hat and put Betsy Parker's glass down on the keyboard, next to the blue bowl powdered with the stale dust of pretzel sticks eaten long ago. He glanced at his wrist watch. It was twenty minutes after eleven.

Driscoll put on his hat and picked up the Val-Pak and he went out, closing the door softly behind him, aware that even in the eyes of his friend Roger he was doing a foolish thing. The knee was beginning to hurt a little as he cut diagonally across the narrow lawns that ran into each other, disregarding the flagstone walks, and headed for the corner around which the taxi driver had said he could pick up, twice an hour on the half hour, the D-2 bus that would get him downtown, pretty near any place he wanted to go or someplace where he could get a cab, anyway. This was not his city, after all. Not yet.

THE PLEASURE OF THE PRESIDENT

Locke didn't want to go but his wife Susan insisted. Locke didn't want to go because he was lazy, and he admitted it, and Sunday afternoon, the only time in the long week when he could forget the Legal Division of the Department of the Interior and lie around the apartment in his pajamas reading the New York papers and indulging his laziness, was no time to go steaming halfway across Washington with a yowling baby to spend several tedious hours with Joe Stockwell, who was inclined to be a little stuffy even on his day off because he was with State, and his wife Hilda, who made a career of reminding people who did not live in Georgetown that she did and it was the only place *to* live, and listen to *their* yowling baby. End of breathless sentence.

If he had to listen to bawling infants, Locke figured one at a time was enough, and he preferred that one to be his own, and if Susan was warming up for her regular weekly routine about how he wouldn't be so lazy and tired Sunday afternoons if he didn't spend his weekday evenings running around town with half the chippies in Washington when he said he was at the Interior Building, working late, she could put on her act just as effectively in the apartment for him as in Georgetown for a larger audience.

But Susan wanted to go because she was cooped up all week with the baby in two small rooms and a bath on Connecticut Avenue, so that even a trip across town on Sunday was an event, and besides, the Pruitts were going to be there and she hadn't seen Ruth and Larry Pruitt for weeks, and Dick Locke knew he liked Ruth and Larry, whether he was willing to admit it or not, and if he wasn't running around with half the tramps in Washington when he told her he was working late, why wasn't he at his office in the Interior Building to answer the telephone when she called him at night, so they were damn well going. "End of *my* breathless sentence," Susan said.

"Okay," Locke said, dropping the *Times'* The News of the Week in Review and yawning himself off the couch. "But if the kid yells, you're the one goes upstairs to shut him up, and if you tear off any witty cracks about how much more attention I'm paying to Ruth Pruitt's legs than to my chicken salad, or whatever the Stockwells will be feeding their guests today, don't expect a beautifully typed affidavit of denial till we get home. I will be stiff."

"No doubt, dear," his wife said.

The baby was fine all the way across town and didn't even cry when they reached S Street and Locke started to swear. Cars were parked solidly down both curbs, and Locke had to leave the Ford at the foot of the block, practically on T Street, and walk back. A dozen or so small Negro children were playing baseball in the middle of the street and, as Locke came toward Susan, waiting with the baby in front of the Stockwells' house, the boy at bat hit a low fast grounder out of bounds. Locke fielded the ball neatly from the sidewalk and tossed it back, and the kids all yelled and cheered, and Locke stopped swearing and forgot that he had not wanted to come.

"Pretty good for an Interior lawyer," Joe Stockwell said with a grin as he pulled the door open for them. The front door of the Stockwell house had a large, curtained, diamond-shaped window in it, and it was Susan Locke's belief, which her husband shared, although he wouldn't give Susan the satisfaction of admitting it, that the Stockwells spent all their time at home, crouched behind the curtain, watching to see who went in and out of the Undersecretary's house down the street. "We're so glad you could come," Joe Stockwell said, holding the beaded silver cocktail shaker away from his blue velvet smoking jacket, keeping the door open with his hip, and shaking hands formally. "Come in, won't you? Dick? Susan? Little fella?"

He tickled the baby's chin and closed the door and took the cocktail shaker in both hands.

"Nothing to it," Locke said, sailing his hat across the room because he knew it would annoy Stockwell. "You should have seen me in my prime, meaning about a month or two after V-J Day, when the Dodgers were after me to quit Washington and go into left field for them. Nice to see you, Joe. Written any good treaties lately? We the first? Those martinis?"

"Why, yes," Stockwell said, looking worried all the way from the center part in his neat black hair to the cleft in his stubby, square chin. "I mean yes, they're martinis and yes, the Pruitts haven't come yet. I can make something else, if you'd rather?"

"I wouldn't have anything else," Locke said. "Just that if they're martinis, that's enough shaking or they'll become malteds. Hilda all right?"

"Swell, yes, she's upstairs with Timmy," Stockwell said, and he stopped shaking. "I always forget you're a stirrer, not a shaker. You can make the next batch. Susan, why don't you leave your things here, in the closet, and take the baby upstairs?"

"Fine," Susan said. "Thanks. Dick, my coat?"

Locke took the coat from his wife's shoulders and Stockwell walked across the room to retrieve Locke's hat, smoothing away the dent the brim had made in the sofa pillow. Then he hung the hat and the coat, over the handles of the vacuum cleaner and the dust mop, in the tiny crowded closet with the slanting roof under the stairs. Susan went upstairs with the baby and Stockwell, still carrying the cocktail shaker, went into the kitchen for the glasses, leaving Locke alone in the ridiculous living room of the ridiculous house.

Locke had the same Civil Service rating as Joe Stockwell and, as a matter of fact, because of the In Grade raise he had received a couple of months after V-J Day, Locke's government salary was five hundred dollars a year greater than Joe Stockwell's but, all through the war and since, Stockwell had continued to receive a substantial income from his junior partnership in the New York law firm he had left in 1942 to come to the State Department for the duration plus one year that he had promised to stay in Washington. Locke didn't have any income from the small practice he had turned over to a friend when he went down to Washington, but he was five years younger than Stockwell and he knew he would get back his practice when he finished his reconversion assignment for the Department of the Interior and returned to New York, so he wasn't really jealous of Stockwell, but Locke did envy him and Hilda their house, even though Locke didn't like it. The house was too damned expensive, and too damned cute, and living across the street and four doors up from the Undersecretary didn't mean a damned thing in Locke's young life. But the two small rooms and a bath and no maid on Connecticut Avenue were murder for Susan and the baby, especially in the summer, and every time Susan acidly wanted to know what sort of legal business he had been transacting for the Secretary of the Interior over cocktails in the Shoreham bar with that frowsy-looking redhead when one of Susan's friends or neighbors happened to drop in and see them, there was a whole lathe-and-fiberboard apartment house full of flopping ears to hear his reply. A house, even a cute one, would have made this protracted interlude in Washington at least bearable. The doorbell rang.

"That must be the Pruitts," Stockwell called from the kitchen. "Would you, Dick?"

Locke went to the door and it was the Pruitts, Larry and Ruth and the baby, plus a tall, rangy blonde with good shoulders and an excellent figure and a pretty mouth and the sort of wise, laughing look that Locke found a little unsettling but definitely attractive.

"You're late but welcome," Locke said. "The host is in the kitchen with the martinis, and the hostess is upstairs with her baby, and Susan is upstairs with our baby, and if the Pruitts know what is good for them Ruth will get the hell upstairs with the Pruitt baby before the trouble starts. Who is your handsome friend?"

"This is my sister, Mrs. Benson," Ruth Pruitt said. "She's staying with us for a few days and don't you get fresh with her, Dick Locke, because she has a husky Military Government major husband who is running half, or maybe it's three-quarters, of the American zone in Germany, and he taught her how to punch before he left. Oh, dear, he's done it again. Larry, the diapers, please?"

Larry gave her the diapers and she went upstairs.

"I'm very pleased to meet you, Mrs. Benson," Locke said. "How about letting me take everybody's things? It's a pretty tricky closet but I've been practicing and I think I've got the hang of it."

"You can call me Ilka," Mrs. Benson said, laughing as she gave Locke her coat and he took Larry Pruitt's hat. "Ruth and Larry told me all about you."

"Yes, sir," Larry Pruitt said. "The wolf of the Department of the Interior. Hello, Joe."

Joe Stockwell came in with the glasses and the cocktail shaker on a silver tray, and Larry introduced him to Mrs. Benson while Locke poured the drinks.

"To the brave major occupying Germany," Locke said. "And to his beautiful wife on S Street."

They all laughed and drank, and Mrs. Benson looked brightly around the room.

"Gosh," she said. "This is cute."

That is the word, all right, Locke thought, grinning to himself as he felt the first long swallow begin to take hold. The house was little more than a two-story box, with a living room and a Pullman kitchen on the ground floor, and two small bedrooms and a bathroom upstairs, and so little closet space

137

that Joe's expensive clothes were kept on an improvised rack behind a waterproof curtain in one corner of the tiny bathroom, but it was in Georgetown, on a fashionable street, and the Stockwells were delighted to pay a hundred and eighty a month for it, unfurnished. Not that Hilda Stockwell would take a furnished house under any circumstances, even across the street, or almost across the street, from the Undersecretary. Hilda had been an interior decorator after leaving Vassar and before she married Joe, and she had done a job on this house. The rear half of the living room was almost completely filled by a Steinway grand, even though neither Hilda nor Joe played, so that you had to walk sideways, with your hands over your head, when you went from the front of the room to the kitchen or to the scrap of back yard that Hilda called the garden; the walls were painted pale blue and hung with gaudy Navaho rugs; and every square inch of horizontal surface in the room, with the exception of the chairs and the sofa, was covered with pottery or hand-woven baskets. It wasn't like anything else in Washington, certainly not like the rambling, roomy, sixty-dollar-a-month clapboard job the Pruitts had in Arlington, but it was cute, all right.

"I'm so glad you like it," Joe Stockwell said. "Hilda did it herself."

The three wives came down in a group, congratulating themselves on the surprising but welcome peace that reigned upstairs, and Ruth Pruitt introduced her sister to Hilda Stockwell and Susan Locke while Larry Pruitt poured drinks for them. Larry, who had taken his Ph.D. in political science at the University of Wisconsin before he came to the Postwar Board of the Department of Agriculture, poured cocktails as though they were beer and you had to watch out for collars, but Locke liked him. Larry Pruitt made forty-six hundred a year and he had nothing to look forward to but an instructorship at Wisconsin, but he was a solid citizen with a brain from here to here and he wouldn't be found dead in a blue velvet smoking jacket on Sunday afternoon, or any other time, for that matter, and he was full of delightful surprises, like this knockout blonde sister-in-law, for example.

"But I can't get over it," Mrs. Benson said to Hilda Stockwell. "It's so, so, so un-*Wash*ington, if you know what I mean. It's so cute."

Hilda beamed, meaning that her thin, bloodless, refined face looked less pained than usual, and the kids upstairs started to cry, all three of them.

"We're off," Locke said, finishing his drink. "On a clear day, Mrs. Benson, you can hear them all the way out at Aberdeen Proving Grounds. Okay, girls, go to it. Mr. Locke will be in the kitchen, making a new batch, stirred not shaken."

"Oh, let me go," Mrs. Benson pleaded. "Please. I think they're so cute and wonderful."

Locke saw his wife's eyebrows go up slightly, and he would have groaned inwardly if he had not had at least one drink under his belt, because he knew he was going to get a caustic earful from Susan about Mrs. Ilka Benson when they got home, but the girls took Mrs. Benson along with them and Locke squeezed past the piano, holding the cocktail shaker aloft, and went into the kitchen. When he came back into the living room, Joe Stockwell was standing in front of the fake fireplace, looking down on Larry Pruitt in the zebra-striped chair, and telling the younger man why he thought the liberals were all wrong in their criticism of Frankfurter's dissenting opinion in the Bridges case. The three wives were sitting on the couch, all in a row, swapping nuggets of misinformation about the polio epidemic and checking up on Dr. Grossveldt, the pediatrician they all used, by comparing notes on the last visits they had paid to his office with their babies.

"What's happened to the soldier's wife?" Locke said. "Glasses, everybody."

"She's upstairs with the children," Hilda Stockwell said. "Just a short one for me, Dick. Thanks. Apparently she's wonderful with them. The moment she came in, they stopped crying, didn't they?"

"They shut up right away," Ruth Pruitt said. "She's crazy about babies. Mother used to leave us all in her care. Not yet, Dick. I'll nurse this one for a while."

"Well, we can't let her do sentry duty on a dry palate," Locke said, filling two glasses on the tray. "I'll take her drink up to her."

"I told her you would," Susan said sweetly. "And you're to call her Ilka."

"Woo-woo," Locke said, picking up the glasses and speaking across his shoulder. "Square me with my wife, Ruthie, will you? This is strictly a Gunga Din act. Honest."

Upstairs, the Stockwell baby was asleep in his crib in the small bedroom and, eighteen inches from the door, across the preposterous hallway, the two other babies were asleep on Hilda and Joe's double bed, which almost filled the larger bedroom. Mrs. Benson sat in the chintz-covered rocking chair near the window, her long, handsome legs crossed, and she was smiling brightly. She put her finger to her lips and took the drink he held out. Locke looked at the sleeping children on the bed, and then he turned to look through the open door at the crib in the other bedroom, and he shook his head admiringly.

"That's the first time *that's* ever happened," he said. "You must have had a lot of practice. How many of these things of your own have you got?"

"None yet," Mrs. Benson said, batting her long eyelashes across the rim of her glass. "But I can't wait to begin."

"What's holding you up?" Locke said. "It'll ruin that wonderful figure, but they tell me it's worth it."

Mrs. Benson giggled noiselessly and almost spilled her drink. "I've been married nineteen months, next Thursday," she said, cupping the glass in both hands. "And my husband's been overseas eighteen months and eleven days, almost twelve." She looked at her wrist watch. "It's six o'clock. In two and a half hours, at eight twenty-five to be exact, he'll have been overseas eighteen months and twelve days. That's what's holding me up."

"Hell," Locke said, wishing he had not asked her, because now his mouth felt dry and uncomfortable, the way it always felt when he found himself at the beginning of something he did not want to begin and, after it was begun, he would not finish. What she had told him was probably true, he had no reason to doubt the facts, but she sounded phony, and the trouble with Dick Locke was that he had an instinct for these phonies, an instinct that he never acted upon but that got him into trouble with his wife Susan just the same. "Why doesn't he come on home?" Locke said. "It's all over. Duration plus six. What's he want to hang around a place like Germany for, with a babe, sorry, girl like you waiting for him? How's that drink?"

"Wonderful," Mrs. Benson said, taking a good long swallow. "Did you ever read one of those commissions? Duration plus *six or* the pleasure of the President. That can mean anything. Occupation for God knows how long. How about another one of these?"

"You bet," Locke said, taking her glass quickly and wishing he were not the only person in the house who knew, God knows how he knew those things, but he always did, that Ruth Pruitt's sister, who was wonderful with children, was also a pushover. "It's the stirring that does it," he said. "Shaking kills them. You hold the fort. I won't be but a minute."

When Locke came down into the living room with the glasses, the three wives and Larry Pruitt were standing in the open doorway, wearing their hats and coats, and Joe Stockwell was pulling his crushed Tyrolean number from the snarl of broomsticks and mop handles in the silly closet.

"Hey," Locke said. "What goes on?"

"We're going over to the Orient on Wisconsin to bring back the supper," Joe Stockwell said. "Chow mein and eggs Foo

140

Young and that sort of thing. They put it up very nicely in containers, you know. We won't be long, Dick."

"All of you?" Locke said. "For God's sake?"

"It takes two or three to carry it all," Hilda Stockwell said. "We're getting lobster Cantonese and pork fried rice, too, and we're all out of cigarettes. They always have name brands there late Sunday afternoon. If we all go we can get two packs each. We won't be gone more than twenty minutes, will we, Joseph?"

"A half hour at the most," Joe Stockwell said, smoothing the hat into shape. "You and Mrs. Benson have another drink while we're gone."

"Aah, now, look," Locke said, feeling foolish and a little frightened and resenting it.

"Don't be a pig and see that Ilka gets one, too," Susan said, far too sweetly, even for Susan. "We don't have to warn you about not waking the babies," she said. "You both seem to be doing so beautifully."

Then they were gone and Locke could hear them, through the diamond-shaped window in the front door, chattering as they piled into Joe Stockwell's huge Buick. Locke went to the kitchen, forgetting to raise his arms when he passed the piano, and he took a nasty crack on his elbow. He mixed the drinks angrily, without quite knowing what he was angry about, and he made them good and stiff, four and a half to one. He went upstairs with two clean glasses and the shaker. The kids were still sleeping soundly and he could tell, from the extra brightness with which Mrs. Benson smiled at him, or perhaps he couldn't tell at all, that she knew they were alone in the house.

"They went to get the supper," Locke said, handing her a glass. "Chinese stuff, over on Wisconsin, and they're going to get on the line for cigarettes. Better take it easy on these. They're spiked."

"I'll try," Mrs. Benson said, and she laughed. "But that's the way I love them. I'm a very weak character," she said, giggling.

There didn't seem to be much to say after that, and there was no place for him to sit, so they drank too fast, and Locke was beginning to feel really foolish, because he could see Mrs. Benson's bright expectancy changing under the influence of gin to puzzled surprise at the way he was carefully keeping his distance, and then to mounting resentment, and he didn't really blame her, because he had gone through all the motions, he had led her to expect that he was going to finish what he had seemed to be starting, even though he wasn't really starting anything; but the pushovers never knew that, they had no way of knowing that Dick Locke was merely flexing his muscles, until it was too late, and when it was too late, and they did know, they were sore, justifiably sore because, even though he had not meant to trick them, that was precisely what he always did, and precisely what he had done now. His feet were beginning to hurt when there was a loud crash downstairs. They both jumped and then the children started to cry, all three of them at once, and Locke saw that Mrs. Benson had spilled part of her drink down the front of her dress.

"It's those damned kids playing baseball," Locke said with quick relief. "Be back in a minute."

He bumped the banister twice going down the stairs, and he stopped short at the bottom. The Stockwells would have a little trouble with drafts for a while, but their view of the Undersecretary's guests was highly improved. The pane was gone, except for a few jagged pieces of glass around the edge of the diamond-shaped window, and the baseball was caught in the sagging curtain as though it were in the net of a lacrosse stick. Locke reached in behind the curtain gingerly and pulled out the ball. He opened the door and walked out onto the front step. The fresh air felt good on his face. The Negro boys were gathered in a frightened group across the street, huddling together as though for protection and staring wide-eyed at the door.

"That's the end of the ball game," Locke called, swept by a wave of exhilaration for his own generosity and kindness and for the narrowness of his escape, and he tossed the ball to them underhand. "You kids better beat it before Mr. Stockwell comes back."

One of the boys caught the ball and they all remained there for another moment, staring at Locke on the front step, before they broke and ran silently down the block, toward T Street. Locke went back into the house and closed the door and, as he started up the stairs, he became aware of the babies crying. He could tell best by his own baby's voice, but it was in the sounds the Pruitt baby and Timmy Stockwell were making, too. They were crying badly. Locke took the rest of the stairs two at a time and his elbow, still sore from the bump against the piano, took another crack as he hit the doorway.

"Hey!" Locke said. "Hey, for Christ's sake!"

Mrs. Benson did not look up. She had clearly passed beyond the stage where all the world seemed cute to her. She was standing over the double bed, shoving and tugging his son and the Pruitt baby with her long lacquered fingers, hauling the infants back and forth savagely, her face contorted by liquor and disappointment and stupidity into a sort of fierce, irritated loathing because the father of one of them had tricked her into revealing herself, and because they would not stop yelling. The harder the babies screamed, the harder

142

she jerked them back and forth. Locke grabbed her shoulder and pulled her away and pushed her back toward the rocking chair, and Mrs. Benson fell into it with a dull plop, losing one of her shoes, and her long, handsome legs sprawled very unprettily.

"Pleasure of the President my eye," Locke said, panting and wishing he were not so drunk and realizing that she was even drunker than he was. "The poor bastard probably doesn't *want* to come back," Locke said. "And if I were in his shoes I'd stay in Germany, or wherever the hell they'll let him stay, I'd stay there forever."

He turned toward the screaming babies on the bed and the screaming baby in the crib in the other room, but Mrs. Benson shoved herself up out of the rocking chair and grabbed him and hauled him around.

"You're a dandy little guesser, aren't you?" Mrs. Benson said, and she slapped his face so hard that his ears rang. "That's for being such a smart little guesser," she said, "you son of a bitch."

Locke blinked and felt his face, which was beginning to sting, and he looked down foolishly at his hand. He was still holding the empty glass. He started to set it down, but there was no place to set it, and he saw that the front of his coat was wet, where he had spilled his own drink, and suddenly there was so much to explain, the broken window and his soiled coat, her soiled dress and the welts on his face, the screaming babies who could never be quieted in time even if they had both been sober, and the years of suspected infidelities of which he was not guilty, so hopelessly too much to explain, even to a level-headed wife who did not really believe the things she suspected, or to a mild-mannered friend who taught political science at Wisconsin and liked him, that Locke dropped the cocktail glass. It shattered noiselessly on the black and red and white Navaho rug.

"Shut up," Locke said loudly, above the noise of the screaming babies, keenly aware of the helpless terror in his own voice, and he slapped Mrs. Ilka Benson across her pretty mouth, hard. "Shut up, you," he said.

There was more to the cable than the first sentence, of course, to make it stick in Reardon's mind, much more. For one thing, it was quite long. It covered two and a half of the blue flimsies used for all incoming cables in the offices of the Halstead-Schick Petroleum Corporation throughout the world. For another, it was the first cable in God knows how long to be received from China in the company's main offices, on lower Broadway. The first cable, that is, to come through from China on Halstead-Schick's private wires since the Japs had taken Hong Kong, and, therefore, clearly an event; the first indication, so to speak—for Halstead-Schick, anyway— that the war was over, really over. And finally, the cable came to the message center, on the fifth floor, from the code room, on the sixth floor, marked "CHINA FOR CARPENTER ONLY REPEAT CARPENTER ONLY." Reardon, who had been chief of the Halstead-Schick message center for eleven of the twenty-eight years that he had worked in the huge oil company's New York offices, had learned one thing during those years: anything marked "FOR CARPENTER ONLY" had to be watched carefully or there was bound to be trouble.

S. B. Carpenter, whom Reardon referred to in private as Sour Ball, was Far Eastern manager for Halstead-Schick and, in Reardon's eyes and archaic language, a thoroughgoing scoundrel—and Reardon had proof.

A couple of months before the war, Carpenter had replaced his private secretary, a middle-aged widow named Hanson who was supporting three children and an invalid sister. Mrs. Hanson had been with the company for twenty-two years and had served as Carpenter's secretary since the big reorganization in 1933, but Carpenter had got rid of her just like that, without giving her a chance to defend herself, because he claimed she had caused him to miss an important luncheon date with the company's Batavia representative, who had been in town for two busy days on his way back to Java after a visit to the company's fields in Oklahoma and Texas. Mrs. Hanson swore, and Reardon believed her, that she had entered the engagement on Carpenter's calendar exactly as he had told her to when he put up his phone after talking to the Batavia man at his hotel.

144

None of the other employees had cared to take sides in the matter, but Reardon was sure that there were the usual number of toadies who accepted Carpenter's explanation that Mrs. Hanson was a sickly old woman and so harried by private worries that she had long ago ceased to function usefully and efficiently in the office and should have been retired on a pension years before. He was certain, too, that they had swallowed this barefaced lie merely because Sour Ball was a power in Halstead-Schick. Reardon, who had never even talked with Mrs. Hanson before, had gone to see the weeping woman at the time and had taken her to lunch in the basement cafeteria of the Halstead-Schick Building, where everybody could see them together. And that night he had tracked the Batavia man from his hotel to LaGuardia airport and managed to have a short talk with him before he boarded his plane.

The next morning, instead of allowing one of the ten routing clerks who worked under him in the message center to make the regular nine-thirty delivery to Sour Ball's office on the twenty-second floor, Reardon had delivered Carpenter's cable to the Far Eastern manager's office himself. He had got by the executive's new secretary with the curt announcement that he was carrying confidential cables that had to be delivered in person, and then, without wasting time on preliminary explanations that would have given Carpenter an opportunity to prepare himself for the onslaught, Reardon had confronted Sour Ball with the Batavia representative's statement that he had arranged on the phone to lunch with the Far Eastern manager on Tuesday, the day for which Mrs. Hanson had made the entry on Carpenter's desk diary, and not Wednesday, the day Carpenter for some reason had assumed he was to lunch with the man from Java.

Reardon still remembered with grim satisfaction the look of astonishment on the Far Eastern manager's face when Reardon presented his evidence. It was a cheerful, friendly, attractive face. The casual observer would have said it belonged to a man who liked children and was sentimental about birthdays and wedding anniversaries. Reardon was not a casual observer. Faces did not fool him, and Carpenter's look of astonishment had disappeared quickly. The middle-aged, well-groomed executive had leaned forward across his large, carved desk, his face now expressionless, and said, "Let me get this straight." His voice, calm and even on the surface, hummed with almost apoplectic incredulity. "You went all the way out to LaGuardia last night after work just to find that out?"

"I did," Reardon had answered firmly.

"May I ask why?"

145

"To see justice done."

"What is Mrs. Hanson to you?"

"A fellow-employee," Reardon had said, staring straight back at Carpenter; the tricks of intimidation used by bullies in positions of power were old stuff to Reardon. "A fellow-employee who has received a raw deal."

"Nothing more? Just a fellow-employee?"

"Just a fellow-employee. That's enough for me."

"I see," Carpenter had said politely. "May I tell you what I consider enough for me, Mr.——? I'm sorry, I've forgotten your name."

"Reardon," Reardon had said evenly, watching his voice with care, avoiding the trap men like Carpenter always set with their own fabricated calm, hoping the false restraint will trip you into the fatal error of losing your temper. "Employee of this company for twenty-three years. Chief, message center, fifth floor, for the past six years."

"That would seem to be long enough for you to know that we do not deal unjustly with our employees," Carpenter had replied with a mildness that Reardon knew was insincere. "Your desire to see justice done does you credit, Mr. Reardon, but I'm afraid it is misplaced in this case. I did not fire Mrs. Hanson, as you put it, because she made me miss an important luncheon engagement. That was merely coincidental. I have been troubled by Mrs. Hanson's—how shall I put it?—by her deterioration, shall we say?—for a long time. The poor woman is too old and has too many private troubles to function efficiently in an office. She has not been fired. She has been retired on a fairly decent pension that should enable her to live in comfort for the rest of her days." Carpenter had paused and looked faintly troubled. "There is one further point," he'd said. "I assume from the assurance with which you burst in on me, Mr. Reardon, that there are some top executives in this company who take instructions from the chief of the message center on how to run their offices. This is something of a surprise to me. My statement that I am not one of those executives may come as a surprise to you, Mr. Reardon. I must ask you to note that the matter of who I want for my secretary is one that I must decide for myself. May I suggest that we'll both be much happier if you go back to your message center and tend to your own knitting, and allow me to tend to mine? Do I make myself clear?"

"Perfectly," Reardon had said. "Would you mind making just as clear what you intend to do about the information I have just given you?"

"Why, I intend to forget it," Carpenter had answered with a friendly smile. "And I would suggest that you do the same."

"The difference in our positions makes it necessary for me to take note of your threats, but I'm afraid I must decline to take your advice," Reardon had said, and then had turned and walked from the office, outwardly composed but inwardly quivering with the fierce and pleasurable excitement generated by the neatly phrased retort the Far Eastern manager had made it possible for him to utter as a parting shot. In Reardon's lonely undertakings, these windfalls came only rarely and for that reason were doubly welcome, but there was always the danger that the selfish process of enjoying them would deflect you from action. Reardon had gone back to his own office, and, even though he made it a point never to do these things on company time, he'd violated his strict code of conduct and had written a letter to the Batavia representative, asking that gentleman if he would be good enough to commit to writing the information he had given Reardon at LaGuardia airport the night before. In view of the fact that the matter was urgent, and because there were opposing forces at work that could only be described as unscrupulous, Reardon had requested that the reply be sent to his home in the self-addressed air-mail envelope he was enclosing with his letter.

The reply, which arrived six weeks later, was couched in the nervous, frightened, equivocal phrases that Reardon had come to accept as commonplace from cowardly underlings, fearful of losing their jobs. The man in Batavia wanted to know what information he had given Reardon, and who Reardon was, and what did he want the information for, and just what was this all about, anyway? The tone of the letter, the obvious backsliding from the clear and forthright statement the man had made at the airport, reminded Reardon grimly of the *bordereau* in the Dreyfus case. The pattern of injustice was always the same.

Reardon had spent all of the next Sunday in his apartment on Bank Street, where he lived alone, composing a long, carefully worded second leter, which was shrewdly designed to allay his correspondent's fears, to elicit the written corroboration of Carpenter's duplicity, and to make the man at the other side of the world feel that he, like Reardon, was embracing a cause that was far more important than any minor embarrassment he might suffer from helping a wronged fellow-worker. It was a good letter. Before it could reach Batavia, however, the Japs had attacked Pearl Harbor, and Halstead-Schick's representative, along with hundreds of other Americans and Europeans in Java, had disappeared. Then Sour Ball Carpenter was granted a leave of absence to accept a majority in the army and left his desk on the twenty-second floor of the Halstead-Schick Building to serve with the OSS

147

in the Far East for the duration. Reardon had lost track of Mrs. Hanson.

Several times during the war the unfortunate woman had crossed Reardon's mind and he had wondered what had become of her, but other and more pressing matters intervened. To begin with, there was the constant battle with the administrative office, on the third floor, which expected the message center to continue making six mail deliveries a day to every office in the twenty-seven-story building, not counting special trips with cables and memoranda marked "RUSH," or for personal attention, even though eight of Reardon's ten routing clerks had been drafted and all the personnel office could provide as replacements were young girls, most of them not particularly bright and all of them untrained. And there was the fight with the ration board that had issued to Reardon a defective book, from which a whole page of red points and two sugar coupons were missing, and then when he had asked to have his book changed, the board had been so dilatory that he was forced to conclude that its members were accusing him by implication of having used the missing coupons to augment his meat and sugar supply. That mess had dragged along for almost four months and brought on a recurrence of the migraine headaches from which Reardon had been relatively free since shortly after his fiftieth birthday, in 1939, when he had successfully carried his struggle for a refund right up to the president of the department store from which he had bought an Alpacuna overcoat for $65.95 two days before the store featured the same coat, in full-page advertisements in every morning paper in town, at $54.50.

Several months after V-J Day, Carpenter had obtained his release from the army and returned to his desk on the twenty-second floor of the Halstead-Schick Building, but even though Reardon had been watching all communications from the Far East with great care and interest, he had seen nothing to indicate that the company's Batavia representative had been found. Reardon had to admit to himself with some regret that the Mrs. Hanson affair, now almost five years old, was a dead issue. This was a pity. If the war had not come along, the Mrs. Hanson matter would have been a beauty, an open-and-shut case, one of the simplest he had ever undertaken. Sour Ball Carpenter, however, was very much alive, and even though the end of the war had returned to their old jobs enough of Reardon's experienced routing clerks to enable him to put the message center back on its feet, he had intensified rather than relaxed his vigilance since the Far Eastern manager had resumed his old duties.

Therefore, even if the cable had not had the striking opening sentence that in itself was enough to make it stick in Reardon's mind, and even if it had not been the first cable to come through from China on Halstead-Schick's private wires since the Japs took Hong Kong, the mere fact that it was marked by the code room "CHINA FOR CARPENTER ONLY REPEAT CARPENTER ONLY" would have been enough to put him on the alert.

One morning, shortly before eleven, as he came back into his office from a visit to the infirmary, on the twenty-seventh floor, where Miss Klauber, the company nurse, had given him a small dose of the barbiturate that sometimes helped his headaches, Reardon noticed Bill Kain, the message-center log clerk, talking on the telephone and, with his free hand, turning the pages of his cable log-book. There was something about the faint flutter of nervousness in Bill's usually slow, drawling voice that caused Reardon to stop in the middle of the office and turn and cross over to Bill's desk.

"What's the matter?" Reardon said.

"What?" Bill said, and then, recognizing Reardon, his face froze and he shook his head quickly. "Nothing much," he said, and, into the phone, "The sixteenth. That's right. . . . No, the *six*teenth. That's exactly three weeks ago. A Thursday. . . . That's what it says here in my log, Miss Sheppard. The sixteenth. Thursday." The mention of Miss Sheppard's name brought all of Reardon's faintly alerted senses into a sudden, sharply focussed knot of awareness that caused his slowly receding headache to throb back to new life. His eyelids flicked, and his thin shoulders straightened just a trifle in the gray alpaca office coat. Miss Sheppard was Carpenter's new secretary, the second girl that the fussy and demanding Far Eastern manager had hired since he came back. "Well, you check, Miss Sheppard," Bill Kain said. "And call me back." He hung up the phone, and seeing that Reardon was still beside him, he said, "Those dumb clucks on twenty-two. Boy!"

"What's wrong?" Reardon said.

"Some damn cable three weeks ago," Bill said. "The first one from China since the war."

"For Carpenter, yes," Reardon said. "What about it?"

"His secretary says he just got an air mail from China mentioning the cable, and Carpenter doesn't know what cable. She called to check and I told her we logged it in on the sixteenth and delivered it right away."

"That's right," Reardon said. "We did. I remember it clearly."

"Boy!" Bill Kain said. "Some of these new secretaries—they must have got them out of the Pentagon or something."

"Don't you worry about it," Reardon said. "If she calls back, switch the call to me."

"I can take care of it," Bill said. "It's part of my job. Be-

149

sides, one thing I learned in the army—I know how to handle these rear-echelon babes."

"No, I'd rather take care of this myself," Reardon said sharply as he picked up the logbook. Since Bill and some of the other clerks had come back, Reardon had noticed a slight truculence, an air of resentment on their part when they were dealing with him directly. Reardon supposed this was inevitable and he tried to be understanding and not hold it against them, but their belligerence, as though they felt that in the three years while they were away they had become too important for their menial jobs and he had grown old and weak and incompetent, was a constant source of unpleasantness. Reardon was fifty-seven years old, but aside from his headaches, he knew he was in much better physical and mental shape than any of these immature youngsters, with all their smoking and drinking and helling around all night and endless babble about experience under fire. "I'll just take this back to my desk," Reardon said. "If she calls, you have it switched to me."

He went to his desk at the far side of the office, near the window from which you could see a sliver of City Hall Park, and sat down. He placed the open logbook on the desk and leaned back in his swivel chair, and as the familiar excitement, the slowly mounting anticipation that was almost orgiastic, began to churn in his stomach and spiral upward, spreading the delicious warm anger to all parts of his body, he looked down on the I.R.T. kiosk on the corner and, very delicately, stroked a throbbing vein in his temple. The phone rang.

"Yes?" Reardon said. "No, this is Mr. Reardon. I asked Mr. Kain to have your call switched to me. What seems to be the difficulty?"

"Oh, gee, I don't know," said Miss Sheppard. "There's some darned cable Mr. Carpenter is supposed to have received from China three weeks ago—a pretty long one, this letter says. This letter he received today that mentions the cable, I mean."

"Mr. Kain has filled me in on the facts," Reardon said. "I repeat, Miss Sheppard, what seems to be the difficulty?"

"Well, Mr. Carpenter says he never saw the darned thing," Miss Sheppard said. "He doesn't know anything about it."

"Do you know anything about it?" Reardon said.

"What?" Miss Sheppard said, and then, "Say, listen, if I did, what do you think I'm calling for?"

"I haven't the remotest idea," Reardon said, putting an edge into his voice. "The records of the message center indicate that the cable in question was delivered to Mr. Carpenter's office at ten forty-five on Thursday, the sixteenth. The responsibility of the message center ends there."

Reardon hung up and, still stroking his temple, waited. At noon, when the first shift of routing clerks went to lunch, Bill Kain came over and asked if there was anything Mr. Reardon wanted of him before he went out to eat. Reardon curtly said no, thanks, not a thing, and then, as the young man was turning away, Reardon said, well, wait a moment, if Bill didn't mind, would he bring along a sandwich and a bottle of milk when he came back, tuna or ham on rye—it didn't matter, anything at all. An hour later, when Bill Kain came back with Reardon's lunch, the phone had not rung. Reardon ate the sandwich and drank the milk at his desk. When the second shift came back from lunch, at two o'clock, the phone on Reardon's desk was still silent. Reardon waited another hour. Nothing happened. At three o'clock he stood up, took the logbook, and walked over to Bill Kain's desk.

"You'd better hold onto this," Reardon said, putting down the book. "If Carpenter's office calls about that cable, you don't know any more about it. Say I'm handling it and I'll call back. I'm going upstairs for a while."

"You bet," Bill Kain said. "Headache bad again?"

"What?" Reardon said, and then, "No, but I think I can use half a teaspoon of bicarb to settle that liverwurst on rye you brought me. I won't be long."

It was ten minutes to four when Reardon came back. He knew what Bill Kain was going to say before the log clerk opened his mouth.

"Carpenter's office called about twenty minutes ago," Bill Kain said. "Three-thirty. He wants to see you right away. About that cable."

"Did he ask for me by name?" Reardon said.

"Well, it was that Sheppard babe did the calling," Bill said. "I told her I didn't know any more about the damn thing than I'd already told her and you'd call her back, the way you said. She got off the phone for a minute—I guess she was passing that on to His Nibs—then she came back on the wire and said O.K., would I tell you to come up to twenty-two when I saw you."

"Let me have the logbook," Reardon said. "If I get stuck I'd like you to stand by till I come back."

"Well, I've got a date for right after quitting time," Bill Kain said, and then, after a moment of rather obvious debate with himself, he said, "You don't expect to be up there *that* long, do you?"

"You never can tell with the Carpenter type," Reardon said. "I'll try not to make you late for your date."

Reardon took the elevator to the twenty-second floor and

151

went through the door at the end of the corridor into the outer office of the Far Eastern manager's suite.

"I'm Reardon, message center," he said to the dark-haired girl who looked at him inquiringly across her typewriter. "Mr. Carpenter wanted to see me."

"Oh, yes." Miss Sheppard's face cleared. "Did you find it?"

"I believe it was Mr. Carpenter who wanted to see me."

Miss Sheppard's face looked blank for a moment, and then, blushing, she stood up and came out from behind her desk. With a short, puzzled backward glance at Reardon, she opened the door into Carpenter's office.

"Mr. Carpenter," she said, "Mr. Reardon is here."

"Who?" the executive said.

"Mr. Reardon," Miss Sheppard said. "From the message center. About that cable."

"Oh," Carpenter said. "Yes. Send him in." Miss Sheppard held the door for Reardon to pass her, and the Far Eastern manager said, "You, too, please." Miss Sheppard nodded and came in, and the door swung shut behind her and Reardon. "I'm sorry to cause you all this trouble and drag you all the way up here." Carpenter said with a smile of apology, "but there's been a small snafu somewhere along the line."

"The efficiency of the message center has never been questioned during the eleven years that I have served as its chief," Reardon said. "Any business you have to transact with my unit, Mr. Carpenter, will be made considerably simpler if you limit yourself to the facts and refrain from unnecessary and unjustified slurs on the people who work for me."

Miss Sheppard, just behind Reardon, made a small, sucking noise, and the Far Eastern manager blinked quickly, like a man who has come unexpectedly around a street corner into a gust of whirling cinders.

"I received an air-mail letter from China this morning," Carpenter said, forcing his cheerful voice, word by word, into a flat, strained monotone. "It refers to a long cable that was sent to me three weeks ago. I never saw that cable."

"That's too bad," Reardon said. "The message center delivered it to your office."

"How do you know?" Carpenter said gently. "I haven't even told you what cable I'm referring to."

"I know the cable you mean," Reardon said. "I remember it clearly."

"You do?" Carpenter said. "How?"

"Very simple," Reardon said. "First, the cable was a long one. It covered two and a half sheets of flimsy. I keep an eye on the cable files myself and I always remember the long ones. Second, the cable had a very unusual opening line and my mind automatically records things like that. Third, it was the first one to come through from China on our private wires since Hong Kong fell, an event that even a man with a poor memory is not likely to forget. Fourth, and most important, Mr. Carpenter, it came from the code room marked for your special attention, and I have always made it a point"— Reardon allowed his voice to drop just a trifle—"to pay particular attention to anything marked for your special attention."

There was a long, almost completely silent pause, during which Miss Sheppard nervously chewed the end of her pencil. Then Carpenter said, "Say, I remember you. You're the man who came steaming in here one day before the war. About that Mrs. Hanson? You followed our Batavia man to LaGuardia? Isn't that right?" Carpenter's voice rose, as though he was pleased with this feat of his memory. "You followed him after work. Isn't that right?"

"That's right," Reardon said. "I fail to see, however, what all this has to do with this cable."

"Reardon, that's your name," Carpenter said. "I remember the whole thing now. My goodness," he said, shoving his arms straight out in front of him and putting his hands on the desk, palms down, "so you're still around." The Far Eastern manager shook his head slowly from side to side with an odd expression of amazed gratitude, as though he were contemplating some astounding phenomenon that, under ordinary circumstances, would be revealed only to more deserving men. "As a matter of fact," he said finally, "it has nothing to do with this cable. I'm sorry that you've decided, for some mysterious reason of your own, to make an issue of a fairly routine and unimportant matter. Having made that decision, however, you leave me no recourse but to talk bluntly. Mr. Reardon, your job is to see to it that cables marked for my attention get to me, not to follow people to LaGuardia or talk back to people who catch you falling down on the job."

"I've done my job," Reardon said. "That cable got to you."

"I say it didn't," Carpenter said. "Now I want to say something to you that is intended in all sincerity and for your own sake, Reardon. I want you to listen to me."

"I'm afraid I'll have to ask you to listen to me first," Reardon said. "You say the cable didn't reach you, but I say it did. I happen to be able to prove my statement." Reardon stepped forward and dropped the logbook on the desk. The canvas binding made a dull thump as it hit the glass top of the desk. With two short contemptuous movements, Reardon flipped the book open and spun it around in front of Carpenter. "We make it a practice in the message center to log all cables as they come back from the code room, not only by their serial numbers but, to ensure accuracy of identification, by their

153

opening lines. Here." Reardon's finger poked at the open page. "There's the serial number and there's the opening line: 'Send four men to Hanoi.' Logged in at ten-forty A.M., on Thursday, the sixteenth, three weeks ago today. In the handwriting of my cable-log clerk, Bill Kain. Here." Reardon's finger moved to the next column. "There's the time, ten forty-five, when the cable was delivered to your office. Here." Reardon's finger jabbed at the last column. "There's the initial of the person who accepted the cable for you, in her own handwriting."

Carpenter looked down at the logbook, then up at Reardon, and his lips worked back and forth several times, as if he had bitten into something distasteful.

"Whose initial is that?" he said.

"Miss Barth," Reardon said, "who was your secretary until two weeks ago, when you fired her and hired Miss Sheppard."

"I see," Carpenter said. "Miss Sheppard." The girl behind Reardon made the sucking noise again and came forward in a frightened jump. "Miss Sheppard," Carpenter said, "was that cable among the papers Miss Barth turned over to you before she left?"

"I don't think so," Miss Sheppard said uncomfortably. "I mean I don't remember. I never saw the thing. Honestly."

"Thank you," Carpenter said. He turned back to Reardon. "The fact remains that the cable is not here. As for the initial, I have only your unsupported word for it that it *is* Miss Barth's. Now let's—"

"I'm not accustomed to having my word questioned," Reardon said. "And I'm sure that Miss Barth will be willing to testify."

"Testify, eh?" Carpenter said. "I see." He pushed himself slowly away from the desk. "You know," he said, "I feel very sorry for you, Mr. Reardon." He turned and said, "Miss Sheppard."

"Yes, sir," Miss Sheppard said.

"Will you be good enough to ask this—this—this gentleman to leave us alone?" Carpenter said. "We've got some work to do."

"Yes, sir," Miss Sheppard said.

She put the chewed end of her pencil back into her mouth and looked uncertainly at Reardon. He leaned over, flipped the logbook shut, picked it up, and walked out. He went directly down to the personnel office and got Miss Barth's home phone number from the records. He called her home, and her mother gave him the phone number of her new job, and his next call reached her there just as she was about to leave. Miss Barth remembered the whole thing clearly. It had seemed so odd at the time, she said, the unusual opening

154

line, the first cable from China in several years, all that. Reardon thanked her and hung up.

When he entered the message center, Bill Kain got up from his desk and came across the room.

"Everything all right?" Bill asked. "You were up there so long, I was getting worried."

"Was it that long?" Reardon said. "Yes, everything's fine. I hope I didn't make you late for your date."

"Heck, no," Bill Kain said. "It's not five-thirty."

When Reardon put his key in the lock of his apartment door, he was surprised to find he had the evening papers under his arm. He did not remember buying them. The apartment—two rooms and a bath, facing an attractive little garden behind Bank Street—looked even neater than usual. On the kitchen table his supper—cold lamb and salad with the dressing mixed and waiting in a small glass that had once been a jelly jar—had been laid out by his part-time maid.

He ate the food, washed and dried the few dishes, and settled down to read the papers, but the headache that had been drumming dully in his temple since he walked out of Carpenter's office seemed to kick at the side of his head, as though it were trying to force its way out into the open. There was no point in further delay. He went to the bathroom. He swallowed two tablets from the bottle Miss Klauber had given him, and closed his eyes to wait for the barbiturate to take effect. When he opened them, the throbbing in his temple was dulled, as though the pain had been wrapped in cotton batting. He was ready.

He went to his desk, uncapped his fountain pen, and pulled a foolscap pad from the drawer. "Sumner Halstead, Esq.," he wrote. "President, The Halstead-Schick Petroleum Corporation. Sir . . ." As his pen moved across the page the pain in his head began to mount again, but he did not feel it. The phone rang, but he paid no attention to it. He was completely absorbed. It was an absorption that went deeper than pleasure. In the composition of such letters there was for Reardon a whole world of secret excitement, the gratification of drawing together, sometimes from a great distance, the pieces of a puzzle that had baffled others, the surge of power that came from bringing to the bar of justice a scoundrel who felt he was safe from detection or punishment.

Reardon raised his head. The doorbell was ringing. He shoved out his breath in a gasp of anger, tried to close his mind against the interruption, and bent back to his task. The doorbell continued to ring. Reardon pushed himself away from the desk and staggered across the room and pulled the door open.

"Boy!" Bill Kain said. "I sure am glad to see you."

"What the hell are you doing here?" Reardon said harshly. "What do you want?"

"He's a friendly guy, isn't he?" said a girl who was holding Bill Kain's arm.

Reardon turned abruptly to look at her. The girl giggled nervously and stepped back, as though she had been slapped. Her hat, a small cluster of green canvas flowers, was askew in her blond hair.

"We been calling you from Keeney's around the corner," Bill said. "We been calling and calling. We thought you were sick or something."

"You're drunk," Reardon said impatiently. "What do you want?"

"Who's drunk?" the girl said. She tugged Bill Kain's arm. "Let's go back to Keeney's," she said.

Reardon started to close the door, but Bill Kain caught it with his toe. "Wait a minute," he said. "Right after you left, just about five-thirty, Carpenter called from upstairs. Not that Sheppard. Carpenter called, himself. He wanted to talk to you."

Reardon became aware of the pain in his head. He tried to grip the door with his other hand and saw that he was still holding the fountain pen.

"What did he want?" he said. "Why did he call?"

"He wanted to apologize to you," Bill Kain said. "He said he was sorry he lost his temper when you were up there in his office, because you were right. Sheppard found that damned cable from China. After you left, Carpenter made her look all over the joint. She'd shoved it in with a lot of other papers in her desk and forgot about it. Carpenter said he wanted you to know and to apologize for everything." Bill Kain stopped, and his face, animated by liquor and the excitement of revelation, seemed to contract. "I tried to call you at home before I left the office, but I guess you hadn't reached here yet, because there wasn't any answer," he said. "I was telling Alice, here—I was telling her about it while we were eating over at Keeney's—all about the fuss Carpenter's office made, I mean, and she said it was a shame, you were probably worrying about it and I ought to call you again. We called you three times from Keeney's, but there was no answer, and Alice said maybe you were sick or something." Bill paused once more, as though he were waiting for Reardon to deny this, but Reardon merely stared at the younger man and listened to the hammer strokes in his head that were blinding him. "We looked up your address in the phone book," Bill Kain said. "You're just a couple of blocks from Keeney's so Alice said let's go over and see if anything is wrong."

He stopped again. Nobody spoke. The girl made an ineffectual attempt to straighten the cluster of green canvas flowers in her hair, and then tugged Bill's arm. "If you ask me, I think he's the one that's drunk," she said. "We come all the way over here to give him some good news, so he won't have to keep worrying, wait to hear it till the morning. We come all the way over here to see maybe he's dead, you'd think he'd say come on in, or offer us a drink, at least say thanks. Some boss you got! Come on, let's go back to Keeney's," she concluded, pulling Bill toward the stairs.

"Anyway, that's what Carpenter said," Bill Kain said, speaking across his shoulder as the girl dragged him away. "He wanted to apologize to you."

Reardon drew a deep breath and slammed the door shut. He leaned his forehead against the cool, varnished wood. The girl's voice came up the stairs.

"Some boss you got," she said. "The cheap—"

Her voice died away. Reardon pushed himself from the door and groped his way back across the room to his desk. He sat down with a thump, as though he had misjudged the distance to the chair, and put the fountain pen beside the foolscap pad. His eyes blurred with anger and disappointment as he tore from the pad the neatly written pages addressed to Sumner Halstead, Esq., President, The Halstead-Shick Petroleum Corporation, but he did not stop. He was not a weak man. The pain in his head made it difficult for him to see, and his rage at having been cheated shook his thin body so hard that his fingers slipped and fumbled, but he managed to find a clip and fasten the pages and put them carefully into the lower drawer and lock it. Nothing was ever really wasted. There would be another time.

SOMETHING FOR LUCK

The alert went as Crayne stepped off the curb. He stopped short, blinking against the warm afternoon sun, and turned up his coat collar. From the corner of the High Road a bus swung into the street, going very fast. Crayne jumped back to the pavement and stumbled into a girl.

"That's right," she said. "Trample me."

The American voice brought Crayne's head around before he recovered his balance. It was Deborah Groot.

"Sorry," he said. "You wouldn't get bumped like this if you didn't wander so far from the Stork Club."

The imminent-danger signal sounded. The retort stopped on Deborah Groot's lips. They both looked up to the clean blue sky. On the third blast of the klaxon they heard the low, grinding roar. She stepped closer to Crayne and, without thinking, he took her arm. The roar grew louder, then began to fade. Crayne's grip on the girl's arm relaxed. The fading roar stopped. They waited in the sudden silence. The klaxon blatted: danger passed. Somewhere beyond the wall of buildings to their right, there was an explosion. The pavement under Crayne's feet seemed to tremble slightly, but it might have been his imagination. You never could tell when they were that far away.

"Not even close," Deborah Groot said. "About a mile. Maybe more." She moved her arm. He took his hand away. "I haven't been within yelling distance of the Stork Club for eight months."

"That's what I heard," Crayne said. "Having fun here in London?"

"It's gotten around that you're a newspaperman," she said. "You don't have to be sarcastic in public." She laughed suddenly. "Are you cold?"

Crayne reached up and turned down his coat collar. It didn't seem to matter how long you had been in it. There were some things, small, silly things like turning up your collar, that you could never remember to stop yourself from doing.

"Only when I'm around certain people," he said.

She was pretty, in a blonde, clean American way that he had grown to appreciate keenly since the war had kept him away from home for so long, and Crayne liked pretty girls; but he did not like Deborah Groot. How much of this dislike was due to the associations with his own fairly recent past as a Broadway columnist, Crayne did not care to go into. Even with himself.

"How's your father?" he asked.

"You ought to know," she said. "You go to his press conferences. I don't."

"For his sake I'll give you a lift. It won't look right if the Munitions Commissioner's daughter is seen on the streets of a suburb as unfashionable as Hexton."

"Thanks. I'm not going your way."

"You don't know what way I'm going," Crayne said. "I'm heading for my office in Piccadilly. I'll tell the driver to go through Grosvenor Square and drop you at the Embassy."

"If you get any kinder, people will forget to mistake you for a gentleman of the press. Thanks again. I'm not going to the Embassy."

She walked away, moving north. Crayne watched her go. The skirt of her thin camel's-hair coat swung neatly around her legs as she stepped along briskly. She reminded him of other girls he had seen when he was younger, hundreds of them, stepping along briskly in the crisp sunlight of Saturday afternoons in October on their way to football games. He wished he could like her, and then, as she turned a corner and disappeared, he told himself he didn't wish anything of the sort. It was almost three years since Crayne had given a damn whether he liked girls like Deborah Groot or not.

"Hey," he called. "Taxi."

The stubby little cab pulled up at the curb several yards ahead. It was one of those funny things about London: the taxis never stopped next to you or backed up to where you were standing. They waited for you to go to them. Crayne walked to the cab and climbed in. He was giving the driver his office address when the imminent-danger signal sounded again. The klaxon drowned Crayne's voice, but the taxi shot down the street in the right direction.

"There it is." The driver pointed upward. "See it?"

He slowed the cab. Crayne looked out the window and saw it, coming in low, a huge, long, ugly cigar with wings and dirty smoke pouring from its tail. The grinding roar made Crayne's teeth ache a little. It passed overhead, going in the direction Crayne had come from, and slid out of sight beyond the line of buildings. A few moments later it cut out. There was the short interval of curious silence, during which the whole world seemed to be frozen motionless, and then the explosion. The windows of the cab rattled.

"Close," the driver said. "What address did you say?"

The klaxon sounded twice: danger passed. Crayne squinted against the sun at the sudden geyser of murky dust that mushroomed higher and higher in the near distance. People were running up the street toward it. Two ARP men in blue uniforms sped by on bicycles. Their wheels leaned sharply as they turned the corner around which Deborah Groot had disappeared a few minutes before.

"How close would you guess?"

"Hard to say," the driver said. "A half-mile perhaps. Might even be a mile. They glide very fast sometimes after they cut out, you know."

Crayne pulled his head in and dropped onto the seat. "Piccadilly," he said, turning down his coat collar. "Anywhere just below Burlington Arcade will be all right."

The United States Munitions Commissioner held his press conferences in the John Hay Room on the second floor of the Embassy. The press corps did not consider them high points in the week's work, but Crayne always went. Sedgewick

Groot was not a colorful man, and there was very little copy in his dry, matter-of-fact reports of the United States munitions allocations to the Allies; but Crayne was more than a correspondent, even though only he and the Colonel knew it, and he did not like to skip anything.

"You're just the man we want," the Colonel had said when Crayne went to see him in his office on Portman Square, several months before, at the Colonel's request. "A good deal goes on in a place like London in wartime that Intelligence misses for a variety of reasons. We can't pick up everything. We need someone to field the balls that go out of bounds, so to speak. You're a reporter. Before the war you were a Broadway columnist. You've got a nose for the small stuff that we miss. Gossip is your business."

"Columnists don't like to think of it quite that way," Crayne said. "You're not being complimentary, sir."

"I don't have much time for compliments now. Look me up after the armistice and I'll give you your full quota." The Colonel smiled pleasantly. "You're made to order for us. Your cover is perfect. We don't have to hire you or put you into uniform or train you or bring you over from America. You're here already, as a correspondent for your paper in New York. All we ask is that you keep your eyes and ears open as you go about your day-to-day work. Whenever you run into something you think will be of interest to us, come and tell me. That's all. It's not much to do for one's country in time of war, is it?"

"I don't think you're being very fair to put it on that basis, sir."

"I'm sorry. I shouldn't have said that. Will you do it?"

"Yes."

"Good. I don't have to tell you to keep your mouth shut. It might interest you to know, though, that I will do the same. Nobody in my organization will know that you're working for us." The Colonel wrote something on a slip of paper and stood up. "I will be your only point of contact. You can usually reach me at this number. If I'm not there, you'll be told when I will be."

Crayne took the slip of paper, memorized the number as he stood up, lighted a cigarette, and touched the match to the paper. "All right, sir." He dropped the bit of charred paper into the ash tray on the Colonel's desk. "I've got it."

"Fine." The Colonel smiled again and put out his hand. "You understand, of course, that you'll get nothing out of this except one man's gratitude."

Crayne shook the older man's hand. "I imagine that will be enough, sir."

He didn't know how valuable were the bits of information

he had turned over to the Colonel since that first interview. The Colonel neither complimented nor criticized. He took what Crayne gave him the way a child accepts his allowance from a parent, without enthusiasm or disinterest, but always with the hint, faint but definite, that it could be larger. All Crayne knew with certainty was that the assignment had caused him to take on a considerable amount of work that otherwise he would have avoided. The Munitions Commissioner's weekly press conferences, for example. You never could tell where you might pick up something. You had to go to everything.

"Hello, Mr. Crayne. Wouldn't you rather sit over here?" It was Stearns, the Commissioner's middle-aged secretary.

"Hello," Crayne said. "Thanks, no. I'm fine here."

He wasn't, but Crayne disliked solicitude that was purely personal. He knew that Stearns was kind to him because he had been wounded in the Pacific two years before and had come to England as a correspondent after being invalided out of the Army. Crayne would not hesitate to make use of Stearns's kindness to get a story for his paper or a bit of information for the Colonel, but he refused to take advantage of it to get a better seat at the Commissioner's press conferences. Besides, they were never very long. This one was shorter than most. After it was over, Crayne caught up with Stearns in the hall.

"The old man seems pretty tired," Crayne said. "When is he going home for that rest?"

"He does look worn out, doesn't he?" Stearns glanced worriedly over his shoulder. "He was supposed to leave the end of this week, but he's had to postpone his trip."

"What's the matter?"

Stearns sent his worried glance up and down the hall. He hesitated for a long moment, then seemed to make up his mind. "Would you come into my office?"

Crayne followed him into a small room and sat down. The older man closed the door carefully, went into the room, then turned back, and twisted the key in the lock. Crayne lighted a cigarette.

"I shouldn't tell you this," Stearns said in his nervous voice. "The Commissioner would be very angry. He hasn't mentioned it to anybody, not a soul, even though I've urged him to go to the police. I'm breaking a confidence by talking to you, Mr. Crayne, but I know you've always been friendly to the Commissioner, and perhaps you can help. You will keep this strictly between us, won't you?"

"Naturally." The siren went: a long, steady, upsetting

whine. Stearns jumped. "All clear," Crayne said. "There's been an alert on since before the press conference."

"Of course." Stearns smiled awkwardly. "I've been so upset these last few days, I can't seem to tell the alerts from the all clears any more." He coughed and waited until the siren died away. "The fact is, Mr. Crayne," he said abruptly, "Miss Deborah has disappeared."

"When?"

"About ten days ago."

Crayne's spine relaxed and fitted back slowly into the curve of the chair. This was Saturday. He had run into Deborah Groot on the street in Hexton on Wednesday. Her disappearance was not due to the bomb that had gone off after he left her. He was not responsible.

"What do you mean by disappeared?"

"Just that, Mr. Crayne. She left the Commissioner's flat in Curzon Street one morning, a week ago Wednesday it was, and she hasn't returned."

"That's why the Commissioner has postponed his trip home?"

"Yes."

"A buzz bomb, you think?"

"No." Stearns shook his head emphatically. "We would have heard."

"Not necessarily," Crayne said. "Sometimes it's weeks before they recover all the bodies."

"No, it's not that. The Commissioner has his ways of checking a thing like that. We know it wasn't a bomb."

"What else do you know?"

Stearns hesitated. He rubbed his lower lip with a bony finger and looked uncomfortable as he stared at Crayne. After several moments he shook his head. "That's all, I'm afraid."

Crayne stood up and punched his cigarette into the top of an empty typewriter-ribbon tin on Stearns's desk. "It doesn't give me much to go on."

Stearns started to run his finger along his lower lip again, and Crayne lighted a fresh cigarette with great care, to give him time; but nothing happened.

"I know it isn't much," Stearns said finally. "But I thought you might hear something."

"If I do, I'll get in touch with you."

"Thanks, Mr. Crayne. The Commissioner refuses to go home without her, and frankly, if he doesn't go soon—well, I don't know what will happen to him. I really don't."

"None of us does. This stuff that's dropping is not confetti."

Stearns turned the key in the lock. "You won't repeat what I've told you?" he said anxiously. Crayne smiled and patted his shoulder. "Thank you, sir." Stearns opened the door. "And if you should hear anything?"

"I'll let you know at once."

Crayne's watch showed a few minutes after three o'clock. He walked past the fish-and-chips shop, turned into the hallway under the sign that said, "Lodgings," and climbed the stairs. He didn't meet anybody. On the third floor he twisted the knob of a door at the front of the house and went in. The room was empty. Crayne closed the door quietly and looked around.

It was a small, dreary place, bare except for a brass bed, a battered wardrobe, two straight-backed chairs that were obviously as old as the house itself, and a scrap of faded carpet on the warped floor. On one of the walls, from which paint was flaking away, hung cheap, framed prints of George VI and Winston Churchill. A white crockery pitcher stood in a basin on one of the chairs. Ten and six a week, Crayne figured, and no questions asked. Fifteen shillings at the most.

Two pairs of stockings were drying on the brass rail of the bed, and three pieces of expensive matched alligator luggage stood in one corner. Crayne felt the stockings. They were still damp. For several moments Crayne considered the problem of opening the bags. He decided finally that the Colonel would not be impressed with his scruples. Crayne tried the catches and was not pleased with his sense of relief when he found they were locked. Either you did this sort of work right, meaning thoroughly, or you had no business doing it at all.

He opened the wardrobe. It was empty. Crayne lighted a cigarette and sat down on the bed to wait.

He could hear the traffic on the High Road at the bottom of the street. Occasionally the voices of customers in the fish-and-chips shop came up through the rickety floors. Crayne smoked several cigarettes. Two alerts went, but the imminent-danger signal did not sound. The sun disappeared behind the church on the High Road. Just before seven o'clock there were footsteps in the hall. The door opened. Deborah Groot came in.

"Oh," she said. She took a moment or two. "It's you."

"I was getting bored," Crayne said. "I'm a bad waiter."

"What do you want?"

"Your father must go home to report to Washington, and he needs a rest. He won't leave without you. His plane goes on Friday. Three days from now. He's not a bad guy. You ought to spend more time with him. I've come to take you down to the Embassy right now."

"Did Father send you?"

"He doesn't know I know you're missing."

"You never did know how to mind your own business." She

163

took off her camel's-hair coat and threw it on the bed. "How did you find me?"

"I used to cover Broadway."

"This isn't Broadway. Please get out."

"You don't have to put it in the form of a request. I don't like it here." Crayne stood up. "In case you haven't thought of it yet, let me point out that I found you in the wilds of Hexton without too much trouble. Others are standing by, ready to take up what has been to me an extremely unpleasant job. The moment I leave this room your disappearing act is over. Your little game, whatever it is, is finished."

"Wait." He turned back. "Sit down. Give me a few minutes to think."

"Don't make it longer. I've got a dinner date near Marble Arch."

Crayne sat down. Deborah Groot moved the pitcher and basin from the other chair, put them on the floor, and sat down facing him. The room was so small that the distance between them could have been filled by a night-club table. It reminded Crayne of the last time he had spoken to her in New York.

It was in January of 1942, the night before he was to report for induction. Crayne went into the Marimba on East Fiftieth Street about two in the morning. The crowd had thinned out. The Marimba was a midnight spot. By two in the morning the real prowlers usually had worked their way west to the Stork. Deborah Groot was sitting at a side table with Joe Herkimer III, the Princeton fullback who had just written football history into the 1941 season. They made an attractive couple. They were young, she was pretty and he was handsome, their families had more money than was good for them, and they were both at the height of their notoriety. They had been in and out of the columns for some time. There wasn't a kid in the country who didn't know about Joe Herkimer and the tattered old jersey with the numerals "11" sewed on haphazardly that he wore into every game, and every stenographer in America was supposed to be familiar with the hairdo and profile of Deborah Groot, number-one glamour girl of the year.

She waved to Crayne and called him over. "You're our friend," she said. "We've got an item for you. We saved it for you. We're going to elope."

Crayne left them and taxied to his office on West Street. In the small hours of his last morning as a civilian, Crayne wrote his last column. Even as he slapped it on the spike and shoved the knot of his tie up to meet the button of his collar, Crayne knew he should not have written it, if only on the theory that you should never write anything while you are drunk. Crayne did not care. The column contained only one item of gossip:

the scoop on the elopement of Deborah Groot and Joseph Herkimer III. But around the three-line item Crayne had placed a thousand words he never could have said aloud; yet it would have left him empty and alone to have gone away without saying them in print. It was not a good column. Crayne was not a sentimental man, but it had been a sentimental occasion: for the first time in fifteen years he was leaving the street where he had spent all he ever would have of his youth. He went into the Army shortly after his thirty-sixth birthday. He was glad he was not on Broadway when he read the column in type a few days later, but for a longer time than that he was glad he had written it.

Months later, in a base hospital in the Pacific, he read that the newlywed Herkimers had parted. No reasons given. A year after that, back on Broadway with a slight limp hidden under civilian clothes, Crayne ran into Deborah Groot. He did not speak to her. Several times during the succeeding weeks she waved to him across a theatre lobby or a dance floor, but he did not wave back. He asked the paper to send him overseas. Broadway was still Broadway, but it was not what Crayne had said it was in the thousand words he had written around Deborah Groot's elopement. Six months after he arrived in London, the Munitions Commissioner's daughter arrived from New York to stay with her father for a while. Like all great cities, London is a small town. Crayne saw her often. Nobody would have mistaken them for friends.

"You don't like me," Deborah Groot said now. "Not one little bit."

Crayne looked at the framed prints of George VI and Winston Churchill on the flaking wall. "That sums it up."

"Just the same, I want to ask a favor."

"Make it short," Crayne said. "My dinner date at Marble Arch is impatient."

She talked quickly, in a low voice, looking past him as though she were addressing the stockings drying on the brass rail of the bed. After a while Crayne stopped looking at her. He continued to listen, but he looked at the stockings, too. When she finished, he lighted a cigarette with great care.

"What makes you think I can do it?" he asked.

"You found me here in Hexton."

"Let your father do it," Crayne said. "He has more influence than all the newspapermen in London."

"He won't. He said it was a violation of security. That's why I walked out and came here."

"Why here?"

"I'm not a secret agent." Crayne's head did not move, but his eyes shot to the right more rapidly than the Colonel would have approved. She was examining the ash of her cigarette.

"And I'm not a newspaperman. But I'm not as dumb as you seem to think I am."

"I don't think about you at all. I asked why you chose Hexton for your hideout."

"I wanted to get as close as possible."

"I see." Crayne stood up and went to the window. There was still some light, but dusk was closing in. Down on the street below he could see blackout curtains being drawn. He spoke with his back to her. "Anything that is a violation of security for the United States Munitions Commissioner is a violation of security for an American newspaperman."

"Not if nobody knows anything about it. I won't talk."

"That's what everybody who ever broke security said before he or she broke it."

"You know I won't talk."

"I don't know it. Promises aren't worth much in this racket."

"I'd give you more if I had it. I have nothing but my promise."

Crayne's back was motionless. His mind was moving quickly. It was possible she was guessing about his work and how much he knew. She probably was guessing. There were no leaks in the Colonel's show. At any rate, Crayne had to work on the assumption that there were no leaks. But she was not guessing about Hexton. She was there. She knew something went on in the dismal suburb north of London. She had been prowling its streets for almost two weeks. How much did she know? That was important. It was even more important that she leave the country before she learned more. Crayne turned from the window. "If I take your promise, I want something in exchange."

"Anything."

"If I do what you ask, you go back to Curzon Street tonight, you tell your father that you've been visiting friends in the country or whatever he'll believe, you go to New York with him Friday, and you never say a word about this."

"I promise."

Crayne picked up his hat. He felt for the torch in his pocket. "Have you got something less American and less expensive-looking than that camel's-hair coat?"

"I have a green one in my bag." She stood up quickly. "Are we going now?"

"Put it on," Crayne said. "Yes, now." He looked at his wristwatch. "After ten o'clock tonight I couldn't do any more favors for you and you wouldn't have to make any promises to me."

She made a curious sound. Crayne looked at her hard, but she did not cry.

166

"If you hadn't come tonight, I would have been too late?" There was the faintest touch of awe in her voice. She opened the largest of the three alligator bags with a key from her purse. "You mean tomorrow I would have been too late?"

"If I were half as smart as you seem to think I am, I would have come tomorrow."

She laughed suddenly, very fast. She may have been laughing at the bitterness in Crayne's voice. She pulled the green coat around her shoulders. "I'm glad you came tonight." She gave him a quick look. "What about your dinner date at Marble Arch?"

"I will be thirty-nine in January," Crayne said. "My dinner date can wait."

The Edward and Lion was at the bottom of a short cul-de-sac between the Hexton High Road and Christ Walk Avenue. It was difficult to find in the daytime. At night in the blackout it was almost impossible. But the owners of local pubs in England do not worry about accessibility. The patrons of the Edward and Lion had been finding their way to its door for years. Neither they nor the proprietors were interested in new customers, especially the ones that the war had brought to Hexton, as to all of England, from every corner of the world.

"Hold it." Crayne flashed his torch on the ground. He recognized the alley by the way the cobblestones were arranged in the road. "This is it." He took Deborah Groot's arm and spoke quietly into the darkness. "I'm repeating this. It's important. I don't know if he's in there. He should be. If he isn't there's nothing I can do about it. This is the only place I can take you to keep my promise. If he is in there, he won't be alone. He'll be in a group. You can't show you recognize him. You can't go up to him. You can't speak to him. All you can do is look."

"That will be enough," she said. "But he'll recognize me, too."

Crayne didn't like her but he was glad there was a blackout. He would not have wanted to see any girl's face while she said that.

"He'll recognize both of us. He won't do anything about it. He's been trained. See that you don't do anything about it."

"I won't."

He led her carefully down the narrow alley, counting his paces. When he reached twenty-four, he stopped. He flashed the torch. They were directly in front of a cracked wooden sign with raised gilt lettering that said, "The Edward and Lion." Crayne snapped off the torch. He pulled aside a heavy black curtain that billowed gently in the night breeze. They stepped into a small, dark foyer, and he let the curtain

167

drop behind them. Crayne pulled aside another curtain, shoved open a heavy door dotted with small squares of stained glass, and they were inside.

"Do what I do," Crayne said. "Nothing else."

"All right."

They faced a large, crowded, noisy, brightly lighted room. A long bar, with mirrors and glass shelves behind it, covered one wall. Black leather benches ran along the other three walls. The floor space in the middle was filled with heavy, round tables. About a hundred people were jammed into the room. The air was fogged with smoke. A darts game was going on in one corner. At a side table, two men were playing push ha'penny for an audience of eight or ten beer drinkers. The noise, after the silence of the blacked-out street, was almost painful. A few people near the door looked up at Crayne and Deborah Groot. The others paid no attention. At the back of the room, around one of the heavy tables, six American soldiers were eating, drinking, and laughing. They wore their pants tucked into the tops of paratroop boots. One of the six was Joe Herkimer III.

"Look," Deborah Groot said. "He—"

"Keep your hands down," Crayne said. "Shut up."

Two men left the far corner of the bar and carried their glasses to the group around the push-ha'penny game. Crayne steered Deborah Groot quickly and skillfully into the vacated space. He placed her against the bar, her back to the room, and took his place beside her. He could see the entire room across her shoulder.

"I'm sorry," she said. "I won't do that again. May I look now?"

"No," Crayne said. "I'll tell you. Two half-pints of bitter, please."

"No more bitter," the barmaid said. "Pale ale and beer."

"Two pale ale."

The barmaid went away. Crayne lighted a cigarette and gave one to Deborah Groot. He blew smoke across her shoulder toward the six soldiers at the far side of the room. Joe Herkimer was lifting his glass when he saw Crayne at the bar. Crayne nodded toward Deborah Groot. Herkimer's glance dropped slightly. He set down his glass, nodded back, and laughed at something the corporal next to him said, but his glance was now fixed on Deborah Groot.

"Thank you," Crayne said to the barmaid. He slid a coin across the bar. The barmaid took it and went away. "We'll pick up our glasses now," he said. "As we pick them up, we'll change places. You want a better view of the darts game. That clear?" She nodded. "All right. Now."

They picked up their glasses and changed places. Now

168

Crayne's back was to the room. And across thirty feet of crowded pub, after eight months of searching, Deborah Groot at last was facing her husband.

"Relax," Crayne said. "You're watching a darts game."

She nodded without moving her eyes. Crayne sipped his ale and watched her face. He felt a trifle foolish, but that was not unusual. He had felt foolish on a number of occasions since he had taken on the Colonel's assignment. It was something you put up with in this work. But this time it was different. Crayne felt foolish now because he realized he was watching Deborah Groot's face with intense curiosity. What did she want? What was she getting out of this?

Crayne knew the facts. At any rate, he knew what she had told him in her cheap room off the Hexton High Road. For eight months she had hunted her estranged husband. By sheer accident she had learned that the army had assigned him to a secret training school in a suburb of London. All her attempts to reach him, to use her father's considerable influence, had been unsuccessful. When the army said secret it meant just that, even to the daughter of the United States Munitions Commissioner. She had not given up. She had walked out on her father and buried herself in Hexton to continue the search. Why? Because she loved her husband after all and wanted to tell him so? A letter could have done that. She had his APO number. But she had not written a letter. She wanted to see him.

Crayne, for his own reasons, had agreed to take her to a place where she could do just that and only that. She could not talk to her husband. She could not even acknowledge by a wave of the hand that she had seen him. Neither could he. Yet she had agreed to all of Crayne's conditions for that small privilege, for the chance to look at her husband for a few minutes across a crowded, noisy bar-room. Why? The obvious answer, which was in her shining eyes, in the taut hungriness with which she stared across the room, did not square with Crayne's opinion of her intelligence, which was high. The thought crossed his mind that perhaps he felt slightly foolish, perhaps he was watching her face with such intense curiosity, because he was seeing in it, or thought he saw in it, something that in his own full but lonely life he always had missed.

"Drink your ale," Crayne said. "Take it easy."

"He sees me. He's talking to the others, but he sees me."

"So does the rest of the place. Drink your ale."

She picked up the glass and took a sip. Her eyes did not move. They did not move when she spoke again. "Couldn't I go over just for a minute?"

"No."

Six months earlier Crayne would have said yes. Six months earlier he would have suggested it himself. Not because he liked Deborah Groot, but because the suggestion was so sensible and seemed so innocent. The six months had made a difference. Crayne knew now that in the work he had undertaken for the Colonel the most sensible suggestions proved the most stupid, the most innocent turned out the most dangerous.

Crayne remembered another group of young men who had completed their training for a mission to the Continent. They had been permitted on their last night to leave their training base, as Joe Herkimer and his five friends had this evening been permitted to leave theirs, for a farewell dinner at a London restaurant. They had been so well trained, so thoroughly coached, that it was considered, as it was being considered tonight at the Edward and Lion, perfectly safe to give them one last evening of freedom. The six young men had done nothing wrong. They had violated no rule of security. After dinner they had returned to their base and had left immediately on their mission. The mission was not accomplished. The six young men did not reach their destination alive. After the tedious, heartbreaking, but necessary task of tracing back their movements was finished, the reason for their death and failure was clear. Toward the end of their dinner one of the young men had proposed a toast to the exiled king of the enemy-occupied country to which they were going. It had seemed an innocent, harmless gesture. But to the ears of an enemy agent in the restaurant, it had been enough. A group of American soldiers in a London restaurant toasting the king of an occupied country had aroused his interest. From the moment those young men left the restaurant, they were watched, followed, and doomed. All the instructions and training in the world cannot prepare men for everything, cannot protect them against the consequences of the unpredictable little things that seem so innocent and harmless.

To the people now in the Edward and Lion, Joe Herkimer and his friends were six American soldiers having a cheerful dinner. They might have been any half-dozen of the many thousand American soldiers in England. They alone knew that they were not. They and Crayne, whose business it was to know. He had taken the risk of bringing Deborah Groot here because she had stumbled on information she had no business knowing, and Crayne felt that by giving her what she wanted he could prevent her from learning more. The Colonel might not approve, but if all went well, Crayne knew that, when he submitted his report, the Colonel would not criticize.

Crayne could not afford further risk. He had given Deborah Groot what she wanted. He could not give her more. Under no circumstances could special attention be drawn to Herkimer and his dinner companions by the arrival of a friend, male or female, by the opening of a conversation and introductions that might lead into the wrong channels. London was full of enemy agents. It was always safer to assume that one of them was always near you.

"If you won't let me talk to him, I think we'd better leave now. Thanks for this much, anyway."

"I was just going to suggest that," Crayne said. "We've been here long enough. Finish your ale."

"You finish it. I don't want it. Is there a little girl's room?"

"At the end of the bar and turn left," Crayne said. "Hurry up."

He picked up her glass and watched her push through the crowded pub, an American girl with a long blonde bob, a well-cut coat, and a large suede purse tucked under her arm. She might have been going to the powder room in a crowded roadhouse near New Haven, where a group of boys and girls like herself had stopped for a bite to eat on their way home from a football game.

The alert sounded. For several moments the noise in the room was drowned by the siren. The wailing scream died away. The chatter of voices and the clatter of glasses rose again until, quite suddenly, the klaxon blatted imminent danger. The glass stopped on its way to Crayne's lips. A hush fell on the room. A moment later Crayne heard the low, grinding roar and, a moment after that, the sudden frozen silence as the robot cut out. People slipped from their chairs. Some fell flat. Others went under the tables. As Crayne ducked below the level of the bar to get his head away from the mirrors and the glass shelves behind it, he saw Deborah Groot.

She was the only person standing in the room that all at once seemed empty. Crayne saw her slide open the zipper of her large purse, pull out a small parcel, and run to the table of the six soldiers. She dropped the parcel on Joe Herkimer's chair. Crayne ran across the room, turning up his coat collar without thinking as he went. He had the parcel in his hand when the explosion came. The room shook. There was a small splattering crash of glass, but nothing came down. It was close, but this one had not had the Edward and Lion's number on it. Crayne swung around, grabbed Deborah Groot, and shoved her against the wall next to the darts game.

"If you say so much as a single word, I'll punch it back down your throat." Crayne spoke into her ear, holding her hard against the black leather bench with his shoulder, his back to the room. Working fast with his free hand he ripped the paper from the parcel and shook it loose. He was holding an old, tattered, faded football jersey. Across it, sewed on

171

haphazardly, were the numerals "11." Crayne stared at the jersey, then caught his breath in a short, rasping laugh of relief and comprehension. "You damned fool," he said softly, crumpling the jersey into a ball. She was staring at him, lips quivering, eyes wide with terror. "You damned fool," Crayne said again, releasing the pressure of his shoulder. "You damned silly little dope."

"I don't know where he's going or what he's going to do." She spoke rapidly, her voice small and pleading. "I don't want to know. I didn't talk to him. I promised I wouldn't. But I want him to have this. He never got hurt in a game when he wore this. He always said if he wore this jersey he was—"

"Shut up," Crayne said. "Get out into that foyer and wait for me. No more tricks. I said wait."

He swung her around and gave her a push. He did it gently. He didn't dislike her as much as he'd thought. She hurried through the room. People were milling about, laughing, helping one another from the floor, examining themselves for minor cuts and scratches, congratulating one another on their escape. The six American soldiers in paratroop boots had separated. They were in different parts of the room, helping people up. Crayne shoved through the crowd. Nobody paid any attention to him. Joe Herkimer was standing alone, near the push-ha'penny board, staring about over the heads of the excited people, hunting for someone. Crayne went to him.

"Here's something you dropped, soldier." He shoved the crumpled jersey into the pocket of Herkimer's tunic "She wants you to wear it. Don't ask any questions and don't worry about her. She's all right."

Herkimer grinned and nodded. He might have been grinning and nodding to a friend across the room. He did not seem to be aware of Crayne at all. He was well trained.

"So are you," Crayne added.

"Thanks," Herkimer said. "Will you tell her—"

"It isn't necessary," Crayne said as he moved away, toward the door where Deborah Groot was waiting for him. There was no more time. The room was beginning to collect itself. "It isn't necessary to tell her," Crayne said again, and added two words that he probably would omit from his report to the Colonel. "She knows."

THE BOTTOM OF THE MOUNTAIN

"Will you have one with us, sir?" The second lieutenant was not drunk but he was not completely sober, either. He looked very young, a boy of twenty-one or twenty-two at the most. There was an airborn flash on the shoulder of his unpressed American uniform that told Crayne, who had never seen him before, almost as much about the boy's recent movements as a less carefully trained observer could have learned from reading all the papers in the boy's pockets. "It's real chartreuse, sir," he said.

He was holding a tall, dark green, dusty bottle as though it were an infant fresh from the delivery room. The girl with him looked even younger. She was very pretty in a shy, almost frightened, breathless, British way. She was quite sober. Crayne would have taken the long end of a reasonable bet that she had never consumed anything stronger than an occasional glass of sherry in the presence of her family, say at Christmas. She and the lieutenant had stopped at Crayne's table, probably because the lieutenant had noticed Crayne's rather obviously American clothes. The British are admirably open-minded about many things, but they have not yet seen the virtues of the shirt with the button-down collar.

"That's very nice of you," Crayne said. "But I'm drinking scotch."

"It's real chartreuse, sir," the lieutenant said. There was a hint of pride in his smile. "I brought it over from Normandy this morning."

D-Day was not so many weeks old that the boy's pride could be considered unjustified or his simple statement unthrilling.

"Thanks," Crayne said. "I'll stick to my scotch."

The boy looked hurt. The girl squeezed his hand reassuringly as they walked back to their own table. Crayne had a moment of anger with himself. It wasn't much to do for an American kid several thousand miles from his home in Iowa or Oregon in the middle of one of the most exciting periods of a great war. Why had he refused to take a drink? The fact that he disliked chartreuse and casual drunks was not the answer. Crayne finished his scotch in a gulp. Apparently it was not as easy as he told himself it was to be facing your thirty-

173

ninth birthday in civilian clothes among kids who wore khaki as though tweeds and double-breasted worsteds had never even been invented.

"Bring me another one of these," Crayne said to the waiter. "Double, please."

The waiter brought the drink. Crayne put the young lieutenant out of his mind. He was not here for fun, even though it was supposed to look that way to the casual observer. Crayne went back to the job of watching the thinning crowd from his side table.

The small downstairs ballroom of the Crescent Hotel in London was not small and it was not downstairs. There were sixty feet of polished dance floor between the ballroom entrance and the bandstand, and diners able to afford the cover charge could reach the ballroom only by climbing a short, ornate flight of stairs from the hotel lobby. It was called the small downstairs ballroom to distinguish it from the larger restaurant at the other side of the lobby, facing the Strand, where the food was the same but the house charge was lower because diners in it could not dance between courses to the expensive rhythms of Cedric Hummert's orchestra. All of London, or rather those parts of it that could pay the price, had been dancing to his music for twenty years. When somebody rang you up and asked you to be in "the Small Downstairs at nine," you didn't have to say, "The small downstairs where?" It meant the Crescent in the Strand. And when you went to the Crescent in the Strand it was not for the food or the drink. You went for Cedric Hummert's music.

"Time, sir," the waiter said. "We're closing the bar. Will you have another, sir?"

Crayne looked at his watch. For the purpose of learning what time it was, the gesture was unnecessary. Since he had taken on this special work for the Colonel, Crayne had acquired a number of interesting skills. One of them was to know always, without having to look at a timepiece, exactly what the hour was. Another was never to indicate unnecessarily, so that an innocent bystander might be impressed into directing his attention toward Crayne, that he possessed these skills.

"Thanks, no," Crayne said. "Bring me my check, please."

The war, which had kept Crayne away from Broadway for nearly three years, had created, or perhaps only awakened, in him a concealed but stubborn patriotism that expressed itself even in small things. Most Americans, after two weeks in London, learned to ask for their bills in restaurants. Crayne, after more than a year, still asked for his check.

"There you are, sir," the waiter said. Crayne picked up his

174

change and pushed a coin back across the table cloth. "Thank you, sir."

Crayne stood up, gave the room a final glance, and moved toward the door. So far as the information the Colonel wanted was concerned, the evening had been a failure. But Crayne was glad to be going. For almost an hour the two small electric signs, in the center of the mirrored panels that flanked the orchestra, had been lighted. Crayne didn't think he was more afraid of the raids than most people in London. It was simply that he did not like to be in the small downstairs ballroom of the Crescent when they were coming over. The room had been done in peacetime by a world-famous decorator who was then in his Oriental Period. There were so many priceless drapes and tapestries on the walls that no sound from outside penetrated to dilute the dance music. Crayne, who had weathered Jap shells and sniper bullets in New Guinea as well as the next man, was all right in London so long as he could hear the sirens. There was something unsettling about being warned that death was overhead by two unobstrusive bits of neon tubing that flashed, discreetly and silently, the almost innocent word "Alert." When he reached the door and put his hand into his pocket for the coat room tab, Crayne realized that he had been jumpy for almost an hour.

"Will you wear it, sir?"

"I'll carry it. Thanks."

Crayne threw the coat over his arm and turned for a last look through the doorway. Very few people were left in the Crescent's small downstairs ballroom. It was late. Three or four couples were still on the dance floor. The waiters were stripping tables of empty glasses and crumpled napkins. The band was playing with the soft finality that meant the next number would be "God Save the King." A young American officer, holding the hand of the girl beside him, stood at the foot of the band stand, talking to the conductor. Cedric Hummert leaned far down from the platform to hear better. Hummert grinned and nodded and straightened up. The young officer turned. It was the boy with the airborne flash and the dusty bottle.

"Would you take this back for a moment?" Crayne handed his coat to the cloakroom attendant. "Some friends I want to say good night to."

He walked back into the room and sat down as the band broke into "Night and Day." When the lieutenant and the girl reached the table they stopped and looked at Crayne in surprise. He stood up.

"I've changed my mind about that drink," Crayne said. "May I?"

The surprise in the boy's face turned to pleasure.

175

"You bet, sir." He took an empty glass from the next table, set it beside the two in front of him, and filled all three from the dusty bottle. Crayne pulled out a chair for the girl and they sat down. "To our side, sir," the boy said.

"To our side," Crayne said. "And to our Allies."

"To our side," the girl said. "And to *our* Allies."

Crayne noticed that she touched the glass to her lips but did not drink. He didn't blame her. The stuff was vile. "It isn't much to do for one's country in time of war," the Colonel had said when, months before, he urged Crayne to take on his curious assignment. It wasn't, and Crayne had taken it on. It had not occurred to him then that drinking bad chartreuse would be a part of the odd duties that nobody in all the world, except the Colonel and Crayne, knew Crayne was performing. The orchestra slid into the second verse. Under the table the lieutenant and the girl were holding hands. The band stopped.

"Great tune," the boy said. "I asked Mr. Hummert to play it for us."

"It's terribly sweet of him," the girl said. "He's such a nice man."

"Yes," Crayne said. "Very."

The boy waved toward the band and Hummert grinned and waved back. The orchestra stood up to play "God Save the King" and Crayne and the lieutenant and the girl rose. When it was over, the musicians snapped off the lights over their music stands and began to pack their instruments. Hummert jumped down from the platform and lighted a cigarette as he came across the deserted dance floor toward them.

"I asked him to have a drink with us," the boy said. He moved forward a step and took Hummert's extended hand. "Thank you, sir," he said. "That was really swell."

"Glad you liked it," Hummert said. "Hello, Crayne."

"Oh," the boy said. "You know each other?"

"Know each other?" Hummert laughed as he pulled over a chair and sat down. The laugh was like his clothes and his manner: very good, very smooth, the best that money and careful study could produce, yet a little too full, just a shade too flashy. "I've known Crayne for donkey's years, long before he got to be a big-shot Broadway columnist. Why, I knew Crayne when he was just a cub reporter around the big street." He nudged Crayne and laughed again. The lieutenant looked at Crayne with quick interest. "I'm just a New York boy myself," Hummert said. He wasn't. He came from Mapleton, Ohio but, after twenty years in London, he pretended, perhaps after two decades of self-deception he even believed, that he was a native New Yorker. Most people mistook him for an Englishman. Hummert did not correct them unless someone like Crayne, who knew he was not, happened to be present. "We're old, old friends," Hummert said. "Aren't we?"

"Yes," Crayne said. "Old friends."

They weren't. Crayne had heard about the older man only vaguely in his cub reporter days, when Hummert was just beginning to be known around Broadway. His name was Charles Hummert in those days. Twenty years later, when Crayne came to London as a war correspondent, Hummert had looked him up. He looked up all the American newspapermen. It was not something you could hold against him. Orchestra leaders were like that. They lived on publicity. It was part of their business to be friendly with the press. Three years had gone by, however, since it had been Crayne's business to be friendly with orchestra leaders. He wanted no part of them. During those first months in London he had not returned Hummert's enthusiastic overtures. He didn't know why he disliked Hummert, but the feeling was strong enough to cause him to stay away from the Crescent's small downstairs ballroom. His obvious coolness had apparently not been noticed by the older man. Whenever Hummert saw Crayne he continued to treat him like an old school chum. Crayne had been annoyed by this attitude. But since the Colonel had assigned him to this job, Crayne regretted his earlier coolness. The chances of his coming up with what the Colonel wanted depended almost entirely on Hummert's belief that he and Crayne were really close friends. Crayne was not sure that he would succeed. He had sufficient self-confidence to believe he possessed a few of the qualities that had caused the Colonel to ask Crayne to work for him, but Crayne felt certain he was not a good enough actor for that.

"Are you an American, sir?" the lieutenant said.

Hummert laughed at the surprise in the boy's voice and he slapped him on the back.

"I'll tell the cockeyed world," he said. "American as apple pie."

He wasn't. There was something wrong about him. Even his slang was dated and false. From the core of his recently aroused and unsuspected patriotism, Crayne wondered if that was why he disliked Hummert. That, plus the fact that Hummert was a naturalized Englishman.

"You'll have another drink, then, sir," the lieutenant said.

"You bet your life I will," Hummert said.

The boy tipped the chartreuse bottle. It was empty. The boy blushed.

"Never mind," Hummert said. "We'll have one on me. For old time's sake, eh, Crayne?" He snapped his fingers at a waiter who was stacking chairs. "How about a quick round for me and my friends, Victor?"

"I'm sorry, sir. The bar is closed, sir."

"To hell with that," Hummert said and his voice echoed loudly in the empty ballroom. "Just tell them it's for me."

"I'll try, sir."

"Step on it, Victor. My friends are thirsty." Hummert laughed. "They always say that," he said to Crayne and the lieutenant and the English girl. "That's the British for you. You've got to know them to get anything out of them. Me, I know them like a book. Inside out. I'm one of them. I've got them in the palm of my hand."

The waiter came back across the ballroom. Most of the lights were out now.

"I'm sorry, Mr. Hummert. The steward's locked up and gone off, sir."

"That's a hell of a way to treat me and my friends," Hummert said. "What's all his rush?"

"There's an alert on, sir. Been on for a couple of hours, sir. I imagine he was anxious to see how things were at home, sir."

Hummert scowled and looked quickly at the lieutenant and then at the girl. Crayne's reaction was divided between his purely personal pleasure in the blustering band leader's embarrassment, and his swift professional awareness that the unprofitable evening had suddenly and unexpectedly taken a turn that might lead to what the Colonel wanted.

"Tell you what," Hummert said. "How about everybody coming over to my place for a couple? I've got plenty of liquor in the house. All kinds. Everything you want. What do you say?"

Crayne crushed out his freshly lighted cigarette, moving his hands to relieve the inner tension. It had taken an effort to restrain himself from making the obvious suggestion.

"That's awfully nice of you," Crayne said. "But it's very late and I don't think we'd want to disturb your family."

"You won't be disturbing them," Hummert said. "The wife and kids are in the country. Sent them down two weeks ago, when these bloody things started coming over. Come on. I'd like you all to see my place, anyway. I've got some interesting things to show you."

"Well," Crayne said and he looked at the lieutenant and the young girl with the awkward, worried hesitation of a man desperately anxious to avoid an imposition. Perhaps he was a better actor than he thought. "If it's all right with these youngsters," he said. During his few months in the Colonel's strange business that was now his business, too, Crayne had learned that, while you could only rarely shape the events

178

with which you had to work, it was always possible to take correct advantage of them when they shaped themselves for you. "I certainly could use a drink," he said.

There were only five or six people in the bus queue on the north side of the Edgeware Road when Crayne came down the street. It was midafternoon, too early for the shoppers and office workers to be going home to Willesden and Maida Vale. The sun, which had finally broken through the overhanging mist, glinted brightly on the barbed wire and the anti-aircraft guns in Hyde Park.

Crayne walked past the queue, turned left, crossed the road, and stopped to buy a paper from the newsboy in front of the Cumberland Hotel. Crayne turned left again, into Old Quebec Street, walked around the block, and came out once more into the Edgeware Road. A bus, perhaps two, had apparently stopped for passengers while Crayne was circling the block. The length and the character of the queue had changed. Now the line included several women with shopping bags, a couple of British R.E.M.E. corporals, half a dozen schoolboys excitedly discussing a movie they had just seen, and an American officer with a white mustache.

Crayne took his place at the end of the queue and read his paper as he waited. A Number Sixteen bus came along and stopped. The schoolboys and the R.E.M.E. corporals jumped in. The bus roared away. Several women joined the queue behind Crayne. A few minutes later a Number Eight bus swept around Marble Arch and stopped in front of the queue. Crayne got on behind the women with shopping bags and the American officer. A few of the women found seats downstairs. Four of them, the American officer, and Crayne climed to the top deck. Several people were scattered about on the seats upstairs. The women with the shopping bags settled themselves up front. The last seat in the rear, a double one next to the stairs, was empty. Crayne took it. The bus lurched sharply. The American officer staggered, clutched at a strap, missed, and dropped into the vacant space next to Crayne. He smiled apologetically.

"Sorry," he said.

"Quite all right, sir," Crayne said. Sitting like that, side by side in the rear seat next to the stairs, there was nobody behind or on either side of them. All the people on the top deck of the Number Eight bus were in front of them. The clippie came upstairs and rapped her ticket rack on the rail. Crayne took a shilling from his pocket. "Two fivepenny tickets, please."

"Where to, sir?" the clippie said.

"The Gaumont cinema," Crayne said. "Kilburn High Road."

"That's right, sir." Americans in London were no longer a novelty. Americans in London who knew the bus fares still were. "Two fives, sir."

She took the coin, punched a couple of tickets, dug two coppers out of the leather wallet at her side, and gave the tickets and the change to Crayne.

"Thank you," he said. The clippie moved on down the aisle toward the other passengers. Crayne said, "We're after the wrong man, sir."

"We can always be mistaken," the Colonel said. "We frequently are." He might have been discussing the weather. Because of the chattering passengers up front and the noise of the bus motor, his voice, like Crayne's, carried only far enough to be heard by the man sitting beside him. "We can't close our files on him, though, until we're certain."

"I think you can close them," Crayne said. "I'm certain, sir."

"Why?"

Crayne turned slightly to look at the handsome, white-haired man beside him. He had first met the Intelligence officer six months before. Then as now the Colonel seemed to know everything about him. Crayne, whose business for years before the war had made it necessary for him to know or know about everybody, had never even heard of the Colonel until the older man sent for him. During the six months that had gone by, Crayne had grown to like the older man. It was a liking based solely on his respect for the Colonel's ability. Crayne had nothing else to go on. Their meetings were infrequent. They were arranged by telephone, and held in odd places, to discuss a new assignment for Crayne or to hear Crayne's report on a current job. Nobody, not even the members of the Colonel's own organization, was aware that Crayne was in any way connected with their work. The Colonel never talked about personal matters. Neither did Crayne. His private life was his own business. The Colonel obviously felt the same way about his own private life. Consequently, Crayne knew almost nothing about his chief as a person. There were times, such as now, when this made their business relationship a difficult one for Crayne. He was certain that the Cedric Hummert case was closed. He was not certain that the reasons for his certainty would be accepted by the Colonel.

"I finally got to his house," Crayne said. "Last night."

"Alone?"

"No," Crayne said. "With a second lieutenant just back from Normandy and his girl. Hummert picked them up in the Small Downstairs. I happened to be with them. He asked me to go along."

The Colonel stroked his mustache lightly and looked out

180

the bus window at the shabby houses of the Edgeware Road. By this small gesture, which Crayne had come to recognize, he knew that the Colonel's interest had been aroused. It was Hummert's practice of taking young American officers to his flat late at night, after the Crescent's small downstairs ball-room closed, and feeding them more liquor than was good for them, that had aroused the suspicions of the Colonel's organization. For a couple of months before D-Day, and during the weeks that followed, there had been a number of small security leaks in London. Bits of information that were not individually important, but which in combination might have been, had filtered through to the enemy. Several of these leaks had been traced back to the small downstairs ballroom of the Crescent. It had been a popular place with the American officers who had been stockpiled in London for the invasion and, after D-Day, with the men who came back from France on missions or on leave.

The Colonel had no real evidence to go on. Merely a hunch. But in this work hunches were often as important as evidence. The Colonel felt there was something peculiar about an American band leader who had left his own country, settled in London, and remained there for twenty years without going back even once for a visit. The Colonel was not given to dramatic statements but it looked, he said, as though Hummert had renounced his native land. The reason did not matter, although it would have been interesting, probably even helpful, to know it. Such men made good enemy agents. There were now in the Colonel's employ a number of Germans who had renounced Germany at one time or another for a variety of reasons. It would have been dangerous sentimentality to think it impossible that an American who had renounced America could not be in the employ of the Germans. There was no room for sentimentality in the Colonel's business. He had assigned Crayne, whose background made him a good choice for this type of job, to the Hummert case.

"How did it go?" the Colonel said.

"Very well," Crayne said. "There was a hell of a raid on."

As he spoke, the sirens went. The bus had just rolled out of the Edgeware Road into Maida Vale. For a moment the women with shopping bags at the front of the bus stopped talking. Crayne stopped, too. Then, in a few seconds, the hum of conversation resumed. There were always a few minutes between the alert and the first robots. It was silly to waste them. They might be your last.

Crayne told the Colonel about his three hours in Hummert's house with the young lieutenant and the girl. He spoke clearly, without emphasis, using as few words as possible, the way he wrote his reports when the Colonel could not get away to see him in person, but his ears were alert for the droning sounds that might be coming toward them at any moment. There was not much to tell. Hummert had spent most of the time showing them his possessions: the piano that had once belonged to the King of Rumania, the set of Swinburne with the poet's autograph on each flyleaf, the liquor cabinet that was a present from someone related by marriage to the royal family, the portrait of his wife by a member of the Royal Academy, the rug that had come from the floor of a bankrupt duke's castle. The young lieutenant, and even the English girl with him, had been impressed.

While Hummert showed and described his treasures, Crayne gradually remembered all that he had known and forgotten about the orchestra leader in those early days on Broadway. It was not much. Hummert had never been a really big name on the big street. He had been just another young man with a band that worked fairly regularly and was paid fairly well. One day he had disappeared. A few questions were asked about him, but not many. Charles Hummert was not missed. Soon he was forgotten. Bigger names and better talents had disappeared from Broadway in Crayne's time with even less fuss. The memory of Broadway is no longer than the memory of any other street in the world. To Crayne it had seemed odd to be remembering all that during the small hours of the night, in the midst of an air raid, in another country, during a war. Odder still was the feeling of embarrassment that came over Crayne as he watched and listened to Hummert. At four in the morning the lieutenant and his girl and Crayne said good night and left Hummert's house. Crayne put the youngsters into a taxi, walked through the blackout to his own flat, and lay awake until dawn thinking the thing out. By the time he pulled the sleep mask over his eyes and took a Nembutol capsule and rolled his face away from the morning sun to get some rest, Crayne was sure he had the problem solved.

"I see," the Colonel said.

The all clear sounded. The part of Crayne's mind that had been in the skies overhead came back to the top deck of the Number Eight bus. The heavy vehicle swayed into the left fork at the top of Maida Vale, swinging the passengers to one side, and pressed the silver eagle on the Colonel's shoulder against Crayne's tweed coat. The bus stopped. The Colonel sat up straight. A couple of women got off. The bus started again.

"I may have it figured wrong," Crayne said. "I don't think so, sir."

The Colonel did not answer. He stared out the window at the queues in front of the fish and vegetable hucksters

182

carts on the Kilburn High Road. He seemed absorbed in the teeming scene. It was the absorption of a tourist seeing a foreign land for the first time. Crayne wanted to tell him irritably that there was nothing remarkable in the sight of housewives buying haddock and potatoes from push carts. The same thing happened every week day on Second Avenue in New York. Crayne was irritable because he felt silly. It was his job to get information. He had performed that job well on previous assignments. On this one he had come up, not with information, but with a theory. It had been an embarrassing theory to explain, in an undertone on top of a bus, to a man about whom he knew nothing except that he was hardheaded and appeared to understand and want to deal only in facts. It seemed, all at once, a little like telling a bunch of roughnecks playing poker in the city room about your secret passion for Shakespeare's sonnets. It was annoying to see that his theory was not even interesting enough to distract the Colonel's attention from a street of fish and vegetable peddlers.

"Of course, all this is based on only one visit to his home," Crayne said. "Hummert could hardly be expected to try to get information out of an army officer while I was present. He wouldn't have invited me to come along if he'd wanted to do that. Just the same I don't think he's the man we're looking for." Crayne regretted that his irritation was coming through in his voice. "I think the files on Hummert should be closed."

The bus stopped. Several people from the top deck got off. A quarter of a mile up the road, three more stops on their fivepenny tickets, were the tall gilded minarets of the Gaumont cinema. The bus started with a lurch.

"I think I'll get off at the next stop," the Colonel said. He stood up and pushed the bell button. "I must get back to my office." He smiled suddenly, a broad, friendly grin that caused a neat, straight gap to appear down the middle of his white mustache. "I'll buy your theory," he said. The bus began to slow down. The Colonel took one of the bus tickets out of Crayne's hand, stepped over to the stairs, and turned back for a moment. "I'm going to close my files on Hummert," he said.

The phone rang on the desk at the other side of the office. Crayne did not get up to answer it. He was trying to finish a dispatch. There had been two heavy raids that morning and his secretary, an English girl who had been blitzed out of three different dwellings in four years, had rushed off to Putney to see if she would have a place in which to sleep that night. The phone continued to ring. Crayne remained at the typewriter. His paper in New York did not know about his work for the Colonel. He could offer no explanation if he fell behind in his coverage of the London news. Crayne saw to it that he did not fall behind. The phone rang shrilly on his secretary's desk. He stood up, finally, and went across the room.

"Hello?" It was a woman's voice. British. "Mr. Crayne, please."

"Speaking."

"Oh." The voice sounded upset. "This is Mrs. Hummert. I don't think we've met. Mrs. Cedric Hummert?"

That explained the voice. It matched the cold, rather silly portrait Crayne had seen over Hummert's fireplace three nights before.

"Yes," Crayne said. "How do you do?"

"I know this is frightfully rude, but could you come around to our flat right away?"

"I'm afraid not. I'm busy at the moment."

"Please, Mr. Crayne. Couldn't you possibly? It's frightfully important, really."

"I'm sorry. I can't right now."

"Please, Mr. Crayne."

The flat, impersonal, superior cadence had not changed, but there was a small, almost desperate increase in pitch. It was enough to cut through Crayne's divided attention. His mind left the dispatch in the typewriter at the other side of the room. His own voice did not change, but now he was paying complete attention.

"What's wrong?" he said.

"Our flat's been hit. This morning's raid. The first one. My husband is asking for you, Mr. Crayne."

"For me?" Crayne was not pleased with the surprise in his voice. "Why me?"

"Yes. I don't know. He keeps calling your name."

"Is he badly hurt?"

"Yes, rather. They rang me in the country at noon. I came up by the first train. It was a stroke of luck that I managed to locate your phone number and find you in. He wants you, Mr. Crayne. Do say you'll come."

"I'll be right over."

"Thank you so much. We're at Westminster Gardens. If you'll just ask any taxi driver?"

"I know Westminster Gardens."

In the taxi Crayne could not decide whether he was more annoyed by the tone of Mrs. Hummert's voice, which had indicated clearly that she thought he lacked the intelligence to find Westminster Gardens without detailed instructions, or by her husband's upsetting summons. The files on Hummert were closed. The colonel had ended the case the day before because Crayne had convinced him on top of the Number Eight bus that they were after the wrong man. Why should Hummert send for Crayne now? Crayne was not one of his friends. Hummert did not know about Crayne's work for the Colonel. He could not possibly know that he had been under suspicion.

Crayne sat up straight on the taxi seat. There *was* a way by which Hummert could have known he was under suspicion. It was the only way: if Hummert was guilty.

The taxi stopped. The street in which Westminster Gardens stood was roped off. Crayne paid the driver, walked up to the policeman on guard, and showed his press card.

"Right, sir." The policeman lifted the rope. Crayne ducked under. "You'll have to use the side entrance. I'm afraid the front has been knocked out, sir."

It occurred to Crayne again, as it had occurred to him three nights before when he came here for the first time with the young lieutenant and his girl, that Westminster Gardens was just the sort of place an American orchestra leader who had gone completely British would choose to live in. It was an expensive, gaudy, modernistic block of flats, with vast sheets of seamless glass instead of window panes, and too many oddly cut mirrors and curiously shaped pieces of onyx and metal tubing in the lobby.

The robot had landed in the street, fifty yards or so beyond the entrance. The blast had knocked out the front of Westminster Gardens and sliced away sections of the smaller blocks of flats on either side. Several small houses across the road were completely levelled. It was impossible to tell whether there had been three or four in the row that was now a flat, smoking ruin. A number of ARP men with *Heavy Rescue* patches on their sleeves were working in the rubble. The pavement was almost hidden under a treacherous layer of powdered glass. The air was sharp with the hard, thin, penetrating smell of high explosive mixed with charred wood and fine mortar dust. Crayne picked his way through the debris to the side entrance. He showed his card to another policeman at the door.

"You'll have to walk, sir. The lift's gone. Back stairs are over there, sir, to your left."

Crayne walked up three flights. The back of the large structure was still standing, but most of the seamless glass on the court was gone. The acrid odors of the street poured in with the draft. The door of the Hummert flat was ajar. The blast had sprung the hinges. Crayne pushed the pearl button on the jamb. He was not surprised to hear the buzzer sound inside. Blast damage was unpredictable. It could wreck a roomful of bronze statues and leave intact a delicate vase on a spindly table in the middle of the chamber. The door was opened by

185

a smartly dressed woman of about forty with a hard, lined face and marcelled blonde hair.

"You're Mr. Crayne?"

"Yes."

"I'm Mrs. Hummert. It's frightfully kind of you to come. This is Dr. Farquarson."

Crayne shook hands with a middle-aged man who wore striped trousers and a wing collar. Mrs. Hummert and the doctor looked at Crayne expectantly, as though they had been waiting for him to arrive with information of great importance. Crayne had come to get information, not to give it. He glanced about as though unaware of the awkward pause. They were standing in the foyer. He could look into the kitchen and the dining room because the doors of these rooms had been torn from their hinges. The beautiful Hummert flat was a mess.

"Mr. Hummert keeps calling your name," the doctor said. "Mrs. Hummert and I were wondering if you know why?"

"I have no idea. Do you want me to ask him?"

Dr. Farquarson and Mrs. Hummert looked at each other.

"I'm afraid it's impossible to question him," Dr. Farquarson said. "Mr. Hummert's condition is quite grave."

"That's too bad," Crayne said. "Is there anything I can do?"

Mrs. Hummert and the doctor exchanged another glance. She nodded slightly.

"If you will come this way," Dr. Farquarson said. "I must ask you not to excite him. He has lost a considerable amount of blood. He is very weak."

"Of course."

Crayne moved toward the bedroom door and stopped. Dr. Farquarson had moved toward the door of the living room.

"The bedrooms are almost completely gone," Mrs. Hummert said. "That's why Cedric was injured. He was asleep when the bomb landed. He always sleeps late because he seldom finishes at the Crescent before one or two in the morning. They found him a couple of hours later and rang me up in the country. I left the children in the country. We've put him in the drawing room. It's the one room that wasn't hit so badly. It faces the court, you see."

Crayne did not like her any better than he had liked her voice on the telephone or her portrait by a member of the Royal Academy, but he admired her self-control. It would have been difficult for a stranger, certainly for an American stranger, to know that Mrs. Hummert was talking about her own husband.

"We must be very quiet," Dr. Farquarson said. "He must not be disturbed."

Crayne nodded. The doctor opened the door. Crayne stared

186

into the room which, when he had seen it three nights before, had been so carefully and laboriously arranged that it had resembled a room in a museum rather than part of a man's home. The piano that had belonged to the King of Rumania was cracked wide open, like a child's toy that has been dropped to the pavement from a great height. The priceless autographed set of Swinburne was torn to bits, the pages scattered like confetti around the room. The liquor cabinet that had been a present from a member of the royal family was recognizable only because the twisted nickel fittings gleamed through the pile of shattered ebony and mother of pearl. The portrait of Mrs. Hummert by the Royal Academician lay on the floor, the frame broken, the canvas slashed in several places as though with a knife. The seamless glass windows had apparently been open at the time of the explosion. The glass had been spared. The windows were now closed and the curtains, which had also been inexplicably overlooked by the freak blast, were partly drawn. Hummert, his head propped up on two pillows, lay motionless in a large bed that had been moved into the middle of the ruined room.

"He's asleep," Dr. Farquarson said quietly. "I gave him a sedative an hour ago."

Crayne nodded. He did not speak. He was shocked by Hummert's appearance. The band leader had changed more completely than the room. His head was bandaged and his left arm, bound in splints, lay stiff and straight at his side. His right fist was tightly clenched. His eyes were closed. He trembled slightly, as though with cold. His heavy, irregular breathing was painful to hear. Most amazing was the fact that Hummert seemed to have shrunk since Crayne had seen him three days before. The large, blustering band leader now looked small and frail under the thin covers. His ruddy face was white and drawn. The weight and the life had been drained from him. All that remained of Cedric Hummert was a bundle of bones in a loose sack of skin. His head rolled an inch or two on the pillow and he opened his eyes.

"Crayne," he said hoarsely. "Get Crayne."

The effort to force the words out left him weaker. His chest started to heave more rapidly. Crayne stepped over to the bed.

"Here I am," he said.

A gleam of recognition sparked for a moment in Hummert's eyes. His parched lips cracked apart in a horrible approximation of a smile and then, as his glance caught Dr. Farquarson and Mrs. Hummert, the smile stopped.

"Alone," he said. "Want talk Crayne alone."

Crayne turned to the others. Mrs. Hummert's hard, lined face was pinched, not with the suspicion that Crayne was prepared for and would have understood, but with a sort of angry, childish petulance, as though a puzzle on which she had been working for some time had been snatched from her grasp at the moment when she felt she was about to solve it. Dr. Farquarson looked disturbed.

"I won't upset him," Crayne said. He did not want any witnesses to what Hummert was about to tell him. "Of course, if you'd rather I didn't?"

The doctor hesitated for another moment or two and then, with a gesture of finality and firmness that surprised Crayne, he took Mrs. Hummert's arm and led her to the door. She stopped and looked across her shoulder. Crayne made a reassuring movement with his hand and they went out and closed the door softly. Crayne turned back to the man on the bed. Hummert's eyes were closed.

"We're alone now," Crayne said. "What did you want to tell me?"

The band leader did not answer. Crayne bent over the bed. Hummert's breathing was weaker. His right fist pulsed up and down, as though he were trying to make it shrink by kneading the fingers into his palm. Crayne pulled over a chair and sat down beside the bed.

"Take it easy," he said. "I won't go away."

Crayne wanted a cigarette badly, but he had neglected to ask the doctor if it was all right to smoke. He was finding it difficult to suppress a mounting feeling of excitement. The Colonel had closed the files on Hummert because of Crayne's analysis of the few facts he had remembered about the band leader. It was true that Crayne would look foolish if Hummert, knowing he was about to die, had sent for Crayne in order to make a complete confession. But Crayne knew that, in this work he had undertaken voluntarily, personal discomfort was of little consequence. Only one thing was important now: to correct a mistake he had caused the Colonel to make.

"Whenever you're ready," Crayne said. "I'll wait."

He watched the man whose life was slipping away before his eyes and wondered where his analysis had gone wrong. Crayne had seen it all clearly three nights before as he watched and listened to Hummert exhibit his treasures to the young lieutenant and the girl. Hummert was like most of the men Crayne had known on and around Broadway. He had wanted success. More than anything in the world, he had desired fame and money, the simple, difficult things for which most men lusted. And like most men, his ambition had been larger than his talent. Hummert never really reached Broadway in the full meaning of that phrase. The competition was too strong. His ability was too small. He reached the fringes of fame and money. He touched the edge of success. He never really held it firmly in his grasp. Success was the pinnacle of a tall, tall mountain. He had struggled and climbed. He had come close, but never close enough. He knew finally that, like most men, he would never reach the top. But Hummert differed from most men in one respect: he faced the reality that if he remained on Broadway he would never have what he wanted. He made what must have seemed at the time a wise decision. He left Broadway. He came to London.

In the British capital the competition was not so great. Here, in London, the mere fact that he was an American was an asset. The talent that had not been big enough for Broadway was big enough for the West End. In London Hummert got what in his own country had been denied him. In London he achieved fame, earned money, became a success. In London he reached the top of the mountain. The air was sweet. It was as he had always dreamed it would be. It was difficult to give it up, to come down from the mountain to the less heady air of home. Hummert stayed on. And the longer he stayed, the more difficult it was to go back. He set about the task of making it impossible for himself to go back. He changed his name from Charles to Cedric. He married an English girl. He sent his children to British schools. He lost touch deliberately with his relatives in America. He cultivated a British accent.

And finally he became a naturalized British subject. Twenty years had gone by. They were good years. It was a good life. There was nothing wrong with it. He was happy. He was respected. He was successful. He had everything he had ever wanted. Everything except the one thing he had always had but no longer possessed: his own country.

"I want you to take a look at this liquor cabinet." Crayne could hear Hummert's voice again as he showed his possessions to the young lieutenant. "It was presented to me by a member of the royal family. Here, let me show you this piano. It used to belong to the King of Rumania."

There had been a pathetic and revealing eagerness in Hummert's voice. For all his hearty British manner, his Savile Row clothes, his fabulous possessions, he had looked and sounded like a small boy explaining how, in spite of his black eye and bloody nose, he had really won the fight from which he had just come home in tatters. Long before he left Hummert's flat at four o'clock that morning, Crayne knew that the band leader did not take young American officers from the small downstairs ballroom of the Crescent to his house and fill them with liquor to pry military secrets for the enemy.

The war, the air raids, the young men in uniform from his own country, all of these things in combination had shaken Hummert's belief in the decision he had made twenty years ago. He was too old to have his belief shaken. It had been with him too long. He was forty-seven. When the robots started coming over, he sent his wife and children to the country. He had to remain in London. Not only because of his work. He was an Englishman now. Englishmen did not run away from bombs. He was alone much of the time. His loneliness had nothing to do with the many people by whom he was surrounded constantly in his work. He had done a good job on himself in twenty years, but it was not perfect. The British knew he was an American, and the Americans thought he was British. He was comfortable with neither. He began to entertain young American officers at his house. To ingratiate himself with them, perhaps to capture their sympathy, he told them he was a native New Yorker. No doubt it was pleasant for them, as it had clearly been pleasant for the young lieutenant three nights before. For Hummert this entertaining was more than pleasant. For Hummert it had become a necessity. The admiration of the young men for his possessions was reassuring. The roomful of treasures was the symbol, the price he had received for giving up his country. Hummert needed reassurance. It was important to be told, over and over again, that the bargain was worth it. It was necessary for him to believe now that what he had done twenty years ago was right.

That was how Crayne had figured it. That was the basis on which the Colonel had closed Hummert's file. Where had the analysis gone wrong?

"Want you do me a favor."

Crayne leaned over the bed. He was about to find out. Hummert's eyes were open. They were curiously alive in that shrunken, inert body.

"What do you want?" Crayne said, trying not to sound eager. He was not completely successful. The confession would clear up the case for the Colonel. It would not answer the question that kept drilling in the back of Crayne's mind: why had Hummert chosen him? Why not his wife? Or Dr. Farquarson? Why had Hummert sent for an American newspaperman who had never taken any pains to conceal his dislike for the band leader? "Tell me when you're ready," Crayne said. "I'll be here."

Hummert closed his eyes and rolled his head weakly from side to side on the pillow. He was telling Crayne without words to wait. He was gathering together whatever was left in him for a final effort. Crayne waited. His glance slid across the room toward the door. He did not want the doctor or Mrs. Hummert to interrupt. Crayne's eyes, coming back to the man on the bed, skipped across the fragments of the shattered room. It was all worthless now, of course. But it had been quite a price. Crayne had known men in his time who had sold more of themselves for less. It was not his business to judge. It was his business to pay close attention and hear clearly what Hummert had to say. He would have to repeat it without error to the Colonel.

"Want you take this."

Hummert tried to lift his hand from the bed, but he lacked the strength. He opened his clenched fist. On the moist palm lay a crumpled wad of paper. Crayne took it and spread it open. It was a tiny brochure, dated 1923, describing the Mapleton Hills Cemetery located on the outskirts of Mapleton, Ohio. Crayne looked at the man on the bed. Hummert's dry lips were moving. Crayne leaned down.

"Family owns plot," Hummert said, forcing the words out one at a time, with painstaking care, like a man trying to make himself understood across a great distance. "Please send cable." His body arched upward in a final, convulsive spurt of strength and Crayne slipped his arm under the thin shoulders. "Cremate," Hummert said. "Send ashes Mapleton. Family will pay. Bury ashes home. Not here. Home."

The stiffness went out of him, from all of his body and all at once. It was as though Crayne had been holding one of those inflated rubber figures with which children play on the beach and suddenly, without warning, all the air had escaped. Crayne lowered the limp body to the bed and straightened up. The Colonel's files would not have to be reopened. Charles Hummert had started his journey back home.

THE PRICE IS RIGHT

by Jerome Weidman

A savagely satiric novel of life—and what passes for love—behind the scenes of New York's fabled communications industry.

"Weidman at his best."   *—The New York Times*

"Cliff-hanging suspense."   *—The Saturday Review*

"Weidman writes just a little bit better than anybody else that's around."—Ernest Hemingway

{75-128}   75c

ONE OF THE ALL-TIME BEST SELLERS

O YE JIGS & JULEPS!

by Virginia Cary Hudson
Illustrated by Karla Kuskin

". . . as colorful as an old-fashioned sampler and lots more fun" (according to the St. Louis *Post-Dispatch*). The author's viewpoint is "much funnier and somewhat wiser than an adult's" (according to the Birmingham *News*). And she has charmed readers from California ("a breath of fresh air"—San Francisco *Chronicle*) to New England ("sheer enjoyment" —Boston *Herald*).

Or, as *The New York Times* sums it up, "delightful is the word for it."

---

66 WEEKS ON THE BEST-SELLER LISTS

60-131   60c
